THE CREEK

Richard France

Disclaimer:

To my wife Anna, who has been a constant source of optimism throughout my life and not least in helping me to complete this book.

Acknowledgement

My thanks go to the staff of Pantheon for their support throughout this project and also my friends Pete and Bill for their initial reviews, helpful reflections and encouragement along the way.

Chapter 1

Lando tried desperately hard to think about how he came to be in this predicament. As he clawed his way to the surface of some dark dream, he realised that whatever drug was coursing through his system was fogging his brain. His right temple throbbed, but he dismissed it as he had far greater worries.

He could not move. His wrists were attached by plastic cable ties to the arms and his ankles to the legs of a hard, wooden chair. They cut deeper into his skin with every twitch of his body. He was naked and marvelled at the amount of hilarity the shape and size of his displayed genitals caused his captors. They really should get out more. The room was small, dirty, and gloomy. Its windows were daubed out with hastily applied black paint, and the smell in the room made him gag, mainly because he thought he might be the cause of it.

These were the three that Hobart had described. Hamza, Abdul and Farouk. Their black and white scarves or "kufiyahs" were wrapped around their faces, and their once-white dishdashas were filthy with all manner of dirt, which appeared to include old blood. He hoped it was not his own. The time of reckoning seemed close as they advanced towards him like a skirmish line. Half smiling, they appeared to be anticipating the degree of sexual enjoyment they would get from damaging parts of his body, no doubt based on some ancient practice. Weird sounds were coming out of their mouths like the ululation of grieving widows as each one, in turn, from behind their backs, produced different objects of torment.

The most diminutive guy spoke first whilst brandishing a large rock with a thick string attached and waved it extravagantly towards his co-conspirators. He had a jagged scar from the crease of his lip up to below his left ear. It gave him a bizarre, permanent half-smile, but only on one side of his face.

"Kafir, you already know me as Hamza. My friends here are Abdul and Farouk." He nodded at each of them. "You are an enemy of the state, and Allah has deemed it necessary for you to find paradise by hanging this rock from your pathetic testicles."

Lando found it challenging to see the logic of the statement or any possible link to anything in the Qur'an and made the mistake of saying so. All three captors lowered their scarves, and each proceeded to hock up a loogie and project it in his direction. However, one of them had not lowered his scarf enough, and his phlegm projectile hung like a slippery snake from his teeth to the edge of his scarf down to his stomach before it finally settled like a speckled slug trail down the front of his already filthy dishdasha. The other two looked at each other and laughed extravagantly. Lando mistakenly joined in. They slowly turned their unshaven faces towards him with menace in their dark eyes.

Abdul was a huge man. He must have been a foot taller than the other two, and Lando thought he could have been a possible basketball star if he hadn't been such a solid heap of muscle. He must have been over two eighty pounds, so the likelihood he could launch himself more than four inches off the ground was remote. He then pointed to his trolley from which a pair of electrodes hung, linked to a large battery. Lando needed no explanation as to where the other ends would be connected. He got one anyway, which did not further enlighten him, after which Abdul had a vengeful look on his face from a previous encounter with Lando, and the other two nodded sagely, which must have been difficult for them given the minuscule gene pool from which they undoubtedly had descended.

Finally, Farouk, who looked as if he had been rehearsing his introduction to his pride and joy, broke into a magnanimous hairy-faced, gap-toothed smile and proceeded to speak about his object of torture that looked like a simple pole.

"Mine will be the final torture," he said with a leer and a trace of dribble on his lips. "To release your soul to beg forgiveness from Allah. You will be bent over the table, and I shall proceed to push this tent pole up your smelly white backside until you scream for mercy. You shall receive none, and then I shall push it further until you scream no more. What do you think of that Kafir?"

"Well, I went to a slightly disreputable boarding school, and this sounds a bit like the initiation ceremony my first week. But may I ask one thing?" They looked at him quizzically. "Would you mind using lubricant as splinters can be a bitch!" He then heard a very non-Arabic chuckle from behind the door.

He often used humour in tight situations and surprised himself with this show of bravado as he felt anything but courageous. He was shaking so much that he could feel his teeth chattering even though the room must have been over a hundred degrees. Strange how he had got into this mess. He regretted his position but could not help thinking that he had never felt so alive. There is something about impending death coupled with a likelihood of intense pain along the way that focuses the mind even through the fog of drugs. Lando's mind was now more focused than he wished, but he had recently acquired a certain relaxed view of life that he had never felt before. He had spent much of his life fending off the tedium of his time in accountancy, and he now realised one benefit of his new predicament. He was not remotely bored!

Chapter 2

A few months before

Roland "Lando" Westwood worked for Wolverhampton University as a lecturer in finance. If it sounded a bit dull, that is because it was, at times. He was thirty-four years old and had been married but only briefly in his early twenties as he and his girlfriend Georgina had decided they would run off to Gretna Green in a fit of tanked-up, romantic zest. The marriage lasted only a fortnight but ended amicably. He was exceptional at Mathematics and had trained as a Chartered Accountant, but he didn't like it. The only maths was basic arithmetic, which did not adequately float his boat. Although Lando never thought he was bright, he rose to a drunken challenge by a friend at the university, Gary Jenkins, to apply to gain membership to Mensa – an organisation whose only qualification to entry was achieving a high enough IQ in a controlled test to be in the top 2% IQ of society. Gary, of course, was a member and constantly goaded Lando that he could never get in as he was too soft in the head, and the bet was that he must either get into Mensa or succeed in dating the voluptuous Amber, the barmaid at the Dog and Doublet where they often enjoyed a pint together on a Friday lunchtime.

Gary prided himself on his understanding of probabilities and felt that the two tasks being achieved by Lando were of similar probability – or improbability. Whilst the barmaid, Amber, was the curviest redhead Lando had ever seen and the most alluring of ladies, particularly after a couple of pints, she allegedly packed a punch like Tyson Fury, so any approach to her in the wrong way could have created a wonderful Friday afternoon's entertainment in the Dog & Doublet. The bet was that Gary would buy Lando's Friday lunches and beers for a month if he succeeded in either task. If he failed both, then Lando would have to do the buying. The only proviso was that Lando had to attempt both tasks and that Gary was present when Lando made his first approach to Amber. Lando's problem was that he was not good at approaching members of the fair sex without being introduced in some way, even though he did not lack the courage. He just felt stupid when he opened his mouth and sensed he had to devise a brilliantly funny line to attract his intended date. He really did not understand women, although he would have liked to. Ten years of all-boys boarding schools saw to that. His only female contacts besides his mother and younger sister were at the occasional young farmers' dances. These were a kind of grab-who-you-can free-for-all which, in the summer, if you were lucky, could have ended up at the top of a haystack – not suitable for Lando's hay fever allergy as too much slap and tickle would invariably result in wheezing and twin streams of snot shooting out of his nostrils with significant force. Not the most romantic way to entice a girl to go further than first base – whatever that was – as Lando never found out. Latterly, he managed the occasional Hunt Ball, where everyone else seemed to be partnered up apart from him. Anyway, he had decided to try the 'bed the redhead' (as Gary put it) task first as he felt the payoff, if successful, would massively outweigh the risk of a few lunches for Gary, despite the bashing to his pride and the humiliation if he failed. For one thing, Amber had a significant vested interest in the proceedings and a reasonable say in the matter.

Lando had worked in the family textile business, Westwood and Sons Ltd., being the fifth generation. He didn't like it, but then his parents died together after a car crash, so the business was sold. He ventured into consultancy, trying to help pick up failing businesses. He didn't like that either. He took time out to do an MBA and learnt how to do reports in five pages that previously took him one page, something else he didn't like. He later joined Wolverhampton University, where he realised he could never have a career in academia without completing a doctorate. He would rather have his plums trapped in a car door than undertake a research thesis on such a subject. However, he accepted a temporary lectureship at Wolverhampton as they were desperate for teaching staff at the time, and he felt this might have opened a few doors – to what, he had no idea, but it was only a thirty-minute train trip from his lovely flat in Shrewsbury.

On his first day at the university, whilst queuing in the staff canteen for his lunch, he had met Gary or Gareth as he preferred to be called, although nobody did. Gary always felt that his full name, Gareth, better emphasised his Welshness and, coupled with his soft South Wales accent, gave him a certain academic mystique to help him stand out in a competitive career environment, a bit like a Scottish accent in a Golf Club bar. One could be viewed with awe as having a supernatural grasp of the game that no one else had.

It was the first day for both of them, the beginning of the university year in September, and a long chatty lunch ensued as, despite teaching different subjects, they were in the same section of the business school. Gary taught statistics, which he loved, and was amazed that others had a different passion for the subject. It was clear to Lando from the beginning that Gary would be an excellent teacher to those who wanted to listen. He had come from another university in London but departed under a slight cloud when a female student made an allegation of inappropriate behaviour against him. Nothing was found against him or on his record, and he said she was not even his type, but he felt he had to leave the university because one or two colleagues treated him with a degree of suspicion. Sometime later, the student had made a further allegation against another lecturer, and she had then been asked to leave as her again unfounded allegations transpired to be a mental health issue. So, it was a new life for both Gary and Lando, and they met regularly on a Friday lunchtime at the Dog & Doublet. They became great friends over the next two years. It was the sort of friendship that held nothing back. It incorporated a mixture of teasing, winding each other up, joking, sympathising, drinking, joshing, ogling, etc., that blokes do when they relax as blokes. Gary, like Lando, was also in his thirties but was happily married with four children, which Lando found impossible to understand as he thought those two aspects of 'happily married' and 'four children' were mutually exclusive phrases. Gary tried to convince Lando that one day, he would find the right woman and fall hard and for good. It had better be quick, as he was becoming just a little less youthful at thirty-four. In his head, like most men, he still felt about twenty years old, which was not surprising as he knew he had never really grown up.

So, it was mid-term and late Friday morning, and Lando had just completed what he thought was one of the best lectures of his life. He met up with Gary, and off they walked to the pub. Gary remarked to Lando that he seemed rather down in the mouth.

"What's the problem, Lando? You seem to have lost your mojo."

"You won't believe this, but I was teaching the Philosophy of Accounting Information and gave what I thought was my finest lecture. Whilst I used some PowerPoint slides to keep me on track, in front of a hundred and fifty students, I paced up and down the front of the lecture hall, speaking into my portable microphone, waxing lyrical, and it was like I was in a dream. As I walked, the words poured from my mouth like a beautiful wavy stream flowing down the rocks of a hill, and I could not stop myself. I talked and talked, and it was like some glorious epiphany as I felt I truly understood what I was teaching for the first time ever. With each sentence, I became more courageous. My voice got louder and more confident, and it was just as if I was riding on a cloud and all the words were coming from some supernatural being.

"So where is the problem in that, Lando?"

"Wait and see. At the end of the lecture, I felt incredible, and as I was tidying up my notes and papers, a dishevelled male student from Lancashire nicknamed Piledriver who would look equally at home on a farm grovelling about under a tractor engine or after a ball at the bottom of a Rugby scrum came up to me and said 'Hey up Lando boy, what the hell was all that about?'"

Gary was almost crying with laughter at this point, and combined with the bewildered look on Lando's face, he could not help himself.

"You know your problem, boyo? One minute, your mood was at the top of the mountain, and next, you hit the depths of the valleys, and do you know why that was? You had not been lecturing to the students; you had been lecturing to yourself and effectively showing yourself how clever you were. I have done that a few times but finally managed to contain myself. Don't forget we also have many international students whose English will not keep up with our expressions. Not surprising, as a few of them have fooled the system by sending friends in to take the English test on their behalf, so we must assume they are slower to assimilate the content."

"Now, Gary, you cannot brand them all the same, besides which this guy was from Lancashire, and we cannot teach to the lowest common denominator; otherwise, we shall need twice as many lectures."

"I agree, Lando, but don't treat yourself so harshly. I'll buy the first pint today."

"You're on."

They walked through the door of the Dog and Doublet. It was more of a scamper as they were eager to round off their week with a good pint of draft Doombar. They had to wait for a few customers and were delighted to see that the voluptuous Amber was serving. Despite her red hair, she had only a few freckles and such clear skin, and when she recognised the two of them, the ready smile on her face made Lando's power of speech turn into that of a three-year-old.

"One minute, boys, I can see you are desperate."

That brought childish giggles from a few folks leaning on the bar. She dealt with it in a way only a seasoned barmaid could do.

"Now now, fellas, we shall have none of that coarse stuff round here, or you shall all be asked to leave, and we don't want that now, do we?"

There was no more ribaldry.

As Gary ordered, Lando asked Amber for a mug with a handle rather than a straight-sided glass. Gary looked sideways at Lando.

"Why do you do that every time, Lando? Why does it matter?"

"Because it tastes different."

"No, it doesn't."

"It does. It also reminds me of the old days when I went for a drink with my old man. We always went to the lounge bar, and they always used dimpled jugs there. The straight-sided glasses were for the public bars."

"Aha, so it is all about your boarding school education, then? Never had you down as a snob," teased Gary.

Lando smiled at him. "You know many town centre pubs don't allow mugs with handles as they are a better weapon than a straight glass if you want to glass someone. A serious fight in that bar is less likely if no mugs are available."

"I guess that makes sense," muttered Gary as he paid for the drinks whilst Lando nodded politely to Amber.

They walked to a table for four and stretched out. It was a haven there. Log fires in the winter, comfortable leather-covered seats, solid hardwood tables that did not rock on the floor, and polished copper and brass implements on the wall, most of which no one seemed to know what they were for. Some looked like instruments of pain, but they all added to the ambience.

"Still like a straight-sided glass, though. You can watch the excess foam slowly slither down the sides and know you will be happy when it hits the bottom."

"Ah, the simple things. Maybe it's because you are Welsh."

"Hey, look you here, boyo. I shall report you for non-PC remarks if you are not careful," said Gary, smiling through his beer glass.

So that was his relationship with Gary. They were like two peas in a pod. They were different in many ways, but when they were together, it was so very comfortable between them, and they could have a good laugh about stuff and then talk about serious things in life, such as the price of beer.

Lando had met Gary's wife, Megan, for the first time when Gary invited him for dinner one Friday evening. She was everything Lando might have imagined. She was very hospitable and welcoming, pretty, cuddly, exuding warmth, and she always seemed as if she was about to burst into laughter at any moment and had that similar, soft South Wales accent like Gary's. Lando could see how they could be happily married. She often knocked Gary off his high academic horse by saying something so logical and straightforward that Gary could be completely floored. Gary had been spouting about mortality statistics that first dinner and said over a mouthful of sticky toffee pudding.

"You are 13.8 per cent more likely to die on your birthday than any other day."

Megan immediately said, "Why?"

Gary replied, after much scowling, that he had no idea.

She then said, "So how can you use that statistic?"

Gary was utterly aghast as he had no idea.

"I suppose you could stay in bed all day." She giggled and then quietly muttered, "Assuming you want to stay alive on your birthday."

While walking through the room, the eldest child, Rhys, having eaten earlier, overheard this and said, "Does staying in bed make you live longer?"

"No," came the reply in unison.

"Is that why you always try to get me out of bed so early in the morning?"

All three chuckled, and Gary decided to avoid his pet subject for the rest of the evening. It was a great introductory evening between Gary's family and Lando, cementing his relationship with Gary.

Chapter 3

Lando thought back to how it all started. He had been working at the university for about nine months when the business school Dean, Justin Crocker, announced in an open forum that the university had established a relationship with the British University in Dubai or BUiD as it was known. It was to become an outreach college for the university. He asked for anyone interested in teaching in Dubai by an all-staff email.

There were four deans in the business school after it became a separate unit of the university in its own right. One dean and three associate deans. They were to rotate, which, surprise, surprise, never actually happened. They were nicknamed the Dean, the Associate Dean, the Co-Dean and the Paracetamol. Typical university humour that did nothing to enhance the stature of the deans, of course.

Gary collared Lando one afternoon in early June during the university exam period after they had been invigilating together, trying to catch students with ever more ingenious methods of circumventing the 'closed book' principle of unseen examinations. They were not allowed outside notes or books to be brought into the examination, which included phones and tablets that could store information.

"Why do they do it, Gary?" complained Lando. "It is so risky and stupid, and some students create such ingenious methods that if they spent the same time on their studies as they did on their cheating methods, they would get a good mark legitimately."

Gary smiled. "It is simple, my little naive friend. They enjoy preparing their ways of cheating more than they enjoy your subject of accountancy. Now, if you taught a creative subject like statistics, they...."

"I am not having that–" interrupted Lando. "In any case, the risk is high to return in the summer and retake the subject. That should be enough incentive. I had one guy writing all the key formulae on a tiny piece of paper stuck to the back of a ruler. Impossible to read, but he could because he also had an extra pair of extremely powerful reading glasses on his desk. I happened to know because he never used glasses at my seminars, and he stupidly dropped his ruler in the examination, which landed upside down, and there was the paper on the back. Silly ass. He was quite contrite afterwards. I felt rather sorry for him in a paternal sort of way."

Over a scone and a cup of tea in the canteen, Gary brought up the subject of the work in Dubai. "Hey Lando, what do you think about a little trip to our new Middle Eastern friends in Dubai? It would suit you down to the ground. They need a lot of accountancy training there to count all their money?"

"No way. I am quite happy here, thanks. It was far too hot for me anyway, and I was not sure I could cope with all the cultural issues. If you know so much about it, why don't you go?"

"No chance. Megan would not like it, and being away from the kids for more than a few days would not suit me either. I would miss them too much. However, they do have some lovely hotels out there, and it is not as strict as some other Arab states as far as dress, behaviour and alcohol are concerned if you don't do anything stupid. I also believe the university will relieve your work here for a while and pay you a daily bonus for all the hours you teach there. The weather is also great during winter, but avoid July and August whatever you do. You're single, so really, there is no better time in your life to go."

Lando's eyes lit up. "How do you know that?"

"I did some work for the university in Abu Dhabi a couple of years ago, so I know how it works. It would be best if you negotiated, however. Justin will pay as little as he can get away with. Less for you means more margin for the business school."

"I get that. Maybe I can at least have a chat with him. I assume it depends on how many others want to teach my subject there."

"I doubt too many," said Gary through a mouthful of jammy scone, some of which was stuck above his top lip. "Colleagues prefer to pick up your work and earn a load of overtime than travel to the Gulf, particularly accountants. They are very risk averse," he said with a goading smile.

Lando let it slide but decided he would at least have a chat with Justin to see how the land lay and booked a meeting for the next day at 9.30 am through Hilda Clench, the Dean's power-driven, dozy secretary who wanted to know why he wished to see him and acted a bit like a doctor's receptionist trying to diagnose the severity of your illness before awarding you an appointment. Legend has it that she put on this act as the Dean had his leg over her at a Christmas party, and she had photographs to prove it. This gave her significant leverage regarding her hours, pay, bonuses and generally what else she could get away with in her behaviour. Amazing are the sources of power! Maybe she was not quite so dozy after all, but after hearing this story for the first time, Lando's estimation of the Dean went down a notch as she was hardly worth prejudicing a career for. Put it this way, if Helen of Troy looked as austere as her, she would have sunk a thousand ships rather than launched them. Come to think of it, Justin was not exactly God's gift in the looks department, so maybe they were suited to each other, at least for two to three minutes at a Christmas party together with a superabundance of cheap alcohol, overcooked Indian samosas, bhajis and dried out ham sandwiches.

Lando arrived in good time for the meeting and sat by Hilda's empty desk, worryingly with no sound of Justin in his office next door. He waited and waited, and at 9.40 Justin walked in straight through to his office, followed a few paces behind by Hilda, who smoothed straight her creased, red skirt with deliberation before sitting down and asking without looking at him what he was doing there whilst she accessed her computer diary.

She seemed flustered, and before he could answer, she said, "Ah, of course, you have a meeting with Justin. I shall see if he is ready for you."

She went to Justin's office, and a series of thoughts entered Lando's mind. Was their combined late entry a complete coincidence? Had they just been at it in the car park, the toilet, the library, the canteen or even on the roof? Had she got the Dean right where she wanted him, and the payoff was to be given a good seeing to on-demand?

Lando shook his head to remove some ghastly images from his mind before his meeting. Looking slightly flushed, she returned and announced regally, "The Dean is ready now."

I'll bet, thought Lando. He ambled through, feeling slightly bemused, but was determined to get the most out of this meeting with Justin.

Justin opened the conversation. "So, Lando, how has your first year been with us? Enjoying it, I trust as your student feedback is positive, and no issues from other staff members have been brought to my attention?"

Did he need that last part? A bit schoolmaster-like.

"It has been fine, Justin. I have felt quite at home here and enjoy the company of colleagues more than I expected. I don't feel as on my guard as I did during my days in the industry. That said, one or two need a bomb up them as I'm not sure they are fully focussed on what they need to teach."

"Oh, who might that be Lando?"

"I couldn't possibly say Justin. I'm sure you can get that from student feedback forms anyway."

There was no way that Lando was going to dump on colleagues. He was sure the Dean already knew who they were. Anyway, he would not do anything about it. He perceived the

Dean did not like choppy waters as he was also open to criticism in other 'personal relationship' issues.

"Yes, quite so. So, you want to teach in Dubai, then? That will be an experience for you. Have you considered what it entails and what time of year you wish to go?"

Underneath his poker face, Lando was smiling. He immediately knew there had yet to be any other applicants, and the only way Justin could encourage staff would be by leaning on them.

"I have been wondering what incentive you would give me for this work. Also, how long is one required out there? Where would one stay? What is the subject matter and level? With whom is the liaison in Dubai? Also... the little matter of... expenses?" He purposely used 'one' rather than 'I' to emphasise that he was not yet committed to taking it on. Rather than mention the word bonus or extra pay, he just left the word expenses hanging slowly in the air.

People do not generally come into academic life for money, but it is fair to say that everyone is up for any extras they can earn. Sometimes, it is because they need the money, but often, it is simply the acknowledgement of extra responsibility and work. Thankfully, Lando fell into the latter category as being single and having spent significant time in industry; he had put a bit aside, together with what his parents had willed to him after their demise all those years ago. When he realised what their old house fetched, coupled with the sale of the family business and added to their savings, he not only cried when he lost them but, having only one younger sister, Jennifer, he cried when he realised that he suddenly had an extra three-quarters of a million pounds even after paying inheritance taxes. He quickly paid off his mortgage on his very expensive flat, giving him the freedom of fewer outgoings. He cried for sadness, and he cried for joy at the same time. He would still rather have his parents back. He still missed them, and losing them before their lives had run their natural course removed that security blanket he had always had. He had closed off a little inside, which prevented him from having any deep relationships with the fairer sex. Probably, he was a little scared of losing that love in his life again.

"Look," said the Dean. "There are a ton of issues to be gone through, and this is an important role for you or someone else and could lead to greater things. The details we can iron out."

Here we go, thought Lando. It's jam tomorrow. No chance.

Justin looked at Lando and saw his face fall. "Firstly, are you interested if we get the expenses right, a quality hotel and clarity on what is required regarding course details and cover for your work here?"

Lando trod carefully here. There was no clear offer, and accepting a vague promise was not good enough, so he laid his demands on the table.

"OK. At a minimum, I shall need clarity of course content, a 5-star hotel, and an extra £300 per day pay, including travel time and weekends. All meals paid for and any other out-of-pocket expenses."

Justin blanched. If he had others who would take on the role, he would not have looked so forlorn. He shuffled his papers together and then went into the side drawer of his desk and pulled out a piece of paper.

"Lando, I understand your request, but it is outside our budget. I cannot clarify the course content today, but that is, to some degree, up for discussion as it will also need to be passed by our quality committee. As for your wage bonus, we cannot go beyond £300 per day, not including travel time and weekends. However, we can give you time off in lieu after you return to England. As for the hotel, the best I can do is give you veto rights. Sometimes the course will be held in a hotel meeting room rather than the college, so we cannot move on that one. As for other expenses, with proper receipts submitted, I do not see a problem. What do you think?"

"Justin, I need to think about it. Can you give me a little time? I shall give you an answer on Monday. How would that be?"

"OK, Lando, that's fine. If you have any questions, email me, and I shall do my best to answer them."

Standing up, Lando thanked Justin for his candour and left. He walked past a smiling Hilda who was up from her desk, briskly striding towards the Dean's office as he visualised her starched underclothes rasping against her thighs with each step. Surely not again, thought Lando, and then he dismissed another ghastly scene from his mind.

Chapter 4

Lando thought about it for a couple of days over the weekend. He rather liked Justin as he was very affable, but he always played the political game, and consequentially, Lando did not fully trust his motives or his word, for that matter. He would promise anything to get a job done, and whilst he may have meant it at the time, he did not have the backbone to make good on his promises if the wind changed direction, a regular occurrence in academia.

He had a relaxing weekend. He went out on a few walks. He watched an old war film on television. He cooked an excellent Sunday lunch of roast duck for himself, which he planned on using as leftovers for sandwiches the following week. He opened a fine-quality bottle of wine, one of the few remaining from his father's old wine cellar. A lovely oaked red from the Languedoc region. All in all, he felt pretty good, so why was that? He didn't usually feel good when he had an important decision to make until he had made it, and he tried to reason why. Then it came to him. He was excited for the first time in a long time about going to a region of the world to work, albeit for a short period, where he could engage with people of different cultures. He only ever saw Arabs depicted on the news as terrorists firing rifles in the air, shouting about Allah and how they were doing His work. Alternatively, they are so wealthy that they can buy whole football clubs in the Premier League from pocket change. They cannot all be like that, he thought. He knew at the back of his mind that he had decided to go, and it fired him up.

***

Monday came along, and although he wanted to confirm with the Dean straightaway that he wished to go to Dubai, he decided to wait until the afternoon to play the negotiation game. He hoped he was still in the pound seats, assuming no other applicants. That being the case, he would be better positioned to confirm terms, mainly if Justin thought Lando was having second thoughts. His main target was to get a written agreement so he could commence his preparation for the trip with a degree of clarity.

He met Justin, who said, "Great news, the other side is paying for your first module to be in an excellent hotel to launch the course, but do not get ideas it will be that good each time."

He always had to put a downer in at the end.

It all went through a little too quickly for Lando's liking, and he felt he might have got more out of the deal, but at the end of the day, he was pleased to go and see a different part of the world. It transpired that BUiD University required his presence in mid-October for one month to cover his module, doing four days of lectures a week on a postgraduate Master's course and engaging in discussions to develop further finance modules. So, he realised he did not have much time to think about it, and he needed to sort his lectures out quickly, and they would print his slide copies and notes in Dubai to save him transporting them all. That sounded like a great idea, and he was given the contact details of two people at the college. One was a Swedish expat named Claes Sundberg, who had lived in Dubai for 10 years. He was the current overall course manager. Lando knew nothing else about him. The second contact was a senior employee of the college, a Dubai national called Qasim Sarawi, who supposedly oversaw the financial aspects of the college and acted as liaison between the academics and the executive board, made up of longstanding scholars led by the college principal, not much else to go on.

He was provisionally booked into the Hyatt Regency Hotel in Deira, close to the Waterfront, a few minutes walk from the Creek. Apparently, this was a natural seawater inlet separating the commercial areas of Deira and Bur Dubai. He would fly out economy class overnight on Friday, arriving early Saturday morning, leaving the day to acclimatise before meeting his Dubai contacts on Sunday, with lecturing commencing on Monday in a hotel conference room, which was convenient. He just needed to confirm it. He could barely wait as excitement was getting the better of him. He decided to go out for a beer with Gary as soon as possible to have a good chat about the do's and don'ts in the Middle East, or more specifically, the Emirates, as he knew nothing about them or even their history beyond anything he may have picked up from watching the David Lean's film Lawrence of Arabia twenty or so years ago on the TV, and that was based on a period a hundred years ago. He vowed to watch it again before leaving to understand the history.

That Friday lunchtime, he met Gary at the Dog and Doublet, and he filled him in on all that had transpired with the Dean whilst struggling to take his eyes off the delectable Amber. She seemed to have such an effortless way of simultaneously serving customers and putting a smile on their faces. Lando was still working on his approach to Amber as he needed to figure out the best way to go on a date with her, or even if that was possible. He knew she was not married, but that was about it. Anyway, he had more important things to discuss with Gary.

He was bursting with questions for him. "Hey Gary, so tell me what you think. Will I survive this trip? How long is the flight? Do I need a Visa? How do I get safely from the airport to the hotel? Are there people looking to kidnap me from the minute I land? What is the currency there? What things will I get arrested for?"

"Lando, Lando, Lando. Slow down. You are not going to Saudi Arabia; you are going to the most westernised state in the Middle East. It has been mainly developed through funding from the government of Abu Dhabi. Dubai has very little oil of its own, but it has refining facilities, which do not bring in anything like the revenue that the oil finds in Abu Dhabi bring in. Consequently, Dubai has become a significant trading hub in the Middle East with fantastic airport capacity, a tourist attraction, and a considerable trading capacity. It is where many well-off people from other Arab states go to have a good time! That should keep you happy, Lando."

"OK, all right. I am just getting a bit excited. Can you tell me anymore then?"

"Well, the country of Dubai is an Emirate, one of seven which make up the United Arab Emirates or UAE. The President of the UAE appoints the Head of State for each Emirate, which in Dubai's case is Sheikh Mohammed bin Rashid Al Maktoum."

"That's a mouthful," interjected Lando.

"Get a load of this then. The president's name is Khalifa bin Zayed Al Nahyan, the Emir of Abu Dhabi. All the heads of state have absolute authority and are Emirs - Monarchs in our language. Hence Emirates"

"So why does the Emir of Abu Dhabi become president of the UAE? I'm guessing it is the largest of the Emirates."

"Bang on, boyo. It occupies over 80% of the landmass of the UAE and, of course, has the most oil and, therefore, the most money. I shouldn't try and take it all in as, for one thing, we will get through at least 5 pints of beer before I'm halfway telling you all about it. I may not even be up to date, but I don't think much has changed since I was there, although the working week has significantly changed from Sunday–Thursday to Monday–Friday.

"Why is that?" Lando asked as he slurped through his beer.

"Friday is their Holy day. People go off for prayer with their families throughout the day. However, the public sector employees tend to finish Friday lunch to preserve this spiritual holiday feel. It fits better with the international trade done on a Friday, which is critical to Dubai's development. Dubai is the name of the main city and the entire Emirate, and I would guess 90% of the population lives there."

"So, what's the population then?"

"Over 3 million. However, only about 15% of the population are native residents. The rest are expats, primarily from Asia. India mostly," responded Gary expansively, like he was leading a student group. "The bulk of the Western expatriates are from the UK. I guess this dates to the entire UAE being under British protection from the 1800s until 1971 when it was revoked, and the UAE was formed."

Lando marvelled at Gary's memory for any statistic, boring or not, but it was all new to Lando. And so they chatted throughout the evening, supping a fair few pints, Gary with his straight glass and Lando with his mug. Both had to get taxis home that evening, and Lando didn't envy Gary's arrival home to a meal that was probably now in the dog rather than the oven.

***

The days came and went quickly for Lando as he was so busy preparing his work for Dubai, putting him under constant time pressure and preparing lectures for his return. He barely had time to keep fit, which he usually did by revisiting his old dojo at least once a week to keep his karate skills up to date. He had no desire to thump anyone, but he always came away drenched in sweat and glad to be alive. He had fewer injuries during karate training than in Sunday league football. For some reason, if he dribbled around an opposition player and did not pass the ball within five paces, he was usually scythed down by the knees.

He remembered one ref saying, "Your mother could ride a tackle better than that." He had got as far as a brown belt in his Shotokan karate style but felt that he would need to push himself too much to take it up to the black belt, and the commitment would increase beyond what he was prepared to give, including improving his chances of getting hurt in a tournament. It always seemed foolish to Lando to train in self-defence and find that you were more likely to be injured as you advanced through your training belts.

That said, it kept him strong and phenomenally fit, sharp, well-balanced and very supple. As for the Mensa or Amber challenge, he decided those needed to be on the backburner until he returned from Dubai. He had procrastinated too long over Amber as he was in no hurry to ruin his lovely relationship with her on his Friday lunches. He had significant doubts about whether he could speak rationally to her on a date without dribbling all down his shirt. He felt sad at how his lack of confidence made him procrastinate over things he wanted to do. Sometimes, he despised his weaknesses.

It wouldn't be long until he left for Dubai, but little did he realise what would befall him, not even in his wildest dreams... or nightmares.

Chapter 5

October came, and he was only a few days away from leaving for Dubai… aaaaah. The Middle East. The Arabic call to prayer, the heat, the sand, the smells, the rich food, the street vendors, the well-stocked shops, the clothing. Lando recognised that he had no clue how he would react to this new climate, people, and way of life.

As he had no lectures to give on Wednesday and Thursday, he took those days off and had a bit of a lie-in. He got up, showered, put on his favourite pair of jeans, and looked in the mirror. He guessed he was not a bad-looking guy, still had all his thick hair, was pretty fit, and whilst his muscles weren't bulging, they were undoubtedly well-defined. He was average height, five foot nine, and thankfully didn't have to wear glasses, and his jet-black eyebrows and hair gave him quite a striking look. At least that was his opinion! He wondered why some gorgeous gal had not made a beeline for him and proposed to him years ago. There again, he probably knew that because he wasn't ready for that kind of commitment, although he liked the idea one day. After flexing his muscles a few times, he put on the rest of his clothing and went downstairs. He looked around and thought he was lucky to have such a luxurious two-storey flat in a lovely area.

It was roomy and had a spare room and a big open plan sitting room, dining room, and kitchen, all rolled into one, and of course, a bathroom, which was all he wanted. What was nice was that Lando could clean a house that size, not that he enjoyed it very much. He had a good breakfast of bacon and egg and some great Brazilian coffee beans ground in his state-of-the-art coffee machine. A gift from his sister, Jennifer, last Christmas. He felt good and decided to get his old travel bag from the loft. He went upstairs, lowered the loft ladder, and climbed up. Unsurprisingly, he found his dark blue travel bag covered in dust. He chucked it down the ladder and followed it. Aargh. The mice had been at it. He unzipped it, and inside, they had just bitten right through it and even had the temerity to set up home there, although now long gone and moved house; what a waste.

One of the wheels was missing from the bag's underside, so he decided to sling it and shop for a new one. He walked into Shrewsbury town centre to seek a large bright red travel bag with wheels and a handle to make life easy for his first trip to the Middle East. Antler was the only brand he had heard of for travel bags, so he bought one. The power of brands, eh? He guessed it would at least give him some minimum level of quality, not least because of its price. It also helped that a young, pretty blonde shop assistant smiled at him as he tried to decide what to buy. She didn't know any more than he did about travel bags. He asked her what she would buy, and she pointed at a pink one. He was not crazy about a pink bag, but he guessed it would be friendly and easy to spot at an airport as the other colours were dark but classier. However, he supposed it would show his feminine side.

"Right," he said. "I shall have the pink one."

"Actually, sir, we call it blush," saying this she immediately blushed bright red, and he struggled not to laugh out loud. He had wanted to make her smile when he made the purchase, which he did, particularly when he asked her to gift-wrap it, and she looked askance at him until she saw he was trying to smother another laugh. If he had more time, he would have lingered and chatted to her as, whilst he often felt awkward with women, for some reason, this girl seemed very comfortable with him, which put him at ease. Of course, she was paid to do that with probably a little sales commission from her £200 sale.

He went home, pulling his bag behind him, and it pulled smoothly. Well, it would do, wouldn't it? It was empty! He was determined to fill it with all manner of things for every eventuality he might encounter in Dubai. However, he did not know what he would need beyond the basics of clothing and other travel requirements like medicines and a sponge bag. If he had known, he would have packed a couple of hand grenades, a machine gun, a flak jacket, a Rambo knife, and a helmet, or maybe he would not have gone at all.

He spent the next day checking over what was needed. He confirmed that BUiD University was happy with his printing requirements, packed one hard copy of his student notes and slides, and ensured a full copy of everything was on a memory stick. He liked to be double covered, which he put down to his cautious training in accountancy. *Prepare for the worst and hope for the best.* Come to think of it, that was pretty much his mother's mantra when he was little. He often chatted with his sister about that, and they had decided that their mum did not want them to be too disappointed in life if it did not go their way. The big problem with that thinking was that it made him slightly pessimistic about life, even before the proverbial hit the fan. The expectation was that the proverbial could not miss the fan! Still, he missed his mother and father, who were good people. They rarely raised their voices to him and never hit him, although he often thought his banishment to prep school at the tender age of seven was tantamount to child abuse. It was not as if he was particularly difficult or naughty. In fairness, he did learn how to play rugby and ignore the pipe-smoking geography teacher who, when he called you up to the desk in class to run through your work, would rub his hand up and down the back of your bare legs in a manner that seemed to be well outside the school curriculum. This guy eventually left the school, no doubt because of his terrible breath from smoking his pipe. God knows what was in it. Lando's mum and dad never understood why he was so excited to return to school when he turned eleven and was allowed to wear long trousers.

He checked his tickets, passport, local currency in dirhams, maps, contact information, hotel confirmation letter, phone, iPad and laptop, and required chargers and adapters. Now, he felt happy in his illusion of control. Excitement tinged with a slight apprehension of going into the unknown. What the hell? It is not precisely Star Trek. Space: the final frontier. These are the voyages of the Starship Enterprise. Its five-year mission: to explore strange new worlds. To seek out new life and new civilisations. To boldly go where no man has gone before! What's so bad about a split infinitive anyway? He was about to find out!

He did not sleep well that night as he pictured everything that could go wrong with his trip. He even got up and had a good slug of scotch to help ease him into his slumbers. At about three o'clock, he fell into a light sleep and dreamt of an Arab lady in full attire wearing a Niqab covering her whole face. Only her eyes were visible, and they were beautifully made up, promising what might be to come. She slowly peeled it back, and her face was like the face of Medusa, one of the three monstrous Gorgons from Greek mythology with venomous snakes in place of hair, and those gazing into her eyes would turn to stone. He awoke again in a cold sweat and got up for another Scotch. This time, he took a slug of his fifteen-year-old Glenlivet. He was shaking all over. Why on Earth would he dream like that? He was not that much of a worrier. That night, he had an overactive imagination. Eventually, sleep washed over him.

The next day, Friday was slow. He slept in, but he was ready to go when he awoke. All he had to do was order a taxi to Birmingham International to catch the direct flight to Dubai via Emirates Airlines, leaving at 9:40 pm. That meant leaving home at around 6.30.

He ate fresh grilled Manx kippers for breakfast, sourdough bread from the German baker, Bakehouse & Co. down the road and a small pot of Colombian coffee. He was ready to go by midday, which left him over 6 hours to kill. He decided to go to his local dojo for a workout. There were no classes that day, but they also had a small gymnasium by the dojo, and somehow, the atmosphere helped him train properly, which never seemed to happen at home. One by one, he went through all his forms or katas, from the first belt up to the required kata for his last brown and white belt. It amused people sometimes when they saw these being done without an opponent, but the key was to completely believe that there was an opponent in front of you, giving you the instinct to perform your kata with total focus. Lando always found this absorbing, leaving him drained but relaxed–quite the opposite of how he felt before. He did a few reps on the weights and showered, and by the time he had walked home, it had turned 3 pm, so he settled down with a cup of tea and an old black and white movie on the box to kill time until the taxi arrived.

It arrived early, driven by a guy who had only been in the country for 6 months, having managed to emigrate from Afghanistan with his family and resettle. Lando did his best to help him get through Shrewsbury, where his Sat Nav would help him get to Birmingham International. He made good time, and Lando gave him an extra tenner, partly out of compassion but mostly because he liked the guy's optimistic view of life. Lando thanked God he did not have to go through what some people went through. He had indeed been fortunate in how he came into this world.

All went well at the airport; the flight was on time, and he settled happily into his aircraft seat until a huge, poorly shaven Arabic-looking guy dressed in jeans and a tee shirt came and sat next to him, and his buttocks flowed off his seat and partly onto Lando's. This did not bode well for the next seven hours. Lando wriggled to one side of his seat by the window in a vain attempt to create space where there was not any. He felt like a planet being sucked into a massive black hole with no chance of escape. The plane smoothly took off–a feat Lando doubted could happen with this guy next to him on board. But take off it did and climbed steeply and levelled out. His big neighbour was sweating profusely, and when the plane levelled out, he was noticeably relaxed.

He turned to Lando, smiling, and spoke while offering his hand. "Hey, up lad, that be a good take-off. They're all good take-offs for me if the plane stays up. Name's Dillon. Dillon Hargreaves."

The broad Yorkshire accent floored Lando briefly, but he held it together long enough to shake hands. "Hi, I'm Roland Westwood. Glad to know you. Looked like you were about to pass out. Sure you are OK?"

"Yep. Just a simple fear of flying. Nay idea why, as nowt else worries me much, but flying, combined with the ear pressure, feels plain horrific. Maybe it is because I am not in control."

"Could be, but you are still doing it. Why are you going to Dubai?"

"I am going to see my mum's family. My dad's from Leeds, my mum is from Dubai, and I ain't seen 'er family in their 'ouse in years." He looked around, turned back, and smiled again at Lando. "We are in luck. The seat by me appears vacant, so I will move into it and give us both room. I really need 1½ seats on an aeroplane as they only cater to Mr Average. I guess it's understandable unless you are my size. Tried for years to lose weight, and finally, I'm cured." Lando looked at him quizzically as he moved seats. The huge frame, the huge backside, the huge arms and thighs. "I thought you said you were cured."

"I am," he replied. "I just don't care anymore."

Lando burst out laughing and knew he would get on with Dillon, even more so now that he was a seat away. They chatted for half an hour whilst the majestic hostesses served their dinner. Emirates certainly had some beautiful ones, and even though the food was reasonable, he was too taken by how graceful and well-dressed they were in their fawn suits, red hats, white scarves, and flawless makeup. He wondered what their real story was. Maybe some were trying their luck, hoping to catch the eye of a wealthy, generous Sheikh.

They both became a little sleepy after dinner, not least because they had a few glasses of very palatable red wine with their dinners. Dillon passed a personal contact card onto Lando if he needed any help in Dubai as he was there for a few weeks; although he did not know much about the place, his mother's family presumably did. Lando reciprocated with his university card, which included his mobile number. He decided to try to sleep, as even though he considered an in-flight movie on the back of the seat in front of him, the rude lout in front decided to recline his chair fully without any reference to the effect on the passenger behind. Lando had a terrifying image of Dillon leaning over the lout and casually sitting right on his face and farting. Sadly, he doubted that would happen but gently laughed himself to sleep.

Chapter 6

Lando awoke with light streaming through his Airbus 380 window. He saw the beautiful blue sky and the waters below. He heard the pilot's proud tone as he chatted over the intercom, giving everyone information about ETA, landing procedures, visas, etc. He wished them all a wonderful visit to Dubai. *Does he really care?* thought Lando. He supposed it was better than being silent before landing. It was 8 am local time and fifteen minutes to go. Thankfully, only a few minutes after the scheduled landing time. He used some spare water to splash his face and wake up. A paper tissue in the seat back was helpful. He did a few deep breathing exercises and hoped that he was not sucking some other person's bacteria into his lungs. He remembered all those ski holidays years ago when several of the party either got a cold within three days of getting there or got one three days after getting home. That recycled air was not very sanitary. The alternative was probably the airlines charging more to capture the scarce fresh oxygen from 30,000 feet up and feed that into the cabins.

What had happened to Dillon? He was not in his seat and could hardly have gone ahead. He was beginning to miss that great big hunk of a Yorkshireman, and he had not known him very long. He missed his crazy laugh and humour apart from anything else. Maybe he had found another seat...or two.

The plane landed with a thump, and the engine reverse thrusters made a terrific noise as they braked hard. Slowly, they taxied towards their allocated terminal, and the seat belt signs went off. Suddenly, Dillon arrived with one of the cabin crew looking most displeased. Lando asked him what had happened; apparently, he felt sick. He had fallen asleep on the toilet and only woke with the thump of the wheels touching down, despite a couple of cabin crew banging on the door.

They grabbed their cabin cases, and Dillon's fell on his head when he opened the overhead locker. There was stuff all over the seat, and he hurriedly scrabbled it into his bag, but not before Lando noticed a map of Dubai with several hand-drawn crosses. Lando remarked on it, and Dillon became rather shifty. He just said they were places he wanted to visit in Dubai. Lando would have thought no more of it, but Dillon's strange look around the cabin with darting eyes concerned him. It seemed out of character.

He put it out of his mind, and they disembarked together, but not before Dillon had to sit down halfway up the aisle to allow a cabin crew member past, as his great bulk would not allow anyone to pass him. He felt the comfort of Dillon's card sporting his mobile number, and they agreed they might meet up in a week when they had both settled in.

Lando disembarked and made his way to the magnificent airport baggage area, and after a short wait, his big pinky-red Antler case plopped onto the baggage carousel and made its way towards him. He breathed a small sigh of relief and was glad he had bought an easily identifiable bag. He grabbed it and felt a little lightheaded but guessed it would wear off. He just needed to navigate the passport entry and find a taxi to take him to his hotel, and then he could relax a little. He looked for Dillon unsuccessfully, so he stood in the passport queue to await his turn. No complications, and his visa was a simple stamp in his passport. This gave him 30 days in Dubai, which was fine, as his teaching ended within three weeks. So, little time to take in the sights afterwards!

He got to the exit doors and wheeled his case through, hitting a wall of heat. It was half past nine in the morning, so he was glad it was no later as he was not used to hot climates, although, like most Brits, he liked to bask in the sun now and again. People were scrambling around to get a taxi at the official taxi rank, although there seemed to be plenty. Then he noticed a tall, powerful Asian guy standing by a barrier with a placard printed as Roland Westwood–Hyatt Hotel. Great! He was not expecting that one.

He introduced himself to the man, who replied, "My name is Gajbaahu, but everyone calls me Gaji." He had a beautiful, melodious Indian accent, and his head wobbled happily from side to side as he spoke with a smile. "Compliments of the Hotel, sir, as it is your first time staying with us. I have a car parked just over there, ready to take you to the cool of the hotel. It is a very good hotel, very, very, very good actually." He grabbed Lando's bag and hand luggage before Lando could object and strode towards the white 6-seater van with Hyatt Regency written on the side.

Lando had packed his sunglasses but had foolishly not kept them with him, having escaped the rainy drizzle in

Birmingham. He shielded his eyes against the morning sun as he approached the car.

"Don't touch the door, sir, very, very hot. By lunchtime, it will be very, very, very, very, very, very, very hot." He grabbed the rear door handle and slid it back, and Lando got in, carrying only his laptop as he did not wish to risk it going out of sight. It could really mess up his teaching if he lost it, despite his backup memory stick.

The door slid back, Gaji got in behind the wheel, and off they went. Gaji could not stop talking all the way, and even though the journey was less than 15 minutes, Lando learnt that he lived in quarters just outside the hotel along with many of the staff, and he sent most of his wages back to his family in Bombay, India. He had been in Dubai only 3 years and was very lucky to get this job as his cousin, a porter at the hotel, put in a good word for him.

Lando raised an eyebrow at the use of the name Bombay, and Gaji responded, "I grew up calling it Bombay, and many still call it that now, even though it was renamed Mumbai in 1995 to remove the British Colonial connections."

"Aha. We have a lot to answer for, don't we?" said Lando apologetically.

At the end of the chat, although chat was not the word as Lando could barely get a word in edgeways, Gaji said, "Anything, anything at all I can find for you, sir–alcohol, girls, places, knock-off watches, pubs, restaurants, more girls, shisha bars–anything at all. I'm very, very, very good at it. Just come to me and no one else."

"You said girls twice," smiled Lando, half-guessing the response.

"I like girls," laughed Gaji.

No doubt Gaji had a deal with the suppliers of all of them. Good luck to him, as his wages were probably embarrassingly low. He was the second good guy he had met on his journey, and he was beginning to feel right at home in Dubai and had not even gotten to his hotel.

Chapter 7

The hotel reception area blew Lando away. There were cushions the size of snooker tables scattered around at the far end just for relaxing on with coffee tables and an enormous what looked like a tropical fish tank embedded into the wall with the variegated patterns on the fish catching his eye as they effortlessly cruised around the tank, no doubt looking for scraps of food on the sandy floor. These fish were way bigger than anything he had seen in a tank back in Blighty. The coolness of the air conditioning was such a welcome feeling. It was still very bright, and he wanted to kick himself again for leaving his sunglasses in his main bag. There was no queue at reception, and he checked in with a very efficient man to his room number 737 and a porter, to whom Gaji had handed his bags after he palmed his card into Lando's hand, followed him with a tall trolley up to his room on the seventh floor.

The porter meticulously and deferentially went through everything in the room. He showed him the bathroom, how the air conditioning worked, how to phone reception, how to get the TV working and pretty much everything he needed. Lando declined his offer to unpack his bags and tipped him a few dirhams, eliciting a big smile, and he quickly left with the door closing automatically behind him.

Lando surveyed the room. It was more of a suite. The double bed was enormous, flaunting four colossal pillows. Strangely, the bathroom was in the middle of the bedroom, visible through glass walls. It was like an island in the room but without a toilet, which was privately separated. He walked over to the main windows, opened the blinds and slid back the door.

It was now 11 am, and the heat was rising, so he quickly skipped onto his balcony, took in the magnificent view of the surrounding buildings, the sea and the azure sky and went back in, speedily sliding shut the door to keep the cool in. His head started to spin, and he realised how tired he was after the travel. He was a little hungry, but he thought he would lie down for five minutes on those luxurious pillows of the elaborate bed before going downstairs to have breakfast.

Three hours later, he woke up still fully clothed and completely disorientated. At least his dizziness had gone, and he was left with a strange spaced-out feeling, but he was also ravenous. He quickly unpacked, had an excellent shower, whilst looking furtively through the glass to ensure he was alone. He put on something casual over his swimming trunks and thankfully found his sunglasses. They were Ray-Bans and one of life's luxuries, which he appreciated every time he wore them. They just somehow felt right. Off he went to the restaurant to be told it had now closed, but there were food snacks at the Club Olympus Pool Bar on the second floor.

He made his way there, found a sunbed under a leaf-shaded structure, and settled in. Within 2 minutes, a waiter arrived. As he laid out the towels, he said Lando could order food at the poolside bar and eat it there, or he would bring it. Lando thought he would take it at the poolside bar and eat sitting down properly. He was not fond of eating in a crouched position. So, after donning his flip-flops as the floor tiles were red hot, he ventured over to the bar. It was indeed a very grand bar for an outside pool bar. The menus looked expensively produced and were all printed in gold on black. One look at the menu and he knew what he was having. Giant battered prawns with a side order of fries and a large glass of Heineken. Just the job.

The beer arrived like a magic trick in front of him, with the froth slowly making its way down the side of the pre-cooled glass. The barman looked at him with pride as Lando took his first precious gulp. He was about 60 years old, of African origin and about Lando's height. However, the bar floor was raised to put him well above most customers' height. It was quiet, and the two of them talked.

"How long you here?" asked the barman.

"Oh, less than a month. Name's Lando, by the way. I should be getting to know you well by the end of it, as I love swimming... and beer, of course."

"I can tell. Watching your face as you took the first sip spoke to me."

"And what did the face say to you?"

"It said, I am a very thirsty face, also a very hungry face. Haii, haii, haii." His laugh was like the bellow of a water buffalo.

Lando laughed with him and asked his name.

"It is Suleiman. S-U-L-E-I-M-A-N," he spelt it. "I was named after Suleiman the Magnificent. He was a Sultan in the Ottoman Empire."

"Oh, why were you named after him then?"

"No idea. I guess my father just liked the old stories about him."

"So Suleiman, I guess that is Soloman in my language. Are you as wealthy as him?"

"Haii, haii, haii," he laughed again. "Not quite yet, sir. However, everyone here calls me Solly, which I am happy about."

"Well, Solly, my friend.' Lando felt magnanimous after nearly finishing his first beer. "Hit me again."

Solly's eyes went wild as he stumbled over his words. "Solly … not … hit you once, sir. Solly does not hit people."

Now it was Lando's turn to laugh like a drain as he conveyed the meaning of the expression to be 'asking for another drink.'

Solly visibly relaxed and they chatted away whilst Lando sipped away at his beer and gorged himself on the newly arrived garlic prawns and fries. They could have been the best he had ever tasted. He told Solly a little of his background and Solly reciprocated. His family had come from Zanzibar originally, going back a few hundred years. He described an island off the East coast of Africa that had been a part of the Omani empire when sailors would travel by sea on the South Westerly trade winds in April/May. His father had taken the family over 2,000 miles up to Oman as there was little work on the island and they had lived and worked in the capital city of Muscat until Solly moved with his wife 30 years ago to Dubai.

"Why did you move?" enquired Lando between slurps.

"Nuttin to do. Dere is work dere, but little entertainment and it not develop much outside Muscat. Boring."

"Plenty of work in Dubai, I guess. I bet you have seen some changes."

"I have. And not all good, sir."

"No formalities, call me Lando, please."

"Don't feel right. Maybe I call you Lando when no one near us. Is that good?"

"Very good." Lando realised he might get into trouble by being too familiar with the guests. Jobs were easy to lose in the Emirate States but not so easy to get unless related to someone in authority or doing building work several hundred feet up with dubious health and safety controls.

Lando signed his room tab with a flourish and left a suitable few dirhams for the happy Solly. He drifted over to where his towels had been laid out, removed his shirt and shoes and dove straight into the pool's deep end. The feel of the cool water skimming over his hot body, lowering at least his surface skin temperature, was an almost ecstatic pleasure, and he did not emerge until he had touched the wall tiles at the other end. He only felt like swimming a few lengths before another wave of sleepiness overcame him, and he longed to return to his luxurious bedroom. He was so glad he had come a day early to settle in. He could at least be clear-headed for his meeting the next day.

He retired to his room at about 3 pm and again slept like a dead man.

Lando woke at 6 pm again a little peckish and in the mood for a little wander into the city. Donning his linen trousers, a nice cool shirt and leather, open-toed sandals, he ventured to the lift and down to the lobby to see the concierge for advice on where to go for a simple meal.

"Well, sir, what sort of food would you like? European, Arabic or something else?"

Lando kept it simple and went for European, and the concierge gave him a little coloured map, marked a few restaurants on it and offered a taxi, which Lando declined as he felt like taking a short walk to clear his head since the restaurants were close.

He departed to a well-practised 'Have a good evening, sir,' and the doorman whipped open the door before Lando could grab the handle. He almost fell through it, and off he went toward the Delicious Dine-In Restaurant, the first name on the map. He had to go down 27th St and left onto Naif St. He didn't like the sound of that. The spelling was OK, but he felt distinctly unsafe when he mouthed the name. He conjured up visions of the old Arabian Nights stories of violent bearded men in swirling robes flashing their curved scimitars and knives. He changed his mind quickly and decided to look for another bar or restaurant on the 4G map on his phone that would better suit him. The Chelsea Arms! He never expected to find the

Chelsea Arms in Deira, Dubai. What a blessing. He followed the dots on his phone map down 27th Street onto Al Maktoum Rd and finally, Baniyas Road. It was a 2½ kilometre walk, which took him about a half hour, and it was right by the humming area of the Creek. He took in all the aromas that lingered in the warm night air, of which many were the cooking smells of street food, which were very seductive. Koftas, barbequed chicken, and plenty of french fries–his mouth was watering.

Once around the bend, he was dazzled by a huge hotel with the Sheraton Dubai Creek Hotel sign. It had enough light for a small village, and then he realised from his phone that the Chelsea Arms was inside the hotel. It was a part of it, which was not exactly the sort of pub he was after, but he was getting a bit peckish now and decided to risk it. A discreet sign inside advertised it as the oldest British pub in Dubai and it was situated on the Upper Lobby level by the Arabian Carpet shop. Lando was warm from his walk and ready for a pint, which he duly ordered. He sat at a table and looked around. Everything seemed brand new: great big TVs for football, no doubt, and probably more accessible and likely to be cheaper to watch the Premier League in Dubai than in England! The pint duly arrived, and it was a special draught beer–Camel's Hump– presumably local and not one he had heard of. Well, he didn't expect a pint of Doombar, which they served at his local in Shrewsbury. A couple of large gulps, and within a few minutes, he felt once more at peace with the world. He took in the velvet-covered seats within the half curtains that made it look vaguely like a train carriage, and in one sense, it was a nostalgic view of 'the British pub.' He ordered a steak sandwich with caramelised onions and a side order of fries. He couldn't help himself. Whenever he saw fries on the menu, Lando caved in.

The waiter was extremely polite, although lacking in the required banter of a proper English pub. Life was suddenly great. Beer in his hand, food on the way, sitting in an English pub. What more could a man want? Well, he could think of something. Rather someone. The voluptuous Amber from the Dog and Doublet sprang to mind. He wanted to win that bet with Gary, not the Mensa one! One date and one smacking kiss would do it. As the waiter walked away, he noticed someone across the room in the half-light at a table by the wall. A large man was talking animatedly to another man, gesticulating wildly. He was extremely upset and then he heard the name Ashiraf used. As the large man turned his head, Lando realised he knew him; it was Dillon from the aeroplane. He would know him anywhere because of his size, but he was not expecting to see him, so he had not put two and two together earlier. He was about to go over to him, but Dillon's expression made him pull back. Lando realised that the expression was one of fear. The two men got up to go, and Lando turned his head away to make sure he was not recognised as Dillon's situation seemed very unusual and not one that Lando fancied being involved with. The other man, although dressed in casual European clothing, was Arabic, with a short dark beard and heavy glasses. He was short in stature and walked with a slight limp. However, there was also a distinct air of menace about him. Lando wondered what Dillon had got himself into, or maybe this guy was just a family member, but he didn't think so. They left, and Lando relaxed, tried to put the little scene out of his mind, and resumed his chilled-out wait for overfilling his stomach, which he fully intended to do.

The meal arrived, and he ordered another beer. Then, he began emptying the contents of his plate and the separate little basket laden with fries. It did not take him long to finish the food, and he became sleepy, resolving to head back to his hotel, probably getting a taxi as he was not in the mood for a long walk. The bill arrived, and he was not sleepy anymore! He hadn't fully taken in the cost of the meal as it was in dirhams, but when he converted the 200 dirhams to pounds Sterling, it was £40 at about five dirhams to the pound. Quite a lot for a snack with a couple of beers. Thank God for his credit card. He took a taxi back to his hotel and went straight to his room but felt distinctly uneasy after seeing Dillon's discomfort in the pub. He would have to forget it; otherwise, he would never get to sleep. He needed to be in his top form in the morning as his meeting with the guys from the college was at 10.00 am in the lobby. He refreshed his knowledge about them from his notes. Little to go on. Claes Sundberg was in the academia; Lando had googled him, and before his 10 years at the college, he had lectured in many places worldwide, including Stockholm, Abu Dhabi, Qatar, Kuala Lumpur and Moscow, primarily in digital marketing, but he had settled in Dubai. He could find nothing about Qasim Sarawi. It was like the guy didn't exist except deeply embedded in the BUiD University website under the administration heading, at least he had an email. He hoped tomorrow would bring lots of information and help him settle, so he showered before getting into his big fluffy bed and opened his John Grisham novel on page one, before falling asleep before page two!

***

Qasim Sarawi leant back in his armchair with an excited smile as he slowly stirred the slice of lemon in his glass of hot sweet tea. He looked at Hamza and Farouk, two out of the other three around the table waiting for his thoughts. Both were in filthy dishdashas, and he was ashamed to be sitting in this old, respectable café with them at the same time as the junior minister.

Shazil Haroun Al Maktoum was a distant cousin of the Emir Sheikh Mohammed. He was desperate to make a name for himself in government and was tasked with tightening security in Dubai. Although he was not actually in charge of security, the responsibility fell on a close family member, Sheikh Massoud bin Rashid Al Maktoum, the minister for Security. There was a mutual lack of respect between them. There had been significant family tensions over the years, and Sheikh Massoud had as good as told Shazil that he was unlikely to progress his career without a marked improvement in his creative ideas to improve the security in Dubai, particularly since the drone attack on Abu Dhabi by the Houthis in 2022.

Sheikh Massoud liaised with friends in similar positions in Abu Dhabi and the UAE Head of Security. Still, he never asked Shazil to accompany him, which irritated him as his family was very keen that he enhance his political and personal reputation by embracing his essential role. However, intelligent though he was, he was always looking for shortcuts as hard work was neither in his DNA nor indeed in his upbringing as he permanently thought the world owed him a millionaire's lifestyle. Having been born just outside the direct lineage of the ruling family, he was constantly irritated by and resented those with higher status and wealth than himself. He consequently found it hard to work within a structured organisation such as the Ministry for Security. He started to speak, addressing Hamza and Farouk.

"Qasim and I have been speaking. He tells me that you know something about the bomb that went off in the toilet in the Royal Meridian Hotel in Bahrain many years ago. Is that true?" This was whilst, with the back of his hand, he gently and effeminately brushed an imaginary speck of dirt off his bright, white dishdasha sleeve.

"Oh yes. That was in 1996," exclaimed Hamza with a big toothy grin. "I was a young boy at the time, and I just followed orders. We were trying to force political change. Sadly, no one was hurt, but it caused quite a disturbance. I planted two bombs, actually, but the other one was disarmed."

"If you had done that here," cut in Shazil. "With your admission, I would have put you inside one of our comfortable rooms in the Ajman Central Jail, never to be heard of again."

The smile died on Hamza's face. He started to jabber incoherently until Shazil held up his hand to pacify him. "Relax, my friend. I have no wish to harm you; otherwise, I would not be here today. I was wondering if, by any chance, you could perform a small service for me?"

Hamza looked warily across at Farouk, and they locked eyes in bewilderment. A look of amusement was on both Qasim's and Shazil's faces.

"No, no, we do not want a bomb planting. However, we believe you have done some work for a certain gentleman named al-Hawiya."

Both Hamza and Farouk seemed to go pale then green.

"Do you know who he is?"

Farouk blurted out shakily, "Nobody knows who he is or even if he exists. What is more, Boss, nobody wants to know."

"Why do you think he is known as al-Hawiya? Go on."

"It means the Abyss. It is a level of hell in the Qur'an which is reserved for Christians."

"Of course, we know that, but why is he called that?" growled Qasim, his face rapidly turning puce with anger.

"Something to do with the degree of destruction he leaves behind, I guess."

There was quiet all around. The atmosphere darkened, and the tone became distinctly stilted. The mood was thankfully broken by Hamza inhaling a biscuit crumb, which then made him do a loud sneeze followed by "Al Hamdu lil Allah" (Praise God), after which they all chorused "Yirhamakum Allah" (God have mercy upon you) followed by Hamza saying "Barak Allah fik" (God bless you).

"Back to the purpose of this meeting, please," cut in Shazil in a rather irritated voice. "We have heard some disturbing news recently that the Houthis, or an offshoot of it going by the name of Wings of Fire, is seriously planning an assault of some sort on the Dubai people. This would be a follow-up of the drone attack on Abu Dhabi early in 2022. This Hawiya fellow is sympathetic to the Houthis and is Iran-sponsored to a large degree. We are seen as the most westernised society in the Gulf and apparently should be made to suffer. I have no need to tell you how important our relationship with the West is, and the effect on tourism, sport and everything else we are trying to build could be catastrophic."

Hamza had found his tongue not least because he believed everything in life had an angle by which he could profit, and he was beginning to feel a small profit for him. His friends were not so distant, although his understanding of international politics was severely limited. "Well, I guess we could use our wide connections to contact Hawiya, if he exists, or at least one of his senior aides. However, it could prove costly, as there may be several people who would appreciate a few dirhams to expedite the process. That said, it won't be easy, as these things take time."

"I'm sure they do," sneered Qasim. "Can you arrange a meeting with him? How much palm crossing will be needed to ensure a meeting?"

Hamza looked over at Farouk, who finally removed the stupid look from his face as he grasped Hamza's enterprising approach.

"Let us say 5,000 dirhams?" said Hamza, lifting his tone at the end, making it sound like a question. He had never previously negotiated anything above 100 dirhams, so he hoped to get 5000 dirhams this time.

He noticed Shazil nod to Qasim, who then said, "Let us not say 5,000; I think 4,000 sounds better." This sum was chicken feed for what was being discussed, but nothing on the planet could stop the Arab desire for bartering, whatever the situation.

Without allowing a counteroffer, Qasim continued, "OK, do we agree, but remember, I know how to find you. Let us down, and you will never be found again in a single piece. Is that clear?"

"Yes, yes," spluttered Farouk and Hamza in unison as they were already thinking about how to spend the money.

"There is one more thing, please," Shazil said gently, almost under his breath. "You will not tell a living soul of this meeting unless you want to die the death of a thousand cuts; we will need contact details within one week." He leaned over very close to Hamza as, upon a nod, Qasim surreptitiously passed him an envelope. "This contains 500 dirhams as a down payment. Use it wisely and report back to Qasim before a week has gone by. Are you in agreement?"

Without taking his eye off the envelope, Farouk dribbled out another "Yes, yes."

At this point, Shazil and Qasim got up and left. Farouk and Hamza sat stunned and staring goggle-eyed at the envelope. They both pounced together, upsetting two empty tea glasses, tearing the envelope open and spreading the money on the table. Discretion was never in their nature or vocabulary, for that matter.

Chapter 8

Lando slept fitfully after the first few hours when he was dead to the world. Tired though he was, he woke up quite early after dreaming about knives, scimitars, flowing robes, bearded growling Arabs, choking underwater, and Dillon's frightened face somewhere in the middle of it. He dismissed it, but it still left a pall over his head until he went under that magnificent shower in the glass-walled bathroom in the middle of the bedroom. It was more like standing under a waterfall than a shower as the volume of water landing on his head threatened to wash him to the floor. He turned the hot water down, and the water immediately became hotter. He had never understood hot and cold tap markings. The plumber had made the blue and red markings on the tap so confusing, as the handle showed blue on top and red underneath. Fine if the handle moved up and down, but it didn't. It moved side to side. Even in 5-star hotels, this happened! Same all over the world.

He dried himself and then noticed the little arrow pointing towards the West in the corner of the ceiling. He realised it was pointing towards the Holy City of Mecca. He knew that Muslims were accustomed to praying facing that direction, and an evil little demon inside his head made him want to climb up and change the direction of the arrow. Why? He did not know, except sometimes Lando could be quite mischievous. Probably not the most sensible thing to do in an Arab country, particularly if he was found out. He had no interest in which direction they prayed anyway. He was not particularly religious himself, although he had an Anglican school upbringing and plenty of Christian history in his background. He had always felt there was something more beyond life, and especially this life for that matter, but he lost whatever faith he had the moment his parents were killed in that car crash.

He walked naked to the big sliding window and looked out towards the sea, pulling it open. What a glorious morning. 8 o'clock, and the air was warming up already. He still felt better, though, and was ready for breakfast and his meeting with the BUiD guys. He donned his linen trousers, a light cotton shirt, and a pair of sneakers. He grabbed his key card and headed off to the lift.

On arrival at the restaurant, he was shown to a table and offered tea or coffee. The waiter gestured towards the buffet area and the open kitchen, where he could order freshly cooked eggs to his liking. Lando decided he would enjoy himself here as he had time, and breakfast was up there, his favourite meal of the day, along with lunch and dinner! He moseyed up to the buffet tables, attempting to look as if he knew the form here and was accustomed to the extravagance of what lay before him. The various types of bread were displayed in an area that could have helped to feed the 5,000 if Jesus had needed it, and he briefly wondered what would happen to it all at the end of the day. He guessed it was probably thrown out, as big hotels were probably so riddled with health and safety laws that they would not wish to prejudice themselves by passing it on to a local charity that sought to help the less well-off in Dubai, of which there were many. The low-paid workers, he guessed, were very underpaid, and slavery was very much alive in Dubai as many of the immigrant workers from Asia had little money for themselves after they had paid for their accommodation and sent money home to their families. He supposed it was maybe a better life than they had back home–but not much.

After another enjoyable breakfast, he retired briefly to his room. The coffee had done its job of reviving him, and after a few minutes on the toilet, he picked up his notebook and information about the course and went back to the lobby to wait for his guests' arrival, leaving his name and those of his two guests from BUiD at reception. He watched the large tropical fish in the embedded tanks in the wall. They had this calm, effortless way of swimming side to side, and he realised why they were there. They help to keep people relaxed, particularly on arrival.

Claes Sundberg arrived independently and was shown over to Lando's coffee table. He was a tall, handsome man in his early forties, clean-shaven with a ready smile and greeted Lando with a strong, welcoming handshake. Placing his briefcase on the floor, he immediately started chatting about anything and everything but nothing to do with the course. Lando heard about his family background and history, that he was unmarried, why he was here, and what he planned for the rest of his life. Within 10 minutes, Lando felt he knew him as well as many friends he had known for years. It was a great start, and Lando tried unsuccessfully to reciprocate when he could get a word in. However, something still seemed missing from Claes's past, and he could not put a finger on it.

After about 20 minutes, Lando was concerned that Qasim Sarawi had not arrived. However, Claes waved his worries away, gesturing that they were on Arab time and that 10 am could mean anything from 9.55 to 11 am, depending on the person. He duly sauntered in wearing traditional Arab dress - a white dishdasha and red and white chequered kufiyah. Upon spotting Claes, he came straight over.

"Greetings, Claes. I trust you are well." Turning to Lando, he said, "And you must be Roland Westwood. I am Qasim Sarawi, and I welcome you on your first trip to Dubai," making an over-ostentatious welcome gesture.

Lando briefly wondered how he knew it was his first time here.

"Well, thank you. Please call me Lando. I was only ever called Roland by my mother when I was a naughty boy."

That seemed to break the ice adequately, and off they chatted about the course content, how Claes managed it, and Qasim's role, particularly in the financial aspects. Lando was assured that all his course materials had been printed and everything was in order. It was all routine and necessary chat, which bored Lando's pants off, and he would be glad when it was over.

Claes confirmed the start of the course would be in the Al-Jafr Conference room at 7.45 am the next day for registration before the 8.00 am start, and each day would finish by lunchtime at 2.30 pm with a 20-minute break at 10.30 am for coffee and another 30-minute break at 12.30 for coffee and prayers. Claes warned Lando that getting them back in on time, particularly the Arab students, could be quite a trial.

"So, what's the story at lunchtime then?"

"Well," replied Claes. "You must finish promptly by 2.30 as the restaurant staff need to pack up after you have finished. You head up to the Al Dawaar restaurant on the top floor, where a table for the full number of students and staff will be already booked, and eat as much as you wish. It is sure to be a delicious meal. Slacken your belt off, mate, as they say. The late afternoon is your own."

Claes was someone that Lando could relate to, and he was glad he was leading the course. Leadership in academic life was unlike most industries because it entailed working with people more than telling them what to do. You could be a leader in one project, and someone in your team could be your leader in another. Consequently, autocratic leaders tended to be shunned. However, thought Lando, the problem with this management style was that a lazy git tended to get away with being a lazy git, and the leader might end up covering their work.

On the other hand, Qasim seemed very intelligent, polite and agreeable to most of the issues raised. Still, there was just something about his smooth, confident, over-polite attitude that Lando could not quite get a fix on. Oily was a word that sprung to mind. Anyway, he consoled himself that most of his contact would be with Claes, and he foresaw only positive aspects of this relationship.

The meeting finished, Qasim Sarawi departed, and Claes and he went for a quick look inside the Al-Jafr conference room in the hotel they would be using for the module and to check on the AV equipment, and then they were finished. All good. Claes checked that there were no burning issues as he had to get back to the university, and with that, he left with a warm handshake and a promise to meet up for a beer or two one evening.

Chapter 9

It was noon, and Lando had the rest of the day to himself, so he decided to spend a little time with his barman friend, Solly, by the pool and chill out until the evening. He kept thinking of Dillon and his strange demeanour when he saw him in the Chelsea Arms and decided to take him up on his offer and meet him that evening if he could. He went to his room, found his card, and gave him a bell. It rang for a long time without any voicemail message and then cut out. Oh well, he tried. Then, his phone rang immediately, and Dillon's name appeared on his screen. Dillon asked who it was in a very guarded tone, and there was an audible relief in his voice after Lando introduced himself. Dillon agreed to meet him after dinner for a beer, and as they both knew it, Lando suggested the Chelsea Arms. Dillon was dead against that and refused Lando's invitation to his hotel for some reason. He suggested a little café/Irish bar around the corner from the Hyatt hotel called Lonigan's. They agreed to meet at 8ish.

Again, Lando put his concerns about Dillon out of his mind and, after donning suitable attire, went up to the poolside bar and met Solly's ever-present grin. His demeanour improved, and Solly asked if he wanted to be clouted with a beer. After Lando tried to fathom what he was talking about, he realised what he meant. "Ah, you mean hit me with a drink, not clouted." This kept them both amused.

He had a few salty nuts and whiled away the afternoon, swimming and sunbathing, although mainly in the shade, as it was just too intense at this time of day.

He returned to his room at 5.00 and had a kip for a couple of hours before proceeding to dinner. He was alone in the lift, and as the doors opened, he was about to leave when in front of him were three Arab women clad entirely in black, wearing niqabs and only showing their eyes. Instinctively, Lando gasped and took a step back. Being faced with three quite tall figures dressed in black with only their eyes visible put him in a state of mild shock. He could not help himself and stammered an uncomfortable apology as he quickly departed the lift. He guessed he would get used to it ... in a year or two. It's their choice, he supposed, or was it?

He had a light meal of a locally caught red snapper, lightly cooked to perfection, and wandered off to his meeting with Dillon.

He found Lonigan's, which seemed surprisingly quiet for an Irish bar, and he ordered a coffee and sat down with his back to a wall to see who entered. Dillon was prominent in every way, so should be easy to spot. Eventually, he arrived and, looking furtively around him, saw Lando and went straight over to him. He wore that worried look and was not the affable guy he had met on the aeroplane. He was sweating profusely and looked very unkempt. He also seemed a bit out of it, as if he had been drinking. He sat down around the corner from the door but with a view of the door like Lando, although opposite each other. They chatted for a while, and Dillon seemed to loosen up as he had also ordered a beer. They talked about all kinds of stuff, including Dillon's family and upbringing in Yorkshire.

"I liked to do a bit of lampin' now and again. It kept me fit in those days and was quite remunerative," he said, tapping the side of his nose, "if you know what I mean."

"No, I don't know what you mean. What is lampin' anyway?"

Dillon was now relaxed. He looked at Lando in amazement. "Well, lampin' or lamping, as the toffs might say, means you are carrying a very bright lamp at night. You go around the fields with a couple of lurchers and...." He saw Lando's eyes glaze over again and sighed with resignation. "A lurcher is a breed of dog or, more correctly, a cross-bred greyhound with something else such as a terrier or sheepdog favoured by the gipsies. It is great for catching a small deer as it can outrun one and bring it down within 30-40 seconds. The lamps are to dazzle the deer until it is too late for them to get a good speed up."

"Aaah," said Lando, tapping the side of his nose as well. "Poaching!"

"I would prefer to call it controlling the deer population. Survival of the fittest and all that."

"I am sure you would," smiled Lando. "Why not call it culling and be done with it?"

"Where's the fun in that then?"

"Where indeed?"

Dillon brightened. "Hey, fancy a bit of Wadi bashing tomorrow evening?"

"I might do if I knew what it was."

"We join a group who go out into the desert Monday nights in Land cruisers and go up and down the sand hills until we feel sick or terrified or both and then on to a camp where we have a barbeque under the stars and are entertained by some belly dancers. Maybe join in. I have a considerable advantage in that department." He said with a grin, jabbing his finger about five inches into his magnanimous stomach.

"Sounds fun but doesn't really explain the name 'wadi-bashing."

"A wadi is a dried-up riverbed, so we are 'bashing' up and down the sides. Great fun. Guaranteed to get your appetite going if you are not sick."

Just then, the bar's double doors opened, and two extremely burly, heavily bearded men in Arab dress came in looking around the room. Dillon shrank around the corner–at least as much as he could. Noticing his agitation, Lando shuffled his chair a bit to one side to block him out–no easy feat considering his size. After a minute of surveying the room and one of the staff offering them a seat, they left quietly. Dillon became visibly calmer, and Lando spoke his mind.

"Look, Dillon. You have no need to tell me anything, but I saw you in the Chelsea Arms last night with a strange-looking gentleman, and you seemed upset and, dare I say it, a little bit frightened. I wouldn't say I liked the look of that guy you were with, either. Who was he? I heard the name Ashiraf used."

Dillon lowered his gaze and was clearly in two minds about how much to say.

"Hey Dillon, best you say nothing rather than make something up."

"I must leave as they will come back, I am sure. Please do not concern yourself as I have had a few debt issues, and these people want their money back." With that, Dillon got up and bumped heavily into Lando, knocking him over and helping him up apologetically and dusting him down in a rather ostentatious way. Lando told him to go and forget the bill, so Dillon quickly left the bar.

"We still on for the wadi bashing then?" yelled Lando but received no reply. Dillon could move very fast, particularly for such a big man. Lando felt a little bemused after Dillon left and meandered slowly back to the hotel, taking in the smells of the night air. It was lovely to wander at night in the warmth, which was so rare where he lived in Shrewsbury. He guessed global warming might give him that pleasure for a few years until the sun cooked everyone to a crisp. He tried to do his bit by recycling what he could, saving water, and buying sustainably sourced items. He just hoped that the research scientists would come up with a source of fuel for electricity that worked effectively rather than being some political hotchpotch. Maybe Putin's crazy antics have accelerated the need, and some good can come out of it.

He retired to his room and was asleep before he knew it.

Chapter 10

Monday am

Lando awoke to his alarm at 6.45. My God, he felt ropy. He was lightheaded and still on British time, so he was effectively getting out of bed at 2.45 am, which was not great. He took his shower as cold as he could in this warm climate, ventured down for breakfast, and arrived at the Al-Jafr meeting room at 7.30 am in good time. A striking, statuesque blonde lady was waiting just inside the room's open door, and she immediately introduced herself with a handshake.

"Hi, I am Lisana, and I assume you are Roland Westwood."

"Bang on, but please call me Lando." He refrained from his mother's naughty boy comment again.

They chatted about the course. She showed him all the printed course material that was very professionally bound in folders branded with the University logo, and all the seating places were laid out in a 'U' shape style with water and a pad and pen by each one. There were expected to be 25 students, of which half were ex-pats, principally from the UK, and the rest were from the Gulf states. Coffee was already waiting, so Lisana poured him one, and then she opened up about herself. She was 30 and had been married for three years. She moved to Dubai from England with her husband, who worked for a Land Rover importer. She could not find a job in radio broadcasting, which she used to do in her hometown of Trondheim, Norway, and this hostess-type job was easy and paid well but did not give her any security of regular income. However, her husband Jack is making a load, but sadly, it 'has gone to his head, and he spends like there is no tomorrow and drinks the same.' She wondered if the pair of them would turn into alcoholics if she stayed much longer. That was a lot for Lando to take on board, but he was a good listener, particularly with someone as elegant and charming as Lisana. She appeared highly vulnerable, so he did his best to keep the conversation positive. He talked a bit about himself, not that he wanted to, but to take the chat away from her personal issues as he thought she might burst into tears at any moment. He needed to be on top form to start the course and to focus on what he was there to do. Thankfully, she got herself together and apologised for dumping too much on Lando, particularly on the first day.

Lando smiled and said, "No worries. I hope things will improve for you, as carrying all that baggage for too long is unhealthy. May I suggest some good hard exercise for at least an hour each day to give you something you have control over and make you feel better? I am no life coach, of course. I have made mistakes and got into plenty of pickles along the way. My marriage only lasted two weeks, probably 13 days longer than it should have."

She laughed out loud, breaking the ice between them just as the first delegate arrived. An Arab guy from Palestine called Najib. She immediately went into professional mode, offered him coffee, pointed to the course pack at the table and requested his signature on her register. *Amazing what a good laugh can do*; he also started smiling without knowing why.

There was a crazy period of 5 minutes when about three-quarters of the delegates arrived all at once, and Lando marvelled at how well Lisana managed, and he thanked God she was there.

Three Arab women arrived together in full black Arab niqabs. Judging by their eyes, all three appeared very young, and he saw all three had the most dramatic eye makeup. They requested to sit close, so Lisana placed them together on the right. This was not before Lando made his first monumental faux pas. He tried to shake hands with one of the ladies, who recoiled as if a rattlesnake had bitten her. She said curtly, "I do not shake hands."

He had been briefed on the etiquette of greeting Arab women, which was to offer to shake hands only if they proffer their hand first. In his eagerness to befriend, he had forgotten and apologised profusely. She did not seem alarmed or upset, and he guessed this happened now and again to her when a Westerner forgot the etiquette. He thought he would remember from now on!

Lando noticed that Lisana found his discomfort highly amusing, and as he grimaced at her, she sported a sympathetic smile. *Ha. At least some good had come out of it.*

"We seem to be five students short," she said, frowning at her list. "But we are past the starting time. Hopefully, they will turn up later. Here are some packs for you in case they arrive.

Weird. This happens often, and they pay a small fortune for these courses!"

Lando did not take it in fully as he was edgy about the beginning of the course.

Lisana opened the course with general housekeeping issues such as fire alarms, where the toilets were, and other dos and don'ts such as timekeeping and reminded everyone to be punctual after the breaks as it disturbs everyone else. It would, of course, not make any difference, but it needed saying anyway. She then gave Lando a great introduction, and even Lando was impressed with himself after that. The course commenced, and Lisana said she would join them during the breaks and lunch. She left Lando feeling distinctly sad, as was every other male in the room whose eyes followed her graceful figure with the perfectly fitted light summer dress and dramatic long blond hair to her exit.

Lando wrenched his eyes and mind back to the job at hand. This was his living, after all!

None of these students were accountants. This was a general business course, so Lando felt comfortable kicking off with whether they knew any accountants and whether they were boring, just to get a bit of light conversation going. One American guy in his thirties introduced himself as 'Hobart G. Lonsdale IV,' which caused a slight stirring among the other students. He said he once talked to his personal accountant in Virginia, and he was so boring, and his voice was so monotonic that he fell asleep in front of him in a one-to-one meeting. Smiles all round, of course. One lady from the UK said she had a good friend who trained as a Chartered Accountant. This guy was so full of fun and out there with pranks and jokes when he was eighteen or nineteen years old. She met him again 7 years later, and it was as if his whole soul had been removed and replaced with a jar of gelatine. That sparked a debate about whether boring people take up accountancy or whether practising accountancy makes people dull. It was a good start and lots of fun, which clearly did not impress the three Arab women who were stone-cold silent. Perhaps the humour or purpose of the debate was lost on them. Lando believed it was a great profession and had always admired those who could do this type of work daily and still stay focused. It just did not light up Lando's life. He yearned for a bit more excitement. Little did he know!

Lando rounded it off. "I often told my consultancy clients that I cannot promise to help make them into millionaires, but I can promise to help them avoid losing a million."

So, they moved through the session to the first break and all dutifully returned in good time for the second session at 10.30. Lando was relieved.

The second session went well, and again, they left at 12.15 for prayers and coffee, with the third session due to start at 12.45. Only thirteen of them had returned by then. All the non-Arabs had returned, plus a few of the Arabs. *Bollocks,* thought, Lando, *Here we go.* He had to play it cool on the first day, and, as they drifted in during the beginning of the session, apologised for the delay as they had been at prayers. Lando doubted one or two of them but let it go on the first day, even though a couple asked to be filled in on what they had missed. Lando politely declined any detail other than referring them to the printed course notes. Finally, the first day was finished, and lunch beckoned at 2.30. They headed up to the restaurant on the top floor. Lando was very hungry and tired. He needed to wind down before eating, but the time frame would not allow that. He returned to his room, put his face in a basin of cool water and changed his shirt. He could have cheerfully lain on the bed for a few minutes, but he knew he would have gone to sleep within minutes. He settled for deep breathing to slow his heart rate. Semi-consciously, he knew what spurred him on to lunch was catching up with the charming Lisana.

Chapter 11

He took the lift to the top floor, and as the doors opened, he was again met by two Arab women who were fully clad in black from head to foot. He was proud of himself as he did not flinch backwards this time as he exited and they entered. *I'm cool with this,* he thought. *Sorted.* He was shown to the table reserved for his course, and Lisana was already there, conversing happily with two delegates.

She waved him over to a chair opposite and gave him the brief. "Basically, lunch is everything you can eat on display over there." She waved her hand towards what appeared to be a feast. "You can dine like a king; the sushi is superb here."

He casually walked to where the food was laid out, and it was staggering. Hummus, lobster claws, lamb koftas, whole beef joints, and all manner of sushi dishes (he had never really got into that at home in Shrewsbury), and the list went on. He filled up his plate for his starter, mixing all manner of things. Flatbread with hummus, a load of prawns, and a few sushi items such as little rice cylinders filled with shellfish. He hoped they were cooked. The thought of lecturing with the trots was low on his wish list. He took a little bowl of soy sauce, a few raw pickled ginger slices and a good spoonful of wasabi paste, which he had never tried. *In for a penny...* he thought.

He returned to the table and sat down and joined the conversation and then the room started to spin. Lisana looked at him quizzically. "Are you all right?"

"No ... the room seems to be moving. Hang on, this really is a revolving building. The whole ocean is moving."

"Just the floor is revolving, actually," interjected Lisana. "Look down there." She pointed out of the window. "See all those little islands?"

"Yes, yes," marvelled Lando. "They look like a palm tree. Of course, that must be the Palms development I have read about."

Lisana nodded.

"What are those large boats doing? There are quite a few of them."

"Aha. They are the Dutch dredgers. They are dredging up the sand, much of which must be replaced to develop the foundations under the water. I don't know the scientific reasons, but basically, it is the wrong sort of sand under the water, and they have to replace it with imported sand."

"Where does the sand come from? Their own desert, presumably?"

"I believe so."

Then, Lando took a large mouthful of neat Wasabi paste on his fork, and his whole body became rigid before the American student, Hobart, could stop him. Lisana and Hobart watched in awe as Lando went puce. Tears rolled down his face, and he coughed briefly, nearly passing out.

The next moment, he said, "Wow. What a rush! That is just the best feeling I have ever had with all my clothes on. What is that stuff?"

The other two were almost apoplectic with laughter. Lisana had to drink a glass of water to calm herself down.

"It's wasabi, real wasabi grown in Japan and not pretend, which I am told is often horseradish mixed with mustard with green colouring. The same family, though," commented Hobart. "After the initial shock, it looked like you enjoyed it."

"You bet. My nasal passages will never be the same again. I had this five-second period of acute pain followed by a massive surge of endorphins. Terrific."

The other delegates had joined them by this time, and everyone seemed very amused by Lando's brief period of discomfort. He could see little pleasure in watching a Chartered Accountant choke. *Or could he?*

Even one of the Arab ladies, named Nadia, gently suggested, "Perhaps you should take a little less wasabi on your fork next time."

"Beautifully put, Nadia. That is, however, the understatement of the year. You have given me an idea, though. Perhaps everyone late for a course session should be made to take a full teaspoon of wasabi as a punishment!" There were smiles all around.

Everyone finished their starters and had their main courses, and no one could move after that. Desserts were not required, although Lisana suggested that the desserts were excellent.

"How do you keep so slender with all these delicious temptations around then?" asked Lando, trying not to sound like he was coming on to her.

"Ah, that would be telling. I do a lot of exercise, but I do not have these types of engagements every week. Otherwise, I would be out here," she said, miming a big humpty dumpty circle around herself. "There is one dessert here which you must try, though. It is called Um Ali."

Nadia's ears perked up at this and she joined in the conversation. "Do you know the origins of this name?"

Everyone shook their heads.

"Um Ali or Om Ali literally means mother of Ali. There are many stories about the origins as they date back hundreds of years. The one I heard was that Om Ali, the mother of Ali, had an affair with a friend of her husband. To prevent him from asking lots of questions, she decided to bake him the most delicious dessert to keep his mind occupied and away from any questions he might have about where she had been. The plan worked, so the sweet became known as Om Ali."

"Ha," said Hobart. "Here is me thinking it was a pudding named after an Irishman, O'Malley." This raised a few giggles, at least from those with some understanding of Irish names.

Nadia continued, "It is like your bread-and-butter pudding but slowly baked in the oven for 15 to 20 hours. It has bread, obviously, cream, pistachio nuts, other nuts, cinnamon, and whatever else you want to throw in it. Delicious."

Everyone was salivating, including Lando. So, he went to the dessert area and found a whole bowl of it on a warming plate. He spooned some out and returned.

Everyone watched him as he took his first mouthful. He put his spoon down, closed his eyes, and quietly uttered the first words that came into his mind. "My God, this is orgasmic."

Smiles around the table, and that ended lunch on day one. *A great start*, thought Lando.

Chapter 12

Monday pm

It was just after three, and Lando thought he would have a few minutes in his room before going to the pool as he was exhausted, what with his brain and body still not fully adjusted to Dubai time and the stress of the first day. He opened the door to his room and saw a note on the floor by the door. It was a note presumably sent from reception on behalf of Dillon inviting him on a 'wadi bashing' trip. Dillon had the tickets, but could Lando reach the Sunset Excursions travel company by 5.30 pm, only five minutes away? *That's put paid to the pool trip*, he thought. *There is no chance of relaxation around here.* He lay down on his bed and was sound asleep within two minutes.

He woke with a start. *Hell, what was the time?* He realised he had 20 minutes to get down to the hotel entrance to get a taxi, so he needed to get going. Thankfully, he had slept for nearly two hours, so he was at least thinking a bit straighter. He had a quick shower and donned a pair of shorts, sandals and a polo shirt. He gathered from his trip planning that it would still be warm enough at night, even in the desert.

Straight down to the lobby, he was about to order a taxi when he saw Gaji, the taxi driver, who had just brought someone from the airport. He waved at him and seemed delighted to see Lando again.

"Hello, hello, hello, Mr Westwood. So good to see you. Are you enjoying your stay?"

"Fine, and good to see you too, Gaji. You always seem so happy."

"That is because I am alive. That is all we need to be happy. Some food, shelter and a good woman help, of course. Can I recommend any of those to you? Maybe... several women?" he said quietly and hopefully.

"Actually, I have to get to Sunset Excursions by 5.30, and I am not sure I can get a taxi in time."

"I am not supposed to take passengers other than from the airport, but I know this place, and it is on my way home as I finish my shift in two minutes."

"Come on, Gaji, I know you live close to the hotel, so why do me a favour? You will be taking me and then must come back. And you could get into trouble."

"No problem, Mr Westwood. Anyway, I must get petrol for the van for many trips tomorrow."

So off they went. Lando got out near a large sign with Sunset Excursions printed on a desert picture and handed over 30 dirhams to Gaji, who had asked for nothing but accepted it happily.

Thankfully, Dillon and one of Lando's students were already there. It was Hobart the American, and they were chatting together, which Lando thought was a bit coincidental as there were about twenty-five people all waiting for the trip. They noticed him, and their conversation became awkward as

Lando came near. There was something about Hobart that Lando could not quite fathom.

"Well, fancy you two knowing each other," said Lando, addressing Dillon. "Now, there's a coincidence. Hobart is one of my students."

They both appeared a little edgy, and Dillon muttered something about the first time they had met and were making small talk about the trip. Lando let it go, and they were then all martialled into four vans emblazoned with the company name in bright colours. They were told it was a thirty-minute journey and to put on their seatbelts. Lando sat next to Dillon, and Hobart was nowhere close as he was in another van. The roads got progressively worse, and soon, they were off-road and driving up a steep sandy hill. They got to the top, and Lando thought they were driving off a cliff as he could see nothing but sky in front of the van, which then nosedived downwards the other side, almost like a vertical drop. He now knew why they were so insistent on the seat belts. He was half standing on the back of the seat of the person in front of him as the vans descended in caravan style down into the valley. Up they went on another slope and then down again, with the Arab driver getting into it, laughing, screaming, shouting and ululating as only an Arab can do. It was terrifying. Lando felt this guy was seriously deranged and getting his jollies by scaring his passengers half to death. Dillon seemed quite impassive. He had presumably done this before. They passed a small camel farm and were encouraged to take photographs through the windows, and eventually, they stopped on a hill overlooking a sort of camp where there were tents and three large campfires in a triangle. Some barbeques were smoking away, and quite a few people were scurrying around, no doubt preparing things. Everyone got out for a leg stretch and was encouraged to take camera shots of the sunset over the desert for fifteen minutes before descending into the camp.

The speed of the sunset amazed Lando, and he was sorry he only had the camera on his mobile phone, but it was better than nothing. It was so beautiful watching this red ball of fire in the sky sink so quickly with the earth's rotation, changing the colours of the wispy clouds and watching the darkening shadows across the miles of dunes. As the sun was setting without the reflective glare of the sand, the scene, peace, and quiet with it was worth the trip alone. It made Lando almost emotional. *So unlike me,* he mused.

They were martialled back into the vans for the final cruise down to the camp. Everyone was talking about the sunset as the darkness descended, and all the camp lights were turned on, making a very festive scene. Combined with the whiffs of the food smoking on the barbeques, people were becoming extremely chatty with one another, and some liquid refreshments of beer, wine, and juices helped. People dined regally on kebabs, koftas, grilled chicken with flatbreads and beautiful salads and were then asked to sit in a big circle around the triangle of fires. Then the music started from speakers, no doubt powered by heavy batteries as Lando could not hear a generator and out came wild dancing men performing a whirling dervish dance spinning around at high speed. A few drinks followed this, and the last part of the evening was a surprise announcement.

There was to be a belly dancing display. Lando was very excited to see this until they were told they would have to join in to be taught how to belly dance.

There were three dancers, and each was announced with a big blast of music and roars of approval from all those helping prepare. The first two dancers did their very energetic dances, but it was the third one who gave Lando a sharp intake of breath, and he would never forget her name. It was Kadri. She was possibly the most alluring woman he had ever seen, including the voluptuous Amber from the Dog & Doublet. She drifted in, owning the floor. If it were up to Lando, she would own the whole desert. Jet black hair in ringlets, fine features warmly tanned, beautifully full lips with deep red lipstick, the curviest shape that no artist could create, and everything held together with a few pieces of string, each doing its job but being strained to the limit. With every shake of her body, her breasts seemed likely to overflow her black halter neck top any moment, her rear had an expression all of its own and was like a pair of smooth footballs fighting to escape the small, bejewelled triangle of cloth, and Lando thought there were probably one or two men there testing the power of prayer for the first time in their lives. If only…The rhythm of her belly in time with the music was hypnotic, and Lando was mesmerised by the large, green jewel in her navel. He did not want the dance to end, and eventually, she went off to thunderous applause. All three girls came together and tried to get everyone onto the temporary dance area for a lesson. Interestingly, Kadri somehow coached Dillon, and they chatted animatedly. She then gesticulated towards Hobart to come and join them, and they were up there for about ten minutes. Again, it seemed a bit coincidental. Hobart epitomised that all-American air of good looks, athleticism, love of his country, etc., who annoyingly danced like a professional. Although belly dancing was not his thing, he had a rhythm that Lando envied. For his size, Dillon was also a surprisingly good dancer. He was a big slab of meat but also moved with considerable grace, and it was fun watching them until Lando was beckoned over. He resisted but played the game, and Dillon introduced him to Kadri. The other two went off after five minutes, leaving him alone with Kadri. She was so lovely, but he struggled to speak to her. He rarely had a good line for a lady but seldom had trouble responding.

"Hello," she said.

"That was a beautiful dance Kadri."

"Why, thank you, kind sir," she replied in perfectly accented English with a little curtsy.

That floored him as she sounded like she was off a BBC period drama. He was expecting someone whose English was rudimentary.

"Yes," she said. "I spent some time in England a few years ago and learned some local language. Did it surprise you?"

"Of course. I was expecting a little more Arabic influence with the belly dancing."

"Most of us are Turkish as the Arab women tend to only dance for other Arabs. I was born in Istanbul but have been over here for three years. It keeps me busy." Then she smiled. Her whole face lit up.

Lando had never seen or talked to anyone so beautiful and engaging, and here he was in the desert under the most glorious starlit sky he had ever seen. It was like a scene from a Steven Spielberg movie, and he was waiting for the shooting star to race across the sky. He was nearly lost for words, and it was all he could do not to stare at Kadri. Until now, he had never believed in love at first sight. He was smitten, and the soft moonlight just added to her beauty, and the flickering flames from the fires bounced off her bejewelled costume and exaggerated her curves almost beyond his ability to cope. He felt like he had died and gone straight to heaven. He said nothing and just watched her as they were dancing. When it finished, much to his anguish, she said she had to leave to pack up her things, but she embraced him warmly and gave him a friendly peck on the cheek and, combined with the scent of her perfume, made him feel like a giddy schoolboy. She also told him that she often worked in town at The Seagull Hotel, which arranged dancing shows many nights of the week. He stammered a goodbye, and off she went as he floated on a cloud to join Dillon and Hobart, who were still talking together.

After that, the evening did not last long, and they returned to the 4X4s. Everyone was very chatty at the beginning of their journey home but soon sank into sleepy postures with a combination of the wine, the swaying of the vehicle and the enjoyment of the trip. Half were sound asleep by the time they reached the drop-off point. Neither Dillon nor Hobart slept as they were chatting quietly but animatedly in the same vehicle as Lando and seated beside each other.

A wonderful thing then occurred. Gaji was waiting for Lando with a beaming smile exaggerated by his glowing white teeth, dark skin and the rally-point lighting.

"I thought you might need a lift back, sir," he said joyfully.

Lando thought he was just so good to be around. They agreed on the fare, and Lando offered Hobart a lift back to the hotel as he guessed he was staying there, but he declined as he mentioned that he 'had things to do.'

"So," said Gaji as he grinned. "Did you have a good night out?"

"Amazing, loved every minute of it."

"Aha, I guess you met Kadri then. All the European men like her. She is a bowl-over, then?"

"What!"

"A bowl-over–she bowled you over." Gaji tittered. "You will indeed be most fortunate to land that one. Most unlikely, sir. Since you are well warmed up, I can find a lady to keep you even warmer this evening. In fact, I know of two sisters who would keep you warm simultaneously, or even three and..."

Lando blanched and interrupted him, "Gaji, I am sure they are all lovely, but I just want my own bed right now as I have a long day tomorrow."

"Maybe another time, sir," he said disappointedly.

"Another time," replied Lando, smiling. He almost considered telling Gaji he was gay to shut him up, but he suspected Gaji would then offer him male partners even though it was illegal in the Arab states.

He was dropped off outside the Hyatt Hotel gates with an energetic wave from Gaji, and he made his way inside and then to the massive bed in his room. He slept soundly but dreaming about Kadri for a great deal of it. He was not sure it was dreaming as he kept directing her into a situation that seemed to find them both naked and in the compromising position from which only an idiot would want to break free. *Que sera, sera,* he thought mid-dream.

Chapter 13

Tuesday

He was up bright and early but not terribly hungry as he had overeaten the previous evening, so he went down for a quick breakfast of a croissant and a cup of coffee and went straight to the Al-Jafr Conference room. The elegant Lisana greeted him with her attendance list, looking efficient, smiley, and accommodating, as well as Claes Sundberg, the BUiD University course leader.

"I just thought I would come and see that you are settled in and students are not throwing stuff at you," he grinned while extending his hand.

"Ah. Great to see you, Claes, and thanks for coming." He shook Claes's hand warmly. "No, they all seem engaged, and I feel pretty good about the atmosphere. Incidentally, a few of us went wadi bashing last night and had a wonderful time. Great food, music and dancing. A great night's sleep after."

Lisana brought them a cup of coffee while they chatted idly, waiting for the course group to arrive.

Claes spoke with a broad, knowing smile. "I guess you met the lovely Kadri then."

"Is there anyone in Dubai that doesn't know Kadri? Yes, I met her. She is what they call in Britain a corker. I even tried to belly dance with her."

Claes spluttered into his coffee. "Is that a euphemism?"

"No, it certainly is not," replied Lando indignantly, which set Lisana off into giggles. Lando thought she was such a charming hostess. He understood why she was there, as she was so much more than decoration on the course. She set the right tone as the students came in, making them welcome and uplifted early in the day.

Day Two of the lectures started with a ten-minute talk about accountants helping find or prevent fraud and error in their work. Then, he asked everyone to spend fifteen minutes talking with their neighbours about their experiences of fraud or error in the workplace. Hobart arrived a little late during this process. Lisana put a coffee in his hand, and Lando told him what the chat with his neighbouring student should be about. Lando thought he looked exceedingly fraught and appeared not to have slept. He also had a large plaster across his left hand, to which Lando decided not to draw attention. Meanwhile, Claes nodded at Lando and quietly left with Lisana, leaving Lando to finish his work.

Claes and Lisana met them all for lunch in the Al Dawaar restaurant, and afterwards, they chatted merrily until 3.30 pm when Lisana and Claes left. Lisana had also remarked about Hobart's sloppy appearance as he sat on his own through lunch.

Back to his room and midway through a short nap before going for a swim, the phone by his bed rang with the receptionist asking whether he would take a call from 'someone called Dillon.'

"Hello Dillon. What can I do for you? Had a great night last night, I really ......"

Dillon interrupted him mid-flow, "Can we please meet soon? I have much to tell you?" His Yorkshire accent seemed to have dropped, his breath seemed strained, fast and shallow, and he was clearly anguished over something.

"Yep. No problem. I need to shower and get some clothes on, and I can meet you. Where do you fancy? Lonigan's again?"

"That would be fine. Please come as quickly as you can." He clicked off without waiting for an answer.

Once again, Lando was deeply troubled by Dillon. It was not what he said but the natural tension in his voice when he said it.

He dressed and ditched the shower in his rush to get off. He headed to the lobby and outside, where his sunglasses immediately steamed up as he came out of the air-conditioned hotel's coolness into the day's dying heat. He wiped them clear and headed off to Lonigan's around the corner and down the street. He would not have wished to walk far in this heat.

Dillon had not arrived yet, so he sat down and ordered a cup of coffee and waited. Half an hour went by, and then an hour. Once it got to 7 PM and darkness had descended, with no word from Dillon, he decided to leave. As he was out, he thought he would take a trip to the Seagull Hotel, where Kadri said she occasionally worked. He checked the hotel's location on Google Maps on his phone and realised that it was only a 20-minute walk away. Perhaps Kadri could throw some light on Dillon's behaviour, as at the desert barbeque, she seemed to know him well enough.

Lando ambled along as quickly as he could without raising a sweat, and his screen seemed to be taking him down a lot of minor roads and alleys, which concerned him somewhat as he wasn't in the mood for being held up in the gloom by some lunatic robber in a foreign country.

He heard sobbing from the street around the corner, and all his senses came alive. He got round the corner, and there in front of him was Kadri sitting on the pavement holding a bloody knife and the immediately recognisable body of Dillon lying on the ground with his stomach pouring blood at an unsustainable rate from a considerable wound. Lando knelt by Kadri and almost fainted. Dillon was alive, just, but taking a better look at the wound in his stomach, Lando nearly vomited. He could smell Dillon's blood. He had never actually smelt blood before, but he instinctively knew what it was, and the sweetness sickened him. Some of his intestines were spilling out onto the pavement like a string of thick sausages, and amidst his pain, he was trying to mouth a few words to Kadri and Lando.

"Take…. this…. note…. to …. Hobart. Tell him…. I've seen him."

Kadri was still holding the knife but shivering and shaking. She managed to get a hold of herself to ask between tears, "Dillon, Dillon, who did this to you?"

"Not matter," he groaned. "Ugly, smelly bastard though." His eyes rolled up to the top of his head, and with that, he lost consciousness. Lando felt his neck for his pulse. Nothing. He was dead. No one could have survived that injury.

Lando guiltily felt slightly relieved at Dillon's last words as he wondered if Kadri had done this, although he didn't seriously believe she could have. He looked across at her, and she looked devastated and in shock. He suddenly felt nauseous, and he stood up, walked three paces and retched violently into a dark corner behind the pavement. He realised life in Dubai would not be the same again. He wasn't that stupid. He also knew that going to the police in this circumstance would not be an intelligent thing to do, and it certainly would not help Kadri. Thankfully, nobody had come down the street, but they had to move fast. His brain was in overdrive, and Kadri was still sitting on the pavement in the darkness, deeply upset and still holding the knife. What was it he remembered from his days at school Corps Camp? *When the going gets tough, the tough get going.* Easier said than done. He had to move the knife, get Kadri out of there, and get hold of Hobart quickly, though why he could not imagine except conveying Dillon's message. What good would a thirty-year-old student be?

Chapter 14

Lando needed to take matters into his own hands. He took the viciously curved knife from Kadri, wrapped it in his handkerchief and jammed it down his waistband. Kadri was unresponsive, and there was little time before someone walked along the dark street and came across the ghastly scene. He roughly grabbed her by the shoulder and almost dragged her whilst coaxing her gently into moving one foot in front of the other to escape the appalling nightmare. Thankfully, she started to respond and began walking with Lando, leaning heavily on him constantly. She was covered in blood, and a good load of this was now on Lando's linen jacket. He, therefore, needed to get her out of her clothes, a situation about which he had already fantasised but, of course, under different circumstances. He also had to dump his clothes and find some clean ones. This could all prove difficult even though a few shops were still open. He thought he would test his luck with Kadri and keep her focused on this single task. Maybe more tasks would help her to come out of her shock as she was shaking uncontrollably.

"Kadri, do you know of any clothes shops around here?"

"Yes," she said breathlessly, "there is an A-a-a-arab clothing shop around this n-n-n-next c-corner. Perhaps r-rather than t-t-trying to change our clothes, we c-c-could purchase a dishdasha each and then w-w-wear it on top?"

"Brilliant idea, Kadri." He was overjoyed that she was now thinking rationally. He asked her to take his jacket, which was highly bloodstained, and he would go into the shop and see what he could do as he thankfully still had cash in his wallet, which would be better for this transaction as he did not want to leave any traces on his credit card of being in this area. His trousers were mucky but only around the waist, and he pulled his shirt out of them to cover the stains. He had a stupid thought that he looked quite trendy. He went inside, and an old Arab was sitting behind a desk, flicking little balls along the wires on his abacus. He didn't think people still used those.

Lando remarked on the old man's dexterity and speed in using the abacus, to which the old chap replied, "It's fun, and I like check numbers shown in the calculator correct." He said with a smile in his broken English. "What would you like, sir? We have fine jackets, trousers, shirts, ties and Arabic garments."

"Actually, I would like two dishdashas with headgear. One for myself in white and one for my wife in black, please. We are wearing them for a dinner invitation one evening, so nothing too expensive, please, as it is a once-only use."

The older man looked very saddened. He had undoubtedly perfected that look to elicit more lavish customer spending.

"We have stock of abayas for wife. This is like a dishdasha but very loose and decorated with embroidery. Here is a niqab; she can always lower the veil if she wishes. How tall she is, please?"

It was all Lando could do not to look around to see if he could spy on Kadri through the window. "She is about 6 inches shorter than me and a full figure," he said with a wink, and the old man grinned.

"I have just the item in stock, and here is a dishdasha for you. That will be 1500 dirhams for both, kind sir."

Lando had a sharp intake of breath and nearly threw up for the second time that evening. The equivalent of £300 did not seem like a great deal for such simple garments. However, this was more than the cash in his wallet, which amounted to 1200 dirhams. The old man looked impassive, and Lando thought everyone in this region liked a haggle, so why not?

"I saw two similar ones this morning, and they were only 600 dirhams."

"So why not buy them?"

"Because I did not have my wallet with me."

"So why don't buy tomorrow?"

"No time."

"What about the next day?"

'Need them for tomorrow night.' The old man looked at him suspiciously and said with a long face, "1250 dirhams then."

Lando needed to get the price well below the 1200 dirhams in his wallet, and he also needed money for a taxi as they could not walk around the town once the alarm was raised. "700 dirhams," he said.

The old man's face got even longer. "How will I feed my children, how will I pay rent, how will wife ever forgive me, or

Allah for that matter? 900 dirhams. That is the best price possible."

"Done," said Lando, offering his hand to shake on the deal. A huge smile lit up the old man's face, and immediately, Lando realised he could have bartered him down a lot more. *You win some, you lose some,* he thought.

The old man wrapped them up, and Lando requested a large carrier bag to hold them. He hurried out of the door, waving thanks and goodbye as he went.

He looked around and saw no sign of Kadri. Where was she? Had she run off or what? He began to feel uncomfortable and wandered around for ten minutes, and then suddenly and gratefully, he heard her calling his name from behind him.

He turned around and saw that she was behind a gatepost. She looked different and not so filthy. However, her eyes still portrayed her pain.

"I needed to get his blood off my face and hair," she said and sobbed. "We were friends. It was horrible, but I found a discarded bottle of water to clean myself up. I can do nothing about my clothes, though."

"You are a courageous girl," said Lando. His heart went out to her as she showed a bit of steel. "I have the clothes for which I was royally stung, but no matter. We need to find somewhere convenient to put them on."

"I know just the place just off the next street. There is an old, disused alleyway with a big archway entrance. May I suggest removing all our foul clothing rather than putting these new dishdashas over the top? I cannot stand to walk another step with Dillon's blood still on me."

"Agreed. I would prefer that, but we shall have to do it quickly. Come on."

They found the alley and went behind one of the pillars in the archway. By the time Lando removed the new garb from his bag, Kadri had completely stripped down to her underwear. Modesty was not in her vocabulary, and despite their grave situation, Lando struggled not to admire her beauty openly while removing his shirt and trousers. He suggested they remove everything except underwear as they needed to get rid of it straightaway just in case they were subjected to a police search in the future. They used the shopping bag to contain the bloodstained clothing and also the murder weapon. He took Dillon's note from his trouser pocket, and they quickly donned their new garments. Lando realised how comfortable he felt in his dishdasha. It was, he realised, a convenient garment in this heat. He looked at Kadri in her long flowing black abaya and wearing the niqab. All he could see were her eyes, but her pain and beauty were still evident. He felt an ache in his chest at the trauma she had just gone through. They scurried off and realised they did not know where to go. Kadri tried to phone Hobart without success and sent him a text. Lando wondered why she needed Hobart and annoyingly felt jealous despite needing help.

"Kadri, would you come back to my hotel for an hour or so until we can contact Hobart and take it from there?"

"All right," she said softly. "Don't know what else we can do."

After folding the dagger up again in his handkerchief, they dumped the clothing bag in a skip and took a taxi back to the hotel. The driver seemed surprised to have a European in Arab dress in his taxi but thankfully refrained from mentioning it, and they were soon back at the Hyatt.

With Lando being obviously European, Kadri suggested they enter the hotel separately, so he gave her his room number 737. He took the lift, entered his room, and went straight for the minibar. Without taking a glass, he unscrewed the first mini bottle of scotch and downed it in two gulps. It found its mark within 30 seconds. He smacked his lips, delighted in the effect, and grabbed a small bag of nuts and a second bottle of scotch. This time, he poured it into a glass with a bit of chilled sparkling water and realised it was a Haig Club whisky. Wasn't that David Beckham's brand? How did he get his name over here as well? There was a knock on the door, and he thoughtlessly opened it with a flourish and a smile, expecting Kadri.

A young man was standing there in his smart hotel uniform, all bright and breezy. "Room Service sir. May we turn down your bed?" Just then, Kadri passed behind him and sensibly continued down the passageway. Lando said it was fine and not to bother and gently closed the door. There was another knock a minute later; this time, it was Kadri. She walked through the door, removed her niqab and sat on the end of the bed. Her face slowly crumpled, and she began to sob quietly. Her breath came in jerks, and Lando sat by her and gently wrapped his arms around her shoulders, saying nothing whilst her sobs slowed.

He returned to the minibar, brought another bottle of whisky, poured it into a glass, grabbed a clean white handkerchief from the bedside table, and sat by her again. He smoothed the hair from her eyes, gently wiped the tears from her cheeks, put the glass in her hand and commanded, "Drink!"

She took half of it in one gulp, and then slowly, it hit her. "Oh my God," she breathed. "What has just happened? I cannot get rid .... of the image of Dillon .... with his insides spread out... across the pavement. He was my friend. A good man, and he died in pain in front of me."

Lando said nothing. He had no words of consolation. All he could do was to look sympathetically at her distressed face. He felt very strange, almost like another person.

There was the Lando he knew, the University lecturer, the guy who joked with Gary about dating the lovely Amber at the Dog and Doublet, the guy who lived in a quiet area of Shrewsbury whose main excitement was going to the dojo every week.

Then there was the Lando of this evening and yesterday. He had been belly-dancing in the desert under the stars with the most beautiful woman he had ever seen. He had nearly choked on a spoonful of wasabi whilst eating lunch in a revolving restaurant overlooking the sea. He had overheard parts of secret, suspicious conversations, and now he had experienced the site of a violent death first-hand. He had smelt human blood for the first time. He had somehow coped and taken the lead with this beautiful Turkish woman. There was a bloodied, curved dagger sitting on his bedside table, and he knew he was in a profoundly severe situation. He most certainly was not bored.

Chapter 15

Hobart G. Lonsdale IV was from a well-heeled, old Boston family and had disappointed his parents by not joining the family law firm. He applied to and was accepted into the CIA after university, aged 25, having had a year out before university working for an environmentally focused NGO in Africa. He had graduated in law from George Washington University, summa cum laude, and combined with his fluency in Arabic through his mother's side, his sporting attributes in wrestling and ball games, round or oblong, he was a good fit for the CIA from a skills and achievement aspect. They recruit from various backgrounds, but critically, they need integrity and the love of the United States. Hobart had this in bucket loads, but sometimes his attitude to life could be taken the wrong way as he tended to shut off from people to relax when not working. He had many acquaintances but few close friends, which was not the worst attribute when working as a field agent.

This undercover assignment in Dubai was his first overseas posting. His cover was as a mature student at the British University in Dubai, as there were thoughts that one or more staff members could somehow be involved in raising finance for Arab terrorist groups. His task was to gather intelligence on any terrorist organisation that might seek to damage American interests in the Middle East or Dubai in particular, and it was stretching him to the limit as he had been struggling to make inroads beyond those of an apparent sympathiser to the terrorists' points of view. His controller, Harold Shrimpton, was based nearly a couple of hours drive away in the Abu Dhabi Embassy and had given him very little support time as he was tied up in a large drugs sting that was coming to fruition.

Hobart had been introduced to Kadri by Harold two months ago amongst a crowd of people at a restaurant. She had a naughty streak, which Harold had noticed as soon as he met her 4 years ago, and he knew she was a potentially good informant, not just because of her looks. The element of danger and the extra money appealed to her. Harold had her checked out to ensure she was who she said she was, and then they put her through a short but rigorous unofficial training program in England, learning the dark arts of the CIA. She was taught elementary self-defence, using a pistol, transferring coded messages to her handler, IT skills, tracing information from digital sources, and simple computer hacking techniques, amongst other things. She was about the only helpful contact Harold had passed on. So, she was already a paid informant for the CIA before Hobart arrived. Her dancing performances took her to various venues, some like desert trips mainly for tourists and some, where private dancers were required to entertain local businessmen. This often placed her in dubious situations, many of which were illegal activities. This made her an immense potential source of information.

Dillon, like Kadri, was one of Hobart's contacts; recruits would be a better term. He had met him in a hotel bar at a promotional evening a few months before. Over the period, they had struck up a relationship as Hobart plied him with drinks and promised financial rewards if he could help acquaint him with the local customs and the major players in organised crime in Dubai. He pretended to be a journalist, authoring a book about exporting organised criminal activity to other countries. Still, all the time, he sought contacts who might lead him towards potential terrorist threats to all things American. Terrorism needed funding, and organised crime, in all its guises, could be a valuable source of income. Dillon had a great deal of local knowledge, and due to his regular trips to Dubai to see his family and his language skills, he had a good cover, so Hobart confessed to Dillon that he was not a journalist but was working for the US government. He did not mention initially that it was the CIA.

Hobart had received a strange phone call from him at about 4 pm. Dillon told him they needed to meet as he had some critical information. He had sounded a little tense, but Hobart put that down to excitement. Little did he know that it would be the last time they would speak. Ever!

He had gone to meet Dillon but never found him at their planned meeting place or any of his other haunts. While walking back, he heard scuffling and loud shouting from the adjacent back alley. He ran around the corner to see Dillon down on the ground with his guts all over the pavement, Kadri with a bloody dagger in her hand and his course tutor, Lando, by her side. He decided to stay in the shadows as the scene appeared incriminating for them both, apart from the apparent horror. He would be more than a bit surprised if they participated in Dillon's untimely death, but he did not want to take any chances.

He reached for the comforting touch of his 9mm Glock 19 and realised he was not carrying it. Those 15 rounds in the magazine would have been 15 pieces of comfort. Still, his controller, Harold Shrimpton, told him to carry it rarely as it was only issued for access by a field agent in a dire emergency. He had picked it up from Harold at the US Embassy in Abu Dhabi, as a batch of them had been shipped from Langley in a diplomatic bag a week ago. He had trained to use one with either hand for many hours until it felt like a part of his anatomy. He desperately needed it now, even though it was not his official, personal weapon. He resolved to follow them at a safe distance until he found out what their game was. He would never have suspected Kadri could kill anyone, and certainly not with a knife, but he did not know Lando's background. He watched them leave the scene, with Lando supporting and half dragging Kadri. After acquiring their robes, he watched them ditch their clothing, and then they got into a taxi, where he lost them as there was not another one immediately available. He took a long walk to the Hyatt Hotel as he felt that might be the only safe place for Lando to take Kadri. It was a gamble, but it paid off.

Chapter 16

In the hotel room, Lando and Kadri spoke for half an hour about what might be going on, and then Lando remembered the note that Dillon had pressed into his hand when he uttered the words, "Take this note to Hobart. Tell him I've seen him."

He walked over to his bag where he had placed the note, and just at that moment, there was a gentle knock on the door. They froze. There was another knock, and this time, it was more persistent. Lando thrust the note into his pocket, shovelled the dagger into his bedside table drawer and beckoned Kadri to lie down behind the bed. He went to the door peephole but could see no one there. He took the latch off the door, and it burst open with Hobart in the doorway. He had his hand in his jacket pocket like he was holding a gun and pushed Lando onto the bed.

"You have some explaining to do," he growled, slamming the door behind him with the back of his heel.

Lando was unprepared for this but wondered why Hobart did not pull the gun out of his pocket. Perhaps he did not have one and was pretending, but Lando was not taking the chance.

"It's a little late for private accountancy tuition, Hobart," he quipped, though why he needed to make a smart Alec comment, he did not know. Possibly stress!

"Quit the wisecracks. Where's Kadri?"

"I'm here," she said resignedly. "Please take your silly hand from your pocket, Hoby. Anyone can see you do not have a gun." She rose majestically from behind the bed like a wraith in the night, which was made more dramatic by her flowing black abaya. Her demeanour was improving fast. She was smiling sympathetically at Hobart's attempt at looking dangerous, and he quickly removed his hand from his pocket and unstraightened his fingers.

"I guess it didn't look like a Glock," he muttered resignedly. "'It certainly did not feel like one."

"Have you been following us?" said Lando, relieved that no gun was trained on him. "Did you see what happened?"

"I only saw you two by Dillon's body with blood all over you and you, Kadri, holding a knife."

Kadri's eyes glared in anger. "Dillon was my friend. Do you think I would have done that to him?" The pain came back to her as she relived the memory of Dillon's suffering.

"No. But I had to be cautious. Think about how it looked, particularly when you took off and both got a change of clothes. By the way, Kadri, they do not suit you. You even less Lando."

"Well, I am not used to wearing dishdashas. Maybe with a bit of practice…"

The night's tension had taken its toll on Lando's gut. So, he produced close to one of his loudest ever farts, surprising even Lando by both its depth and length, and after an apologetic expression from him, all three of them descended into laughter. It broke whatever doubts remained, and it was clear that Hobart was now judging them with his heart and not by what he saw… or smelt, for that matter.

Lando decided to go on the attack. "What about you? You still have a plaster across your hand. What caused that? Been in any knife fights?" he prodded aggressively.

"Yes, I have. You may have noticed I had this at lunchtime, so it cannot be related to poor old Dillon. As it happens, I was doing some exercises in my bedroom last night after I got in, pretending I was in a knife fight with some cutlery in my room. I stabbed myself in the process. Hurts like hell."

They smiled sympathetically, like parents at a child.

Hobart scowled and said, "So where is the knife then, Lando? I saw you take it from Kadri."

Lando went to the drawer in the bedside table to retrieve the knife still wrapped in his handkerchief. Hobart took it and placed it on a small table at the end of the suite and, lifting one end of the handkerchief, slowly rolled it across, revealing it as it unfolded with little bumps along the way. The vicious, short, curved blade was caked in Dillon's blood, which had now turned to deep brown as it had dried. Hobart was careful not to touch it.

"Well," grunted Hobart. "This is a lead of sorts. This knife is a jambiya and originated in Yemen although common in the Middle East."

"It's sharp on both sides," noted Lando.

"Yes, that is normal." Hobart's head lowered for a closer look. "The hilt looks to be made of carved horn, probably from a rhinoceros, and there is a red stone in the middle." He carefully turned it over, revealing a matching red stone. "I guess these are semi-precious stones, but the knife itself could have symbolised wealth or status. However," he said with dancing eyes. "You know the most valuable thing about this jambiya?"

Kadri and Lando looked up with anticipation.

"If you can find the matching sheath," he paused for a dramatic effect, "you have probably…"

"Found the killer!" they chorused.

"I shall take it to the Consulate in the morning. They have private local connections to give a full forensic report on it, and although I doubt much will be revealed, you never know."

Lando got up and meandered over to the mini bar. "Anyone for a wee dram?"

They looked at him quizzically.

"Sorry. Scottish. It means a small measure of whisky, also called a snifter."

"I'll have another snifter, please, if there is one?" chimed Kadri.

"Bourbon for me," Hobart said with a smile while Lando grabbed another Haig Scotch.

They sat around the small table, digesting the day. The only sound was the sipping of the drinks, the crunching of the nuts and the distant sounds of music from the pool bar outside.

Lando decided to plunge in with both feet as he had a big question. "Hobart, would you mind filling me in on some things? Why would you, as a business student, firstly follow Kadri and me and secondly carry a Glock pistol when you remember, of course, and thirdly talk about Consulate connections? Are you some kind of Private Eye?"

"No."

"Come on, Hobart. Tell him," said Kadri.

"No."

"Go on. If you won't, I will."

Lando was bemused now as Kadri obviously knew something he didn't. This was becoming irritating. "Am I the only one in the dark then?"

Hobart then said with a resigned puff of his cheeks, "Ok. I give in. I am with the CIA. This is my first assignment. The student thing is because we suspect something is going on at BUiD to do with terrorism, although it is unlikely to do with British management. I am trying to find out what is happening, and things are heating up. My controller is of no help as he is too busy working on another operation in Abu Dhabi, and I feel a bit like a fish out of water."

Lando's mouth dropped as he turned to Kadri. "So, what about you? Are you a spy as well?"

"I resent that," she said. "I am a part-time informant, though."

"Goodness gracious," was all Lando could say. He almost followed it with 'great balls of fire.'

Hobart took another gulp of his bourbon. "I suppose Dillon did not say anything to you before he died?"

"My God, Hobart, he did, and I had forgotten the note he gave me."

"Go on then."

Lando narrated the exact situation, "Dillon said, 'Take this note to Hobart. Tell him I've seen him.'"

"Seen who?"

"No idea," said Lando.

At this point, Lando removed the note from his pocket, stained with a streak of Dillon's blood, and placed it in front of Hobart.

Hobart unfolded it and read it repeatedly. He looked up, and his eyes shone. "Do you realise what this could mean?"

"We have not had a chance to read it," Kadri exclaimed indignantly.

Hobart was still determining how much to say as Kadri and Dillon were known to the CIA, but Lando was not. He decided to risk it.

"For years, we have been on the trail of a man named Ashiraf Nasruddin. He would appear to be the chief henchman and strongarm of the Spiritual guide of 'Wings of Fire' whom no one has seen. It is an Al-Qaeda or Houthi-affiliated terrorist cell. The leader is called al-Hawiya, which means 'The Abyss' in the Qur'an. Something to do with hell."

"Ugh. I thought Al-Qaeda had been severely degraded since Osama bin Laden was eliminated. Anyway, that does not sound like a charming name," muttered Lando.

"It isn't. A neat term, though, 'degraded.' We use that often in 'The Company.'"

"The Company?" questioned Lando.

"The Agency, the CIA. We do not know if this Hawiya exists or if he is just a bit of folklore. Still, if we can remove this Ashiraf Nasruddin fellow, then we are getting somewhere as without him, we believe this Hawiya chap, again, if he exists, would be effectively neutered."

"Neutered?" queried Kadri.

"Castrated, emasculated, rendered powerless," Hobart replied. "Sorry, I could have used a better description."

"Come on, what does the note say?" implored Kadri.

Hobart looked down at it again. "It says, *'Finally met Ashiraf. Wants to accelerate terrorism campaign. Thinks I am a sympathiser being a Sunni Muslim and offered me a chance to prove it. I asked for a reward as I felt it might strengthen my case. Said he had a stream of finance controlled by someone in a local education establishment. Got to see him. At last, we are getting somewhere. Will send a picture of Ashiraf from the phone.*

—Dil"

There were a few seconds of silence, and Hobart looked around with a glum look. "We were so close. I still have no picture of this Ashiraf and can only guess it was on his phone. I assume you two did not see it around Dillon's body?"

Both shook their heads.

"Pity. I am guessing that picture is what cost him his life if they had tapped into his phone. Tried to track his phone without success. At least we have some useful information."

Lando suddenly went rigid and burst out, "Hang on. I may have seen this Ashiraf fellow."

Hobart and Kadri looked at him expectantly.

"I have just remembered. I was at the Chelsea Arms pub in the Sheraton Creek Hotel on my first night. As you know, I met Dillon on my plane flight into Dubai and recognised him across the room in the pub. I would have approached him, but he seemed upset with the other person at his table. No, not upset... frightened. I am sure I heard the name Ashiraf used, but I could not be sure it was to the man at his table."

"Could you describe him at all?" said Hobart, who could hardly contain himself.

"Yes, he was Arabic-looking but dressed in casual European clothing. He had a short black beard, thick-framed glasses and a definite menacing look on his face."

"Anything else? Was he big, fat, tall, short? Is anything else distinctive? Please try. Think back."

"Well, yes, he was short. I would guess only a little over five feet. Medium build. Oh, and he had a limp, although not very pronounced."

"Aha!" yelled Hobart, leaping from his chair. "That could be him. We heard he was wounded years ago in some situation or other. Would you recognise him again?"

"Definitely, but more because of that look of menace on his face. Not pleasant."

"Would you care to come to the embassy and look at a few mugshots or try to help us create an artist's impression of him?"

"Of course, I would. Not a problem."

"Okay, we shall set it up. It may be better if we do not go to the embassy. I shall speak to Harold and let you know."

"Who is Harold?"

"Sorry. He is my controller in Abu Dhabi. Not been much help to me, but on this, I think he will be."

Through all this chat, Kadri had been noticeably quiet. Hobart and Lando looked at her simultaneously and observed her shallow breathing. She had fallen asleep in the chair.

"Not surprising with what she has gone through," whispered Lando, and he gently lifted her off the chair and placed her on his bed with the enormous pillows all around her, making her seem like a bird in a nest. He looked at her compassionately and turned to see Hobart smiling at him.

"I see someone has lost his heart, and you have only been in Dubai for a few days," mused Hobart.

"Well, who wouldn't? Just look at her. She is like a sleeping angel."

"No, I'm not," she yawned through half-closed lips and drifted off again.

"I think she had better stay here for the night, Lando. That is if you can keep your hands off her."

"I am sure she would have a say in the matter, Hobart. Anyway, I am not like that."

"Like what? Are you gay or something?"

"What on earth does 'or something' mean? I'm not as it happens, but what's it to you? Why? Are you gay? You are not propositioning me, are you?"

"Absolutely not," retorted Hobart, laughing wildly. "Well, look after her. She has been through it. I will get off home now, and I need to put in a report for Harold before morning. It has been one hell of a day."

Hobart thought it beat practising law, remembering the old family law firm he might have entered. Not as safe, of course.

"You need to function as if everything is normal, which means you are doing your lectures as usual. We cannot, for a moment, change our routines; otherwise, the other side will pick up on it. Also, hide those dishdashas from the staff in the morning." He glanced at his watch. "It is past midnight, so see you in the morning. Sleep well if you can."

He left with the knife wrapped up in Lando's handkerchief and secured in his pocket.

Lando looked over at Kadri. He loosened her clothing as delicately as possible and wrapped a side of the duvet over her. The problem was where he would sleep. There was plenty of room on the great big bed next to her, but he needed help figuring out how to play it, as there was nowhere else in the room he could sleep other than on an uncomfortable floor or sitting in a chair. He decided to undress down to his underclothes and sleep on the bed next to Kadri but with his head at the other end. At least he would preserve a little modesty and make her less embarrassed when she woke up.

He had a quick wash, set his alarm, and lay with her on the bed with his head near her feet. They called it top and tailing at Uni. He did not remember falling asleep.

Chapter 17

At 7.00 am, Qasim was in his office at BUiD drinking his favoured sweet tea with lemon from his Arabic style, slim-waisted, glass teacup and saucer. He gave it a stir with the long steel teaspoon. He picked up his second cell phone used for his 'clandestine' calls. It rang with the silly ringtone of the 'Teddy bears picnic,' which he used for Hamza, the only one of the three brigands allowed his number.

"What have you got to tell me then, Hamza?"

"Ahaa, Qasim Effendi. How are you?"

"I have told you I do not like that Turkish gibberish. Mr Sarawi will do nicely. I hear you have been a naughty boy, Hamza. Who do I blame, you, Abdul or Farouk?"

"But, but, but..."

"Now listen to me; I want you to tell me exactly what happened last night. Exactly, do you hear? Otherwise, as Clemenza says in the Godfather film, you will be sleeping with the fishes."

"Well, you told us to quietly silence that chubby lump called Dillon, which we did."

"We? So, all three of you are responsible for that fiasco? What do you not understand by *quietly silence*?"

"But he did not make a noise. It was on a quiet street."

"Hamza, quietly silence means quiet in the publicity sense as well. This was all over the newspapers this morning. It even made the national TV and radio. Wallahi (I swear to God), his intestines were all over the pavement!" Qasim was losing his cool. "You father of stinky smells. You stupid, smelly, ugly son of a thousand whores, how do you think this looks to outsiders? It looks like there is a deranged, bloodthirsty killer on the loose in the streets of our country. The police are everywhere. I presume you used a knife. What have you done with it?"

There was a loud silence.

"Hamza, tell me you retained the knife."

"The silly fat bastard would not let go of it after I stabbed him, and none of us could yank his fingers from around the handle, and we even tried to cut them off with another knife."

"You what? You left the knife! You are the most completely cretinous goat-shagging waste of a dirty dishdasha. You would not even be worthy of a landfill or embedded in the corner concrete pillar of a multi-storey tower. You scraping of filth off the sole of a dirty shoe. May both of your father's bollocks explode in his sleep, and may your sister be shagged by one hundred syphilitic dogs with filthy arses. May the stepladders fall when you are halfway through shagging a camel, so your pathetic wang is wrenched from your body. Finally, may the TV news catch you on video with your dick embedded in a sloppy baba ghanoush. Do you know how long it will take me to cover this up and how much it will cost?"

Hamza had a visual imagination and was still trying to recover from the multiple curses.

"A great deal is the answer. Now, give me some good news. Have you made any connection with Hawiya?"

Hamza did not like giving negative news, so he tried to counter it with some hope. "We have made inroads into our connections but cannot find any way to engineer a meeting for anybody with Hawiya. However, we have good news."

"Okay. What is it? Let me have it quickly."

"We have found out the name of his most dependable man. His name is Ashiraf Nasruddin. This man is like a general but participates in strategic planning, outcomes, and tactical operations. He appears to be the one that makes the wheels of the organisation turn. I think we can get to him to arrange a meeting, but after that, it is up to you to decide whether you are happy dealing with him because Hawiya, if he exists, has seen nobody apparently outside his inner circle in the last 20 years."

"Well, wonders never cease. That is not a bad start, Hamza, and it compensates slightly for the mess you have made over eliminating this Dillon. I shall speak with Shazil Haroun Al Maktoum and see how he wants to take it from here. Meanwhile, please get word to Ashiraf Nasruddin and let us know when we can meet him. Where would it be? Please assure him there could be significant compensation for him if he can help us. Tell him that a minister of government would like to talk to him anywhere of his choosing."

"Thank you. Thank you. I shall get word to him straight away. I am sorry about the issue with Dillon."

"Hamza, it was more than an issue, you son of a pig." Qasim could not resist further abuse as it made him feel more in control. "I trust you will let me know within 48 hours if, when and where we have a meeting."

Chapter 18

Lando woke up with his 7.15 am alarm. He was muzzy in the head and realised that he was facing the wrong end of his bed. He recalled the previous evening with horror and turned over to wake Kadri. She was not there, although her side of the bed was still faintly warm and retained her heady scent. She must have gone early and had not wished to wake him. A good thing, as she could leave more surreptitiously in the early hours than when the hotel was busy. He hoped she was all right. From what Hobart had said, he knew they must act normally; otherwise, the game would be up. There were far too many eyes about, and if less of them were focused on Lando and Kadri, the better. He wrenched himself out of bed and dived into the shower. It still seemed strange to shower in front of the bed and the main windows, looking out over the buildings, but it was also strangely enjoyable. He turned the tap onto the full cold, the opposite direction, having learnt from day one in his room. He fancied a freezing cold shower so that he could grit his teeth and focus on the pain until the cold numbed him. No chance. He forgot for an instant that he was in the Middle East and the coldest the cold water could get was fundamentally tepid. He assumed Wim Hof would not have a significant following in hot countries as a cold shower or bath was out of the question unless they froze their water. The only way was to order a shed load of ice and chuck it into a tub. So, he turned the shower to a gentle warmth, covered himself in soap suds and tried to melt the previous day's memory away, apart from sharing his bed with Kadri. Even though the circumstances were horrendous, he could not forget her vulnerability as well as her attraction.

He skipped breakfast and headed straight to the Al-Jafr Conference room, hoping Lisana would be waiting to greet the students with a strong cup of coffee. Now *that* he could cope with. He dressed smartly in a jacket and tie, although he did not know why he took a jacket, as it would be taken off immediately and sit on the back of his chair all day. At least it held his wallet and smartphone. He supposed the alternative was to carry some kind of man-bag, but he couldn't bring himself to do that. He welcomed change, but there were some traditions from his old days of working in the family business that he liked to keep. He kept his shoes clean, ensured his flies were done up and didn't carry a handbag!

How did she do it? Lisana looked as classy and efficient as ever and he had a cup of coffee in his hand almost before he had finished asking for it. She reminded him of a character called Radar in the Mash TV series.

"My word, Lando," she said. "You look tired. You look like you have just seen a dead body."

It was all Lando could do not to choke on his mouthful of coffee. He forced it down even though it was scalding hot and tried to turn his response into a weak joke. "How did you know? The body has only been cold for three hours. I have been an assassin for five years, and you are the first to have caught me out."

"Okay, Lando. Everyone is allowed a night on the tiles occasionally. Where did you go?"

"I didn't go anywhere. I briefly walked around last night and returned to bed quite early. I didn't sleep, however. I guess I am still on UK time." Lando had regained his composure and was quite pleased with himself for not completely falling apart, despite Lisana's humour being unwittingly bang on the truth. She gave an understanding nod as the students filed in. Hobart nodded knowingly in his direction when he arrived, and the morning proceeded as it should. There was one thing Lando always enjoyed about lecturing—at the lectern, he was in control and entirely in the moment, which took his mind off other things. It was beneficial on this occasion, and as they proceeded out of the room to lunch, Hobart quietly congratulated him on how he had handled himself this morning. Hobart seemed quite unruffled himself, as if he dealt with murders every day, although Lando presumed it had been a big shock to him as well, but he was coping no doubt due in part to his training. They all arrived at the Al Dawaar restaurant, and Lando had a silent prayer that the mechanism of this fantastic revolving restaurant would not go into overdrive and spin them around at two or three times the normal speed. He was still feeling a bit delicate in the head. However, having not had any breakfast, he realised his stomach was grumbling a little, and he could manage a reasonable lunch. He kept it simple with freshly cut beef, crushed potatoes and a green salad. He tried a little wasabi on the meat but did not make the mistake he made before. Just a little bit was enough. In the middle of a conversation with the students around him, Nadia, who had become quite chatty as the course proceeded, brought the conversation to a standstill. "I heard on Dubai TV that there was a horrible murder close to here. A man was stabbed and left in the street."

Lando blanched but continued eating.

"Yes, I read it on Gulf News on my computer this morning," said one grinning Arab student. "Apparently, his intestines were on the pavement, and two dogs were chewing away at them." He loved the effect of the shock on the others. "He was a large…"

Lando interrupted quickly, "Hang on, guys, this is a bit of a fruity conversation over lunch. Could we at least get to the Om Ali before going into detail?"

That lightened the atmosphere, but Lisana looked distinctly pale and only picked at her food afterwards. "Does anyone know who he was?"

"It was not mentioned on the TV," said Nadia quietly. "May Allah have mercy on him."

Lunch was quiet after that, and everyone departed in a sombre mood. Hobart and Lando could barely look each other in the eye. Lando proceeded to his room and lay on his perfectly made bed. He marvelled at how well housekeeping made the room look as if it had barely been lived in and was like a showroom. He looked up at the arrow on the ceiling pointing to Mecca and thought back over the last 24 hours—it was a disturbing experience being a witness to a most horrendous murder and fleeing with a beautiful woman and wearing Arabic clothing. Indeed, it was not your average night at the Dog & Doublet, although a picture of Amber briefly flashed through his mind wearing a belly dancing outfit! A part of his brain had been aroused like nothing had in years. He closed his eyes and drifted off into a disturbed sleep with horrendous images of Dillon, and he woke with a start. He had only dozed for about a half hour but felt so awkward and unbalanced that he got up, donned a polo shirt, swimming shorts and flip-flops, and headed for the pool. A challenging, long swim would help stabilise him, he hoped. He opened the outside door, reeling at the wall of heat that hit him, which steamed up his sunglasses again. He had to stop quickly before he tripped over the beautifully manicured hedge that lined his walk to the pool. He wiped his glasses and headed straight for the bar, and he was pleased to see his friendly bartender, Solly, with his ever-present smile.

"Hello, Mr Lando, sir. How are you today?" he sang out happily whilst wiping and putting glasses away. He immediately placed a frosted beer glass on the countertop.

"I am fine, Solly," he lied. "But I will be even better after having one of your fine beers."

Solly commenced pouring an ice-cool bottle of beer into the frosted glass with a look of pride. He glanced up at Lando, and a frown came over his face as he saw his withdrawn expression.

"Now, Mr Lando, sir. You need more than a beer to put your head in a better place."

"Very perceptive of you, Solly. I have some difficult things to think about."

"Ha, you think you have the big problem, sir. There was a man killed near to here last night. He perished in a very messy way. They think he was stabbed. Not a pretty sight, I believe." He gently handed the filled glass of beer over.

Lando turned away so Solly could not see the hurt on his face. He remained silent for a full minute before replying quietly, "I heard about it. Yes, very tragic."

"This happened many times when I was a child in Zanzibar. Many bad people desperate for food or money. That is why my father took us all to Oman." He raised his eyes from wiping the spilt beer froth from the counter and saw something in Lando's eyes. "You knew this man, Mr Lando, yes?" His eyes were full of tenderness.

Lando was utterly taken aback. How could he know that? He decided to face Solly head-on whilst there was no one within earshot.

"I saw the report and picture on the news, and yes, I knew him. I had travelled over from England on the aeroplane, sitting by him. He was genuinely good and came over to see his family."

"I am so sorry, Mr Lando." He looked him straight in the eye, and Lando realised that he meant it. The compassion that had developed throughout his hard life showed in every crease and wrinkle on his face.

"Yes, I did not know him well, but even so, he made the world better. He was a big man with a big heart, and I cannot think why anyone would do that to him or any human being for that matter." Lando did not want to give away any further information about Dillon if he did not have to. He thought he was learning for the first time in his life what it was to be involved in an undercover operation. He found it difficult as he was an open and honest guy, so holding back on personal information about somebody seemed slightly like he was lying. It did not sit well, particularly with Solly, as he regarded him as a friend even after such a short acquaintance.

They continued to share stories until Lando's beer glass was empty, after which Lando got up from his stool, beckoned goodbye to Solly, stripped off by a lounger and dived into the pool, hoping to wash his bad memories away. He swam hard for 20 lengths, nearly drowning a little boy who was splashing around in the shallow end and had to apologise to his mother profusely for being careless. He realised he was living in an unfamiliar world. A world of violence, a world of death, a world of lies but hopefully not a world of drowning little boys, although he could think of one at his prep school called Horace, who had an enormous head and was nicknamed 'Head-butt Horace' because no one wanted to be head-butted by him. On a school walk, Head-Butt Horace shoved him headlong into a prickly gorse bush. He had little thorns in him all over. Lando still remembered the pain. He could cheerfully have drowned that one.

He knew he needed to understand himself better and compartmentalise things, not least the last couple of days; otherwise, he would not get through whatever was to come.

He returned to his bedroom after a deft wave to Solly. He turned around and almost clattered into that same little boy standing behind him on the way out of the poolside area. Another load of apologies to his mother, who looked at him like he had crawled from under a stone. He did not blame her or stick around to convince her that this was not his usual way of treating little children. He almost ran to the glass door and got in the elevator but was not quick enough to avoid sharing it with the little boy and his mother, who was also going to his floor. He could see a regular relationship building with this lady, but not one he wanted. They did not speak, but he took the time to look at her in the lift, and she avoided his gaze. She was skinny and had decided to go to the pool covered in jewellery as if she had emptied her whole jewellery box onto her body. He was surprised she could keep her head up with the weight of the numerous pendants with large, ornate stones around her neck and dangling onto her dark-tanned chest, which had seen better days. He mused at the thought of her taking the jewellery off in a while and finding the patterns on her skin that had not been tanned by the sun. He could not stop himself from smiling.

"What are you smiling at?" Her voice was like the squawk of a bird of prey. "Do you see something funny?" She was clearly up for a confrontation, and he did not wish to satisfy her, so he had to think of something to say quickly.

"Oh, nothing really. I was only thinking of something the barman said." It was the best he could do off the cuff.

This was not good enough for her. "Are you sure you are all right in the head?" She would not be outdone and tried to needle Lando sufficiently to create an argument.

Lando thought quickly, the elevator would arrive soon, and he had two ways to go with this one. His instinct was to apologise profusely if he offended her or her child, but his childish desire to get one over on her was a force he could not resist.

"I, er, er, haven't got a bike, so I need to find my shorts, and the barman said lunch tomorrow was on the piano, and he clearly knew what he was talking about, so he advised me to find as many little boys as possible and knock them over." Lando had no idea where this gibberish sentence originated, but it had the required effect. The jewellery lady looked at him with complete astonishment just as the lift reached the floor.

The door slid open, and she almost ran out, dragging little Willie or whatever his name was, along the landing. The smile returned to Lando's face, and he felt lighter than air as he walked towards his bedroom door. He was almost crying with laughter before he could get into his bedroom and had to muffle it as said lady was only a few doors down trying to get into her own room, and she looked back with a slightly frightened expression.

It was 5:30 PM, and Lando had a cool shower in the room. He still could not shake the strange feeling of showering in the bathroom in the middle of the bedroom, stark naked, turning slowly in every direction, staring through all the glass walls. However, now he was beginning to enjoy it. He dried himself, lay on the bed with his damp towel wrapped around him, and decided to have dinner in his bedroom and assess the room service.

The next thing he knew, it was 7 PM. Amazing how quickly sleep came to him when he had so much on his mind. All this excitement was tiring. He checked the room service menu and craved something filling and simple, preferably with fries. He fancied a Wiener Schnitzel but not a proper one as he had few scruples with food, but the treatment of the calves did not appeal, and he often made his own version at home using a pork steak hammered thinly. He doubted he could get a pork version here, so he opted for a breaded half-chicken and seasoned fries. He guessed it was their upmarket version of a KFC.

He grabbed the phone by his bed and dialled room service, who picked up immediately, and he ordered it for 8 pm with a chilled lager. His mobile rang from across the room when he replaced the hotel phone. He hopped off the bed and seemed to spend an age finding it. He looked at the screen and instantly smiled, and he felt his heart skip a beat. It was Kadri. He was so eager to accept the call that he dropped the phone. By the time he had retrieved it, the call went dead. He was almost apoplectic with rage but pressed the return call more in hope than expectation. Joy! She answered immediately and asked him what he had been doing. He almost said he was having a wank, but realised that his humour would not necessarily translate across cultures or even genders, for that matter.

"Sorry, I couldn't find the phone even though I could hear it, and when I finally found it, I dropped it. You see what you do to me?"

"Why is it my fault?" she replied in her breathy Turkish accent. He could tell she was laughing as she said it. At least he had broached the idea in a slightly amusing way that he was rather fond of her.

"Just kidding. But I think you know that. How are you? What have you been up to?" he asked as if accusing her of something very naughty.

"I wondered what you were doing this evening and whether you fancied meeting for a chat and maybe some food?" she said hopefully.

"Well, I have just ordered room service. I didn't fancy going out, but I could cancel it."

"Or I could come to you and join you. As much planning is needed, we could talk more freely in your room." The word *planning* did not sit well with Lando as it sounded too business-like. "Anyway, what have you ordered?" she continued.

He told her, and she straightaway said, "I'll have the same plus a side order of coleslaw and double up on the lagers, please."

"Great. See you as soon as you can get here. I'll order it for 30 minutes. OK?"

She rang off, and he could not understand why he was trembling slightly. Maybe it was because he invited a woman who liked beer to his room. He was sure James Bond did not tremble before he had a beautiful woman come to his room. He put that out of his mind as too many of Bond's female friends seemed to end up dead. They were not real anyway. This was real.

He re-ordered from room service and lay on his bed waiting. He lasted about 30 seconds. He was too excited. He got up and checked himself out in the bathroom. Bad idea, as usual. He got a handful of Aramis and splashed it all over his shirt and neck. He coughed himself hoarse, sat in the chair in the small suite area by the table, and read a book for a while. After twenty minutes, he could not remember a single word he had read. He had just been staring at the words. He started to think back over the last few days. Then he heard a gentle knock on the door.

Chapter 19

He leapt out of his chair and wrenched the door open in excitement, little realising that Kadri's hand was on the door handle, dragging her in with such speed that she fell straight into him, taking them both to the floor. He briefly sensed the warmth of her body and then saw the surprise on her face changing to a smile, followed by an infectious giggle. There was no ice to be broken in this conversation.

They got up and patted themselves down, and Kadri looked him straight in the eye, saying, "Should we start again?" She then leaned forward and gave Lando a lingering kiss on his cheek. He felt his face burning. He was more than a little embarrassed but hid it by turning around and gesturing to the small, velvet couch by the table. Kadri sat to one side, leaving room for Lando, and looked up at him with a playful expression on her face.

She could not resist it. "You sure know how to show a girl a good time." They giggled together, and there seemed little he could say in return that adequately expressed his feelings of desire, embarrassment, stupidity, pleasure and self-humiliation. So, he didn't. He just stared at her lovely form.

"How about a glass of water or a beer?" It was the best he could do with a brain about as chaotic as a bag of dropped ping-pong balls.

She nodded gently. "Water, please."

He walked to the mini-bar and took out a little green, distinctively shaped bottle. "Looks like Perrier. Will that be ok?" She nodded again as he also removed a bottle of lager. Heineken. They get about a bit, he mused.

Lando was about to pull up a chair just as Kadri patted the seat by her. He looked down at her, quickly taking in all her splendour again. Her jet-black hair in falling ringlets framed her faultless light brown face. The subtle, sparkly earrings that shimmered as she moved. The perfectly shaped eyebrows highlighted the intense, deep brown eyes. Her perfect poise whilst sitting in the chair seemed to accentuate her magnificent, shapely bosom, which stretched the top of her white silk blouse beyond reason and her long, muscular legs wrapped in a pair of black, floaty harem trousers, gathered in at her ankles that were uncrossed but modestly together at the knees and drawn up to one side. He felt himself on the verge of dribbling, which would be very uncool, as he took up her offer.

It was a small couch, so they were, of necessity, touching at the hip, and her bodily warmth radiated through to him like a bolt of electricity, and he needed a cold shower. He got one because Kadri came out with a load of questions.

"We must plan our next moves as there is so much to do. It will not be long before we are linked with Dillon. After all, he was on the desert trip and spoke to us as well as Hobart, so we need to be ready to answer the questions of the Dubai security services. Then there is the knife, there is the way he was killed, the why he was killed and how much he knew, and how do we find out any of that anyway?"

"Hold your horses, Kadri. I only pray no one saw us anywhere near Dillon's body in the street; otherwise, we shall be thrown in the slammer and not see the light of day. I guess Hobart would probably get away with it through his embassy."

"What is this slammer?"

"Sorry, it is a slang word for prison. I assume it is because when you go to prison, they slam the door shut."

Just then, there was a double knock on the door, and a light call of 'room service' was heard. Kadri looked at Lando with a half-smile playing across her face. "I'll go onto the balcony as the less I am seen around you, the better for all our sakes. I hope you are not going to give him the same treatment you gave me."

"Depends how pretty he is, if it is a he," mused Lando as he walked to the door. He looked through the peephole. "He is!" he said as he laughed and opened the door to reveal a smiling waiter.

The young man placed the tray on the table, and Lando tipped him enough dirhams to keep him happy but not enough so that he would remember him from any other person he delivered to. Lando detected a knowing look from the waiter as he glanced towards the balcony. He could not think why, as whatever he thought he knew, even Lando did not see how the rest of the evening would go. He was delivering a meal for two, which rather gave some of the game away. Lando closed the door behind him, and Kadri floated back from the balcony.

Their eyes lit up as they viewed the platefuls of breaded meat, fries, and coleslaw with two large, frothy beers on the side. They tucked in and left nothing. Then they both reclined with satisfied stomachs and still with half their beers to finish.

"Elinize sağlık," whispered Kadri with a dreamlike look on her face. "I have not eaten properly for 24 hours. Fantastic."

"Go on then. What does 'knees are salak' mean?"

"It's pronounced El.. neezer... salik. Elinize sağlık. It is Turkish for complimenting the food and the chef who made it. He is not here, but my praise goes to heaven for him... or her, of course."

"Yep. I can drink to that. I have probably had a better meal, but it was exactly what I wanted tonight, and the company made it taste even better." He thought a bit of flattery would not go amiss.

It was not lost on Kadri as she looked sideways at him knowingly. He had recognised how consistently perceptive she was, and subtle gestures were never lost on her. This could have been more subtle, but it did the trick. She suddenly changed the tone of their idle chat.

"Do you have a lady back home in England?"

This was unexpected.

"Not really."

"What in the name of God does that mean? Do you have a boyfriend?"

"My God, no," he voiced a bit too loudly. "I mean ... er ... it's ok for some ... er ... people, but it is not for me."

"So, what does 'not really' mean then?"

"Well, I was married years ago for about two weeks, and I have not had a meaningful relationship since. However, there is a barmaid back home called Amber, who I have my eye on."

He thought he had better come on with some lad stuff to ensure Kadri was aware he liked women.

Just then, she leaned over so close to him that he felt her warm breath on his face and said, "Kiss me."

My God, he thought. I do not even have to make the running.

"Kiss me," she breathed at him again.

He was usually so slow on the uptake with the ladies, but he could not help himself this time. Her perfume invaded his whole being as if the heat of her body had just caused whatever scent she was wearing to wash over him like a tidal wave. He kissed her lips softly, and then he became a hostage to her. He could not help himself; his tongue tasted hers, which was equally exploring. Their hands encircled each other's bodies, and he felt the old familiar bulge in his trousers grow. He almost tried to hide it, but her hand reached down, lay on his lap and slid upwards, gently stroking him until he began to lose control.

He plucked up the courage and whispered in her ear, "May I take you to bed?"

She nodded a breathy "Yes, Please," and he picked her up like she weighed nothing and almost ran towards the big fluffy bed, tripping over a pair of his carelessly strewn shoes on the way and tossing her across the bed. She would have been clear off the other side of a normal-sized bed. Thankfully, she laughed out loud, which turned into a giggling fit that she could not stop. It took all the anxiety out of Lando's situation, but then he remembered the need for protection. He leaned over to his bedside table drawer and scrabbled around wildly before Kadri gratefully deemed it unnecessary. It was a significant relief as he last used this packet before the Covid outbreak, and it had probably biodegraded. He knelt on the mattress beside her while gently undoing the buttons of her blouse. With both hands, she opened it wide, and Lando bent down and gently kissed each of her breasts through her lace brassiere. His lips lingered over her nipples, which he felt harden through the material. He leaned over her, dimmed the lights and kissed her again tenderly on the lips. Their tongues explored each other, and Kadri's hands went for his belt buckle and expertly released it in one sweeping action.

Before he knew it, they were both naked, and she marvelled at his male hardness under the covers. She did not want to let it go. In the room's half-light, they made love energetically and desperately. Kadri started to moan whilst her hands were stroking his body all over, and it was all Lando could do to wait for his orgasm until she was there. It seemed to happen in seconds, and as Kadri enjoyed being ravished by such a sensitive man, she completely let go as he took her to heaven and back. Not a word was said by either of them beyond their gentle groanings of pleasure. Afterwards, they lay in each other's arms for half an hour until Kadri smiled as she felt him hardening again. Lando marvelled at his manhood, which appeared to have a mind of its own. The second time they took it more slowly and with a tenderness that Kadri had not experienced in a long time as he sucked her toes, kissed her feet and then the back of her knees and tummy. His male muskiness aroused her as he kissed her on the side of her neck. He kissed her on the attractive little dent between her nose and forehead. She responded to this man's care for her needs besides his own and gave herself entirely to him.

Afterwards, despite the cool of the air-conditioning, they were both extremely hot, sweaty and thirsty. Lando smiled to himself and suggested they raid the mini bar. He walked over to it and returned with a couple of Heineken tins, dropping one on the way. He brought them over to the bed and looked at Kadri's half-covered body and how lovely she seemed.

"How long will you hold that smile on your face, Lando?" she said as she laughed. Lando had no idea he was even smiling. It was a wholly involuntary reaction.

"Maybe a week," he muttered as he got his finger under the tab of the beer can and flipped it. Sadly, it was the one he had dropped on the floor, and a jet of ice-cold beer shot all over Kadri's bare breasts, causing her to shriek with both shock and pleasure. He offered to lick it all off, which she thought about briefly before declining and suggesting her thirst was greater than her current need to have Lando inside her.

"Shame," he grunted. "I thought we had something going for a while." They both beamed, and they compromised, with Lando taking a clean white handkerchief from his bedside table and wiping her face, followed by her perfect breasts, whose nipples had reacted powerfully with the cold beer. That did it. They both took a long swig of beer and within thirty seconds, he was kissing and sucking her nipples. He moved his tongue down to her tummy button and beyond, leaving her completely helpless, and, grabbing his hair with both hands, she forced him to continue his explorations until she came violently in wave after wave of orgasms. A minute's quietness ensued until her breathing became normal, and her hand went down to Lando's still throbbing member. She caressed him rhythmically as she kissed his chest. It seemed about three milliseconds to Lando until he came, creating bolts of lightning throughout his head, his hands and the soles of his feet. He had nothing left to give, at which point she nestled into the crook of his neck before her breathing slowed. She fell asleep. They were in a heaven where nothing else existed besides the two of them. They surfaced, and Lando reached for one of the cans of beer, sloshed it around his mouth, and proceeded to let some seep out onto Kadri's breast. She casually pushed him away as he feigned disappointment, but neither had anything left to give.

"What just happened?" mused Lando. "I have… never…. had… an experience like that."

"I should hope not," Kadri replied as she feigned hurt in her expression.

They sat up in bed in silence for several minutes, supping their beers until they were empty. He stared at his crushed can and imagined that was how his balls felt. Mangled and drained.

Chapter 20

That evening, Kadri had left soon after their tryst. They had agreed that little planning could be done as they both needed a good sleep and trying to plan what to do next, with the Dillon situation, did not do it for them.

Lando slept like a log, and he could not get his energy up for his lectures the following day as much as usual. It did not seem so important anymore. Hobart stared at him with a vaguely quizzical look on his face all morning, and when they conversed over coffee, all Lando could think about was the night before with Kadri. Accordingly, he struggled to speak coherently with Hobart. He would never know how he got through the rest of the morning.

Just before lunch, Lando took a breath of fresh air around the hotel and received a call from Qasim Sarawi, who requested Lando to come over to BUiD as he needed to check out student numbers to sort out the fee payment to Wolverhampton University. Lando thought this a bit strange as this was more of an administrative issue, and surely it was something Claes Sundberg would have at his fingertips. He headed down to reception and asked for a taxi, and who showed up within five minutes, but Gaji, his friendly airport driver, still wearing his predictable smile.

"What can I get you, Mr Westwood? Alcohol, girls, places to go, knock-off watches, pubs, restaurants, girls, shisha bars?"

"Gaji, when will you ever learn? I need a trip to BUiD, the British University in Dubai. Do you know where it is?"

"Of course, sir. It is about a half-hour drive away."

"Why are you taking me as I was expecting a public taxi to pick me up?"

"I have no airport trips for a couple of hours, so the hotel turns a blind eye to us doing private trips to earn a bit more. Comes in handy."

I'll bet, mused Lando, and he would bet his life that Gaji had a deal with reception to refer taxi trips to him when he had no airport runs. *C'est la vie*, he thought.

They left the reception, and the stifling air walking through the glass door exit hit Lando with a thump in the face. Once again, his sunglasses steamed up. He removed them for a minute while they warmed up to match the temperature of the air outside.

"The car is over here, sir." Gaji waved him over to the right towards the taxi area by the hotel exit.

"Who are you seeing at BUiD?" asked Gaji, which seemed a strange question to Lando.

"I am seeing a gentleman by the name of Qasim Sarawi."

Gaji went noticeably quiet, and the atmosphere in the car seemed to change.

"What's the matter, Gaji?"

"None of my business, Mr Lando," he replied curtly.

"Come on, Gaji. Don't hold back. How do you know him anyway? You do know him, don't you?"

"Yes, Mr Lando, I do. He is often in our hotel and comes around regularly to check student numbers. He always makes a point of telling me that, as if I care.'

"I get the feeling you do not like him very much."

"None of my business, Mr Lando."

"Look, Gaji, he is not a friend of mine. I only met him for the first time a few days ago. He does not make me comfortable, so what's the problem?"

"He is insulting, and I have heard him abuse many people on the telephone. He speaks to people about things he does not want me to hear. I once found him a woman for the night, and she said she would never go with him again as he was cruel to her and gave her so much pain after he tied her up."

"Ok, Gaji, that is immensely helpful as I like to know the kind of people I am dealing with. I guess you would not trust him then?"

"Not in this world or the next, Mr Lando."

"Thank you, Gaji; I appreciate your honesty. Perhaps neither of us speak of this conversation to anyone else as I have similar reservations about him."

Gaji pulled an imitation zipper along his lips, and Lando copied him before Gaji nearly ran someone off his bicycle. There were loud Arabic expletives exchanged before Gaji's smirk returned.

"Here we are, Mr Lando. The British University in Dubai."

"Well, thank you, Gaji. A most informative journey. What are you doing now?"

"I guess you will need a lift back. No problem, Mr Lando, but I must leave within an hour as my next shift starts in two hours."

"Gaji, you are a living, breathing, walking miracle of a friend. That will be enough time, I believe. Perhaps I can give you a ring?"

Gaji gave him his mobile number or at least one of them, and Lando paid him the fare along with a handsome tip and a handshake, and off he walked to the quite understated front door of the University.

At the reception, he asked for Mr Sarawi and was told he was expected to go straight upstairs on one floor, and his office would have his name on the door.

He went up in the lift as, despite the air conditioning, he still felt a lack of energy in this foreign climate and seemed to perspire rather easily, even in the cool of the building. He spied Sarawi through the glass wall with his back to him, talking animatedly on a mobile telephone. He picked up a few words about student numbers on the course, and the expression 'ghost students' was mentioned several times. As he turned around and saw Lando, Sarawi hurriedly finished his phone call and beckoned him in.

"Greetings, Lando. How are you going on?" he said in a slightly nervous fashion. "Just trying to correlate the student numbers with the fees received. All seems good now. Fancy a coffee?" He ordered two coffees from his desk phone without waiting for a reply.

"That would be good," said Lando. "By the way, I had a call from my university about their finance fee receivable from BUiD, which they were trying to match up with the student numbers as the statement from yourselves did not seem to match up."

"Aah, we often have this problem." He deftly brushed it off. "It includes the cover for lecturer's fees, hotel costs and your travel, and the fee for each student. I shall send a full reconciliation at the end of the month."

They chatted further about the fee structure due to Wolverhampton University for another 10 minutes or so, but Qasim seemed very cagey, and Lando was left wondering why. He felt something was just not quite right. Qasim soon changed the subject and asked Lando again how everything was going.

"All good, thank you. The hotel and the food are lovely, and Dubai is amazing. I shall not want to go home." He blatantly did not wish to discuss the student numbers any further, which confused Lando, and he could see the discomfort on Qasim's face, so he asked him where Claes's office was so he could catch up with him about other course matters. It was on the floor above, and fortunately, Claes was at his desk. He beckoned him in whilst replacing his phone and walked briskly towards him with his hand outstretched, and they shook hands. Claes had a firm grip, which comforted Lando as he felt uneasy about his brief chat with Qasim.

"So, my friend," said Claes. "To what do I owe this pleasure of a visit from the English lecturer when he should be sunning himself by the swimming pool?"

"Jealousy, jealousy. Qasim Sarawi summoned me to discuss the program's student numbers and the fee due to Wolverhampton University. We only had about 10 minutes, and then he kept changing the subject."

"That is a strange one. He should have briefed me if there were any issues and then left it to me to deal with them. It is a part of my job, after all. Maybe it is because I keep giving him a roasting for creating administrative chaos. I have to cover all the courses for him as he is 'supposedly' monitoring their costs and income."

Lando frowned and suggested he should not be in his job if he cannot control the simple ins and outs of the course income and expenses.

"Easier said than done, Lando. He was placed in that job by someone with great influence outside the University. It is one of the drawbacks of working in an Arabic state. If someone is related, even distantly, to a member of the Dubai ruling family, they automatically have a passport to success because everyone is too scared to say 'no.' I believe he is paid two to three times what I am, and he does nothing useful that I know. He can pull strings in high places when something needs to be sorted, so we put up with him because of that. Anyway, I cannot balance the number of students again with those who have signed up for the course. I get no sense out of Sarawi, so I do not know where to go now as he processes their applications and paperwork, and it reaches me last minute, in an appallingly messy state."

"So why are you so worried? You receive their money, don't you?"

"Yes, that is why I am bothered. We seem to have around 10% extra students paying for a course they do not attend. It happens too often."

"So, this has happened before then?" Lando cut in excitedly.

"Yes, every course. I do not know what the hell is going on. I would not worry if it were occasional, as we often get the odd wise guy booking on the course, paying and then wanting a signed qualification at the end of it without even attending and learning anything."

"May I have a look at the booking information for your courses from last year, please?"

"'Of course, but what use is it to you?"

"I think you are forgetting …. I am an accountant!"

Claes smiled, downloaded all the figures from the previous year's database, and scowled. He removed a pair of spectacles from his pocket, looked up at Lando, shrugged, and muttered, "Just for computer work," as he put them on.

Lando nodded, recognising the effects of staring at screens too long for so many years. "These do not look right," he said under his breath, throwing his glasses onto the desk in evident disgust.

"Let me have a look," Lando went through the database course by course, showing all the bookings and the money received. They matched up precisely. "Just as they should do. A perfect reconciliation. All the income matches the students enrolled."

"But that cannot be right," exclaimed Claes animatedly. "None of them matched. I remember."

"It is clear to me," said Lando as he grinned. "Someone has redacted names from the registers to make them balance. I think your friend Mr Sarawi has some explaining to do."

"You mean he has been keeping the money from the students who did not come on the course."

"That's it, Claes. That's it," yelled Lando, almost beside himself with joy. "Ghost students!"

"What are you on about?" Claes's eyes had widened at Lando's excitement.

"'Ghost students!' I know what he is doing. I heard him on his mobile phone. I could not hear much and was not trying to, but he used the term 'ghost students' several times."

"So?" exclaimed Claes, getting slightly irritated.

Lando was now wondering if he should say anything more to Claes. Claes was safer if he did not know, but Lando desperately needed a friend to share it with. He decided to risk it.

"Claes. How good are you at keeping a secret?"

"Well, I am perfectly capable of it unless it relates to child abuse or terrorism," he retorted rather sharply and then saw the look of shocked surprise on Lando's face. "Oh my God. Child abuse?"

Lando shook his head from side to side.

"Not terrorism?" He registered the nod from Lando. "Herregud!"

"What is that? I guess it is an expletive."

"Sorry, it is Swedish for 'Oh my God.' Sometimes, I need to curse in my native tongue. Makes me feel better."

"Forgiven. Look, I need your word not to mention this to anyone. Not your mother, father, wife, children, dog, anyone. At least for the time being."

"You have my word," Claes responded earnestly. "I could not tell my wife anyway. She died 6 years ago. Cancer, if you must know. Hence, I often move jobs when bored and like to test myself in different countries. Having no children at least gives me that freedom," he said without a hint of self-pity, making it easier for Lando to respond.

Lando now realised that this was the piece missing from Claes's past, which he had felt at their first meeting. He also identified with the suffering he had gone through, like Lando had when losing his parents so young. He declined to mention this, though, as the last thing Claes needed was someone to compete with him for losing a relative. Another time, maybe. However, he showed one of his better traits, which was empathy and looking him straight in the eyes, he said, "Claes, I am so sorry. I hope the future holds better things for you."

Claes was moved by Lando's genuine response, which was neither awkward nor long. He dismissed Lando's comment with a wave, which seemed to say *Don't worry, I'm O.K.*

Lando continued slowly, "What I think Sarawi is doing is making dummy or 'ghost student' registrations, which do not raise any eyebrows as the money is coming into BUiD, so I do not think anyone would care. The ghost students then mysteriously cancel their reservations before the course, and again, no one bothers. Still, after the course, the money from those students is transferred into another University account, and who knows what is done with the money then? I suspect Sarawi knows. The money transfer is not investigated because the income received on a course reconciles with the number of students physically on the course."

"Herregud," muttered Claes again under his breath.

"Herregud, indeed," echoed Lando.

"Where do you think the money comes from then?"

"No idea. With all the international students anyway, it will not stand out. It could be any bank account in the world, and I guarantee it will not be all from the same account, as that would be too easy to spot. Claes, we need to be extremely careful with this information. I cannot impress you enough with its importance."

"Do not worry, my friend. I will cover my tracks. I already think someone could trace my download of last year's student numbers, so I shall deal with that immediately." He smiled and, tapping his nose, said quietly, "I have not worked here all these years without learning much about its data processing system. I will delete the search file as soon as we are finished. There will be no audit trail. After all, I was a computer hacker in my other life years ago."

Lando filed that one away in his memory.

Claes then became severe, looked Lando straight in the eye, and spoke quietly, "Now tell me. What is going on? How could you possibly know about terrorism issues? Is there something you are not telling me?"

Lando replied inappropriately with a joke, "Well, if I tell ya, I've gotta kill ya," all in his best American drawl.

It made Claes smile, and Lando decided he could not tell him too much yet.

"Look, Claes, we have the same views on life, and I cannot tell you everything. At least not just yet, but I desperately need a friend as I am alone here. Do you remember that horrible murder a couple of days ago?"

"Yes, I do. You mean the one where the guy was stabbed in the stomach in the street?"

"Yes. His name was Dillon, and I met him on the aeroplane coming over. What I can tell you is that I believe he is one of the good guys, at least he was. I found his body that night. It was horrible and I cannot get that picture out of my mind. I have got caught up in this quite by chance. I am struggling to piece it all together, but this is much, much bigger than a murder. I believe it is of national security significance."

Claes frowned. "Why could it not just be Sarawi lining his own pocket?"

"He could, but why was he discussing 'ghost students' with someone on the telephone? I also know there are other issues which, as I said, I cannot discuss with you yet. Sorry."

"So where do we go from here?" Claes responded in an upbeat manner. "I would not know where to begin with this."

"May we stay connected, Claes? As I said, I desperately need a friend as I am unsure who I can rely on. I think I have someone who can help, but I need their OK. Please try to act as if everything is fine, particularly with Sarawi, until we find out more."

"All right. Sounds good to me. At least we have each other's numbers. May I suggest that if we text each other, we delete the text immediately just in case we lose our phones? They can still trace texts through the phone companies, but that would need police intervention."

"Damn good suggestion. Thank you."

"Well, as I said, I was a computer hacker years ago. I might add it was all above board. Several institutions paid me to try to break into their systems. I would receive nothing if I could not break in but a big bonus if I could. I managed to win some incredibly good bonuses, but the work was too unreliable, so I moved on. Perhaps it will prove useful now, eh?"

"Darn sure it will," said Lando, clapping him on the back. "I guess we are done now."

Qasim Sarawi rushed past the glass door and stopped to look through.

Lando held his hand out to Claes and winked as they shook hands. He opened the door and nodded politely at Sarawi, who came in as Lando left.

Sarawi addressed Claes, appearing a little furtive. "What did he want then? Was everything all right?"

"All fine," replied Claes. "He's a very irritating fellow. Seemed quite upset that all the figures for students and income balanced up. I suppose it is because he is an accountant and likes finding things wrong rather than right." He noticed the mild relief on Sarawi's face and was pleased with himself for conveying to Sarawi that he had a negative view of Lando. Sarawi rushed off again, and Claes texted Lando to that effect.

Lando left the building, read the text with delight, and deleted it. Claes really was a top guy. He then rang Gaji, who arrived with his customary sunny disposition, and back to the hotel they headed.

The only words he spoke to Gaji were, "Well, that has now confirmed that my view of Sarawi is even worse than yours, Gaji," who nodded with a sage-like expression.

Chapter 21

Whilst Lando was leaving BUiD, another more chilling meeting had just started.

Hamza, the witless Arab thug, had managed to gain through a friend of a friend the contact details for Ashiraf Nasruddin, the strategic leader of the 'Wings of Fire' terror organisation. Although friendship would always remain a questionable term for any of Hamza's relationships, his persistence, at least, was his sole redeeming feature motivated by his desire for money. However, his desire for money was continually at odds with his acute lack of willingness to work honestly for it.

Hamza had been put in contact with a man called Yusuf by his associate Farouk. He had promised to arrange a meeting with Ashiraf, conditional upon his palm being crossed appropriately. It turned out that greasing Yusuf's palm cost him nearly all of the original 500 dirhams downpayment he had received from Qasim, which frustrated him. Still, he was intelligent enough to know that his life would not be worth living if he did not deliver on his promise to Qasim and the minister Shazil Haroun.

The meeting was arranged in The Fadak café, a small coffee house down a side street near the border with Sharjah. A large, rough, round table was wedged into a corner of the room in the half-light due to the blinds being drawn. Seated around it, apart from Hamza and Yusuf, were a very hot and agitated Qasim Sarawi, the junior minister Shazil Haroun, well hidden behind a red and white, tightly pulled kufiyah and a smallish man with a short, dark beard and thick-framed glasses. Next to him was an extremely broad, muscular, dark man of African origin named Bongani, clean-shaven with hands so large and meaty that they appeared as if he wore gardening gloves. He had a permanent half-smiling expression displaying two rows of perfectly white teeth, one of which housed a glinting, diamond-like stone. All six were dressed in white dishdashas, although Hamza's stood out because his dishdasha was so filthy that it looked like an Arab version of a tie-and-dye fashion statement. Shazil, by luck not of his own choosing, was seated next to him and tried to keep himself as far away as possible. Apart from the noxious emanations, he did not wish to catch anything horrible, whether it was hopping or of a bacterial nature.

Beyond brief formalities, at which the smallish man with the short, dark beard and thick-framed glasses was introduced as Ashiraf Nasruddin, little was said until Turkish coffees and chocolates arrived, of which Hamza approved enthusiastically. He ate half of the dish before the conversation started, at which point Hamza and Yusuf were requested to sit elsewhere out of earshot. They promptly left the table, Hamza palming five more chocolates on the way, and the conversation began with Ashiraf.

"So, my friends, to what do we owe this pleasure, and how can we be of service?"

Qasim looked across at Shazil, who immediately sprang into action. "We thank you for meeting and trusting us with this location. It is indeed an ideal, out-of-the-way spot, and we appreciate the appropriateness of the surroundings."

Ashiraf nodded politely and beckoned with a raised eyebrow for him to continue.

"I will get straight to the point." Shazil leaned forward and continued to talk in a hushed voice, "I would like you to use your good offices with the Iranian government to procure some drones to mount an attack on a building in Dubai."

Qasim watched Ashiraf and, at that moment, could have given him a big hug of congratulations. Ashiraf did not even bat an eyelid. His calm, reptilian stare at Shazil was almost surreal, and, at that moment, Qasim saw the wheels turning at breakneck speed and knew why this was a man to be feared. Everyone held their breath, waiting for Ashiraf's answer, which came in a measured and respectful tone.

"I assume there is more to this than simply destroying a building," he said slowly in a monotonic voice.

Until then, Bongani had not uttered a word, but now he sought to laugh. The "ha .... ha .... haaaa" came out of his mouth like three deep grunts from his bowels, which split the atmosphere in two. It was chilling, and Qasim could not take his eyes off the gem in his tooth, which sparkled through the half-light in the corner of the room.

"Yes, of course," replied Shazil rather too quickly. Bongani's low-toned laugh noticeably disconcerted him.

"We need you to attack a building with drones that are armed and programmed for attack. I shall ensure we are well prepared to defend the building against them, shooting them all down."

There was a pregnant pause before Ashiraf spoke, "Let me guess, Shazil. You will become a hero because you have saved the building, whichever one it is, and it will also enhance your position in government. You will undoubtedly receive some public award or reward. You will become untouchable politically for the rest of your life."

"You have got it in one, Ashiraf. You appreciate the Arab ways. Of course, this will be good for all my friends."

"Shazil, do you know the cost of these drones? Do you understand the risk to life of these drones crashing in a crowded city? Not that I care, of course. Do you understand that there is no guarantee that, whatever your defences, a drone could get through to the building? We would need all the financing upfront, of course. How would you manage that?"

"We have a fund that we could dip into for just such occasions. That would not be a problem. As a matter of interest, what would be a ballpark figure of half a dozen drones?"

"That depends on what the drone is to do. If it is simply a case of filling up a load-carrying drone packed with explosives and it is to fly kamikaze style into a building, that is one thing. If it is to be a recoverable, full-on attack drone fully weaponised, then that is another. The difference is tens of thousands or even millions of dirhams."

Shazil was encouraged by the way the conversation was going until Ashiraf spoke. His eyes narrowed and became ice cold as he spoke, "You appreciate that I am accountable to our spiritual leader, Hawiya. Why should he trust a man with no objective except to enhance his reputation at the cost of potential significant loss of life?"

Shazil immediately backtracked a little by explaining his desire to limit the loss of life, although saying some loss would be a good thing to enhance the reality of the situation and show what greater catastrophe would have been prevented. Finally, he finished by saying he would pay significantly over the going rate for the drones and only wished to get an agreement with Ashiraf that there would be no attacks by his organisation on the country of Dubai for the next 10 years or at least during Shazil's term of office in Dubai.

"Why not just plant a nasty little bomb in this building, as that would presumably have the desired effect? Much cheaper, would create a limited loss of life, and I'm sure you could find some patsy to take the fall for it," said Ashiraf, glancing across the room at Hamza and Yusuf with a twitch of a smile across his face.

"No!" muttered Shazil immediately. "The threat must be both credible and potentially catastrophic. A drone attack would rock the nation to the core, and nobody anywhere in the country would feel safe, but if I can be the one to prevent or limit the result, then I would be in a position of considerable influence. A bomb is just a routine prevention exercise. Another aspect is that the security within this iconic building is second to none, so mounting a drone attack would be simpler from a security viewpoint."

"Iconic, you say?" Ashiraf glanced up questioningly at Shazil.

Shazil lowered his eyes as he knew he had said one word too much. "Now, what would be an iconic building in Dubai? Let me see." He pretended to search the ceiling for an answer. "Now, the Burj Al Arab in Jumeirah is the most iconic building in Dubai. Could hardly miss a building like that!"

"That is one of the buildings I have considered but have not settled on which building yet."

Shazil was now gritting his teeth and casting furtive glances at Qasim, who was doing his best to avoid eye contact. They both knew it was the only building he had considered, being iconic, magnificent and at the core of the 'Dubai brand.'

The meeting continued for another 20 minutes, ending with neither side committing one way or the other but with an in-principal agreement by Ashiraf to take the proposition to Hawiya and confirm whether they would continue the discussion any further. They all returned to their various abodes, and Qasim and Shazil walked a few hundred metres to pick up a taxi far from their meeting place. Shazil was more preoccupied with looking for hopping creatures on his robe than with the meeting's possibilities. He knew it would take a little time to organise, and this was the first rendezvous with these ghastly rebels. He was pleased he found nothing living on his robe, as sitting next to Hamza for any length of time made him itch and scratch automatically. He decided Hamza would be treated as 100% expendable when this was over. His only value on this planet was as a breeding ground for small, hopping insects. He laughed inwardly at his ability to abuse his power to correct the way of things.

Chapter 22

After the trip to BUiD, Gaji deposited Lando back at his hotel and, with an apology, ran inside ahead of Lando just in time for his next airport trip.

Lando was pleased to get inside and retire to the cool air-conditioning in his room as he was boiling hot and tired after his stressful, although rewarding, trip. He had taken Claes into his confidence and was comfortable with the risk of that decision. He felt mentally lighter. He needed that crutch and knew he had an affinity with Claes from the moment they had met. Of course, he doubted that trust would stand up to torture like most people, but that was a risk he had decided to take. A problem shared is a problem halved, as his mum and dad used to say, so he just hoped Claes was never tortured.

He had a quick cool shower, which woke him up, and he decided to drift down to the swimming pool for a dip and maybe one of Solly's ice-cold beers from the poolside bar. He only hoped he did not meet the squawking lady with all the jewellery and her irritating little Willie. He got out of the lift and opened the door to the pool area when said little boy cannoned straight into him, causing him to trip onto the tiled floor. He was unhurt but looked up into the child's face and then at his mother's and instantly felt sorry for the boy as she looked at Lando as if it were all his fault again. He was torn about how to respond and decided to continue as he left off and started barking like a poodle at the mother. She dragged little

Willie off as fast as she could with an anguished look on her face and muttering all kinds of threats. Lando noticed little Willie desperately trying not to laugh as his arm was almost dragged out of its socket. At least she was leaving the poolside.

Solly missed nothing and had a cold one waiting for Lando as he approached the bar. He was grinning away as he spoke, "Hello, Mr Lando. Your exploits by this pool will be repeated for generations amongst the staff in this hotel."

"Hardly the stuff of legend Solly." He took a long, slow draw on his beer. "Aaaaah. It just gets better and better," he said as he wiped the froth from his top lip and relished the coolness that flowed down his throat.

"So, how has the rest of your day been, Mr Lando?"

"Tiring. It is hard when you do not know who you can trust." He realised he had said too much and waited for Solly to question him further, but it never happened. He just strangely looked at Lando.

"Forget I said that, Solly. Just been a difficult day."

"No problem, sir." He immediately pulled an imitation zipper along his lips and looked him pointedly in the eye.

Lando remembered his conversation with Gaji and realised the two must have conversed. "Are you friends with Gaji by any chance?"

"Well, we are not related or even from the same country, but yes, we are good friends. Please understand, I disapprove of how he makes his money, but I trust him very much as a friend."

"So you share a lot then," Lando said in more of a statement than a question.

"Everything, sir."

"So, the zipper only works except for Gaji?"

"That is correct. I am sorry." He looked a little downcast. "Sometimes, a promise of silence has to be broken to protect the innocent."

"I can go along with that."

Lando did not want to talk anymore. He acknowledged Solly, took himself off for a few lengths in the pool, and returned to his room. He was getting dressed and dwelling on how to handle the relationship between Gaji and Solly when his bedside phone rang. It was Hobart.

"Can we meet? Soon?"

"Sure thing, Hoby. Lonigan's?"

"Lonigan's it is. Fifteen minutes."

****

Hobart was already sitting at a table scowling when Lando arrived.

"Who told you to call me Hoby?"

"Dunno. It just slipped out. I think I remember Kadri calling you Hoby once, and it seems a little less formal than Hobart. Who would introduce himself in a course lecture theatre as Hobart G. Lonsdale IV? A trifle stiff, don't you think? Particularly for an American."

"OK. OK. I was only trying to stay in the character of an arrogant, brash, cartoon-like all-American tosser."

"You do it extremely well."

"That is because I had the best teachers. My family. Much as I love them, that is how I was brought up. Enough said, eh?"

"Enough said. May I still call you Hoby?"

"If you must," Hobart growled.

"So why are we here? What's the rush, Hoby?" Lando liked to twist the knife a bit. Not because he was trying to be annoying, but by scratching under the surface, he hoped to get to the real Hobart.

Hobart brightened from his self-absorbed funk. "I have some rather better news for you." As Hobart leaned forward, Lando noticed the handle of a gun in a shoulder holster peeking out from under his jacket.

"What! You are going to shoot me with that canon in your pocket?"

"Of course not." Hobart quickly leaned back and ensured his pistol was well hidden. "Things are getting more dangerous, and my controller, Harold, has now authorised me to carry it."

"Is that the better news then? You Americans always seem to like to solve things with a gun. At least in the movies."

"Come on, Lando. Be serious for once." Hobart paused for dramatic effect, then leaned forward and whispered in a conspiratorial fashion, "We found Dillon's cell phone." His eyes widened, and he repeated it with a bright excitement behind them. "We .... found .... Dillon's .... cell .... phone."

"You mean his mobile."

"Yes, yes, cell phone, mobile what's it matter? Same thing."

"Of course. Great news. Tremendous news. What did you do? Ring it?"

"Lando, you're at it again. You continue like this: I am leaving the table, and you can pay for the coffee. I rang it as soon as I found out he had been murdered, but there was no signal, so the embassy thought the other side had got it." Hobart could barely contain himself in his chair. "I asked for a detailed search to be done of his flat, and of course, it was not there. We thought the murderers had it, but I decided it was worth a chance to do a more comprehensive search of the area in which he was killed and guess what?"

"You found it, I know. Come on, come on."

"It was only a few feet from where his body lay. It had gone down an open street drain. Can you believe it?"

"Why would it do that?"

"We can only assume it was in his hand when he was stabbed, and it fell or more likely, when he knew he was critically injured, he had managed to get it out of his pocket and threw it down the drain before he died to prevent it being taken by the wrong people. He was a true hero to the end."

"Yes, he was," whispered Lando. "A true hero. I could do with a stronger drink. I'm getting a scotch. Do you want one, Hoby?" His voice cracked with emotion.

Hobart declined, and Lando rose quickly, keeping his eyes averted. He returned with his scotch, downed it in a couple of gulps, and waited for that click in his head when everything seemed better.

"So, what was on the phone?"

"They are still trying to get the information off both the sim card and the phone as it was all broken and damaged from water ingress. But we did get this." Hobart showed Lando his phone with a picture on it.

Lando nearly leapt out of his seat. "It is Ashiraf. That's Ashiraf. That's in the Chelsea Arms. I recognise the furniture and walls. Look at him. Those thick glasses. You cannot see how short he is, but I would recognise him anywhere." He was so gleeful he could barely contain himself, particularly in that public place.

Hobart was now smiling broadly. "We suspected it was him but hoped you could confirm it. Do you realise what this means?"

"Presumably, it can be circulated to all the CIA field agents in the Middle East, which has got to be a good thing."

"Yes, coupled with his limp and short stature, this will severely restrict Ashiraf's freedom of movement at the very least and, at best, could lead to his capture or preferably early demise."

"You mean get him terminated."

"What would you rather have? Some long-drawn-out, tit-for-tat negotiation to release him in return for some random hostages or financial incentive instead of taking him out of the equation with immediate effect?"

"The end justifies the means, eh?"

"Not always. But in this case, it will set them back significantly. This Hawiya fellow is only a spiritual leader. Still, Ashiraf is the 'Head Honcho' regarding the tactical decisions, and I believe most of the strategic ones where violence is central."

"Does not leave much left for the Hawiya guy to do. That assumes it is a guy?" Lando mused.

Hobart went quiet for a moment. "Interesting point. We never really thought about him being a woman. So uncommon in the Arab world to have a female leader, particularly a spiritual one. Unheard of, but I guess we should keep an open mind."

Lando noticed a pensive look on his face as if he were wrestling with something and immediately said, "C'mon Hoby. Spit it out. What's ailing you? Is it good news or bad?"

"Actually, I will have a drink. A bourbon on the rocks, if that is ok?"

Lando went up to the bar, ordered a Jim Beam, and bought another scotch for himself, this time with a little water. He looked quizzically at Hobart.

Hobart took a slug from his drink, then leaned forward again, emphasising the importance of the information he was about to impart. "We have had the results back from the autopsy with no significant information beyond what we already knew. Dillon died from severe internal and external haemorrhaging from a large sharp instrument."

"Brilliant. The knife was already in him. What genius produced that piece of evidence?" said Lando sarcastically, almost spitting the words out.

"However," continued Hobart, undeterred, "traces of blood were found on the knife."

"Are you having me on Hoby? Traces of blood?" Lando was struggling to keep a lid on his response pitch.

Hobart was beginning to enjoy this. He realised Lando expressed his anger at a situation through sick humour or sarcastic comments. *A pity he could not express it in violence*, he thought. *We could use him in the Company.* Little did he realise.

Still leaning in towards Lando, he whispered, "The blood was not only that belonging to Dillon." He sat back with a smirk, allowing it to sink into Lando's now overcooked brain.

"You mean?"

"Yes. It is the killer's, almost certainly. No doubt caused by him trying to remove the knife from Dillon's gut. We already have it on our DNA database. We believe this person is responsible for several other murders that we know of. The problem is that we do not know who he or she is."

"So, you still think it could be Kadri then," stuttered Lando, aghast.

"No. Not for a moment. However, we have suspicions about the character. He goes by the name of Hamza Badawi. He was born into a Bedouin tribe, and many years ago, we believe he participated in the bomb that went off in a toilet in the Royal

Meridian Hotel in Bahrain in 1996. We could never prove it, though, as we do not have Hamza's DNA. If we did, it would be contaminated with something, as he is about the filthiest human being on the planet. He also has a scar from under his left ear to the corner of his mouth, apparently received in a knife fight. Makes him distinctive. He is known to have two associates." Hobart scanned his phone for information. "Abdul Iqbal and Farouk. Abdul is a very tall and heavy man and is used as an enforcer, a physical frightener against anyone from whom they wish to extract money. Farouk appears to have no known last name but is probably the most intelligent, although Hamza is unofficially their leader." Hobart muttered a bit as he skipped down the page to get the more relevant facts about them. "They tend to work as a team on diverse nefarious projects such as extortion, robbery with violence, etc. They are clever enough not to get caught but not clever enough not to leave trails or find a way of living that does not harm others."

"So why not arrest them if the DNA matches?"

"Well, Lando, funny you should ask that. Firstly, we have no jurisdiction in Dubai. We work to aid the local police, particularly where American interests are at risk. Secondly, the DNA only matches these other records, but the records do not identify the name. We could do with corroborating evidence that we could take to the Dubai Security Services."

There was a long minute's silence between them, and then Hobart said what he had wanted to say all evening. "This is where you come in, Lando."

Lando looked up partly in shock and partly in excitement. His heart was thumping. "Go on."

"I am known to Hamza and his associates. He would recognise me immediately, and I would get nowhere except dealt with down a back alley somewhere or floating face down in the Creek. How do you feel about collaborating with me to find out what they know? Remember, if they still have the sheath that matches the jambiya used to kill Dillon, then we have our evidence."

There was another long silence whilst Hobart downed the last of his bourbon and then, in a quiet voice, said, "So what do you think?"

"What exactly are you asking me, Hoby?"

"Ah, of course, I was getting to that. We need someone to befriend himself to Hamza and his associates somehow and try to establish what they are up to, as our guess is the killing of Dillon is only the beginning."

"That word 'somehow' does not heighten my desire to work with you on this. It sounds like you do not really have a plan. We must find these guys first, and they are not exactly, by the sound of it, 'my type' of guys. How would I befriend a bunch of apparently very smelly Arabs as a moderately well-heeled English-speaking temporary visa lecturer?"

"By the way, only one of them is very smelly, but it is funny you should ask me about that as I have an idea. They will not be hard to find, though we don't know where they live. We can find where they hang out, however. I have a colleague working on that right now. I suggest we fake a robbery from them in the street near you, and you manage to disarm the robber and return their purse or whatever is stolen. They will feel beholden to you, and no Arab likes to receive help without the opportunity to return the favour. That even applies to scum like them. At the very least, they would wish to buy you a drink to say thanks."

"Sounds like a plan of sorts... a pretty crap one if I may say so. I thought one of their guys, this Abdul fella, was an enforcer and built like a tank. Surely, he would deal with the robber?"

"Yes, but he is so musclebound that he cannot run. You would need to disarm the 'robber' but allow him to escape after he has dropped what he stole. Otherwise, Abdul would tear him apart."

Lando thought for a while whilst Hobart's expression indicated he was willing Lando to help. Lando's heart was racing with excitement and fear, but he could not stop himself. "Ok. I'll do it, provided I am in the eyesight of someone on my side the whole time. I have no desire to die as Dillon did, and I am not equipped or trained as some kind of spy, exciting as it may sound." Lando thought about his karate expertise but decided not to inform Hobart of this as who knew what Hobart would use him for otherwise? Anyway; he had never used it outside his dojo.

"I shall watch and follow you myself, Lando. I promise. Finding out where these guys hang out might take some time, but we have reason to put resources into it now. You will need to keep everything as normal with your work until then. I shall contact you as soon as we know their whereabouts."

With that, they parted company. Lando left first as Hobart suggested they depart separately to help reduce their apparent association with outsiders who may have seen them enter. From then on, it was clear to Lando that they must assume they were being watched, particularly Hobart, as he was known to Hamza and his merry men.

Chapter 23

The night is still young, or so Lando thought as he returned to his hotel and the coolness of his room. His mind swiftly returned to Kadri and his beautiful night of passion with her. He was hoping she felt the same, but his age-old paranoia regarding his relationships with women was beginning to kick in once more. He felt jumpy and was twitching and clenching his jaw. It was as if he had imagined their night together. Then he tried to change his mindset as he hoped their physical attraction to each other was more than needing closeness during an extremely tense situation and their shared shock and horror over Dillon. That fluttering in the stomach he remembered from his teens returned, so he decided to contact her if he could.

Her phone was engaged as he tried three times in as many minutes and decided it was not to be, so a shower before ordering room service seemed like the best idea. He set the shower to maximum coldness, trying to give himself some energy and remove the lascivious thoughts of the kind of evening he could have with Kadri when his mobile rang out. He leapt out of the shower, grabbed a towel, and skidded on the wet, tiled floor headlong into his bedside table where his phone lay. He picked it up off the floor, rubbing his bruised chin, saw it was Kadri returning his call, took a deep breath, smiled, and answered as coolly as he could.

"Hi. This is a welcome surprise." *My God, I'm a prat,* he thought.

"So, what are you up to tonight, Casanova?" She giggled infectiously. She just seemed like an easy road to follow despite his lack of confidence.

"Well. It is funny you should say that. I am at a bit of a loose end, and I was wondering what you were up to."

"So," she replied in a playfully cross-tone. "I'm a fill-in for a loose end now, am I?"

"No, no, not at all. I ... uh ... I was er," and then he realised happily that she was messing with him. "I would love to have your company around a dinner table tonight. Is Mademoiselle free?" he said, adopting his most pompous, public-school accent, at which it was her turn to smile.

"Strange, you should ask that. Ten minutes ago, I was not free as I had another dancing event in the desert, but it was cancelled as the group booking fell apart. So, shall I come up to your room? Also, I would like to know what we shall have for afters."

"I take it you mean the dessert course," he replied, as she giggled again, her breath sounding heavy in his ear.

"To be honest, I was thinking we could go out somewhere special, on me, of course."

"Aha, the traveller has an expense account," she fired at him pointedly.

"Actually, for what it is worth, this would be out of my own pocket." There was a short silence, and then he said, "Of course, if you prefer another room service meal like before, that is fine. Perhaps we can improve on the previous dessert?"

After they both stopped tittering like children, Kadri said breathily, "Lando, I would love to go out with you on a normal, how you say, …. date? I do not often have the opportunity to go somewhere special."

"So special it is, then. Put on your glad rags, and I shall find some suitable ritzy nosh."

"Sorry, I have no idea what you just said. Glad rags…. ritzy nosh? I am not wearing rags. If you think …"

Laughing again, Lando said, "Hang on a minute. I did not mean offence. It is slang and means wear your best clothes, and I shall find a special restaurant for us."

"Nothing too expensive, please," she pleaded. "I like something more intimate than these big showy places."

"OK. I shall text you an address and meet you there in an hour. That would be 8 pm. It's better than coming here and travelling away again. Just give me a half hour, please. Hasta la vista, baby." Lando closed the call and wondered what psychotic worm had got into his brain to use an Arnie Schwarzenegger quotation to a Turkish belly dancer he wished to impress. Sometimes, he despaired of himself.

He wore a bright, pale blue, lightweight suit that he had never expected to wear, a crisp white shirt, no tie, and a pair of light brown loafers. It was the first time that he had gone out without sandals. He briefly looked in the mirror and realised he had gained a slight tan, buoying him up. He was planning to ask the concierge for a restaurant recommendation, but just as he was a few metres away, he spied Gaji out of the corner of his eye. Gaji nodded at him and came over.

"Good evening, Mr Westwood, sir. How are you this beaaaaautiful evening?"

"I am fine, Gaji, but I could use some help."

"Anything at all. What would you like? Alcohol, girls, places, knock-off watches, pubs, restaurants, girls, shisha bars."

"Here we go again, Gaji. I'll tell you one thing: you are very resilient. I am meeting a lady for dinner, and I would like to find a quality, reasonably priced restaurant with great food and an intimate ambience. Any ideas, my friend?"

"I could do it with just a little more information than that, sir. What kind of food would you like?"

"Oh, I do not know. Mediterranean, seafood, maybe, Asian?"

"Aha, I know the perfect place not too far from here. The other side of the Gold Souk across the Creek. It's called Al Khayma Heritage Restaurant. Rely on me, sir. I know everyone in this city. Shall I book it for you, sir?"

"Yes, please. For two for 8 pm."

Whilst Gaji was chatting animatedly, Lando watched him. Gaji would undoubtedly have a little payoff from the restaurant, but Lando had no problem with that. He earned it. He checked the hands on the dark blue face of his Omega Seamaster, which gave him a half hour. A gift from his father on his 21st birthday. He just loved that dark blue face and bezel. He smiled in remembrance of his father. He would have envied Lando his evening out with such a beautiful lady. Although, he hoped she was not too much of a lady tonight.

"We are in luck, sir. I have, with my magnificent abilities and connections, managed to negotiate a perfect table for you and your lady for 8 pm and curiously, it was the last table available, and I have described you to them so they will greet you like a long-lost son or I shall never recommend anyone else to them in this life or the next. Fortunately, my shift has finished, and I have no more airport transfers, so I am free to take you."

"I thought I would walk there if that were all right with you. I could use the fresh air." Lando got out his phone to check Google Maps for the distance. "How long a walk is it?"

Gaji opened the exit door of the hotel, and a hot blast of air hit him like a wall. He came back inside whilst his body unsteamed itself.

"It will take you an hour to walk there, and my car is parked up over there and cool inside, Mr Westwood."

Lando double-checked the distance; sure enough, it was at least a fifty-minute walk. "OK, Gaji. Once again, you are my saviour. My lady would not be happy if I was that late and all sweaty as well."

His face lit up. "Thank you, sir. Then let us go. We cannot be late for Kadri."

"How did you know I was meeting Kadri?"

"It was that look on your face that only Kadri can generate. She is so beautiful with lovely black curly hair, a figure to die for, and...'

"Ok, ok, ok. Enough said."

"I also saw her in this hotel a day or two ago, so I had a guess."

Lando texted Kadri the address, followed by an emoji of a fish, and she texted a thumbs-up emoji with a big X in return. Encouraging. So off they went to Gaji's vehicle. They travelled to their destination, and Gaji commented on the route.

"Here's the police station; now we are approaching the Gold Souk. Do you want to buy any gold, Mr Lando?"

"Not for the time being, thank you."

"What about for Miss Kadri?"

"Hey up, Gaji, we are only having a meal together."

Gaji chuckled to himself.

"We are now crossing the Creek. Right onto Al Falah Street and heading for the Dubai Museum. It's worth a visit, Mr Lando. Here we are. The Al Khayma Heritage Restaurant."

"Thank you, Gaji," said Lando, and then joked, "Don't wait up." Gaji gave a knowing wink.

Lando got out of the car and was immediately greeted before stepping inside the restaurant like a long-lost son by a tall Asian man who was one of the owners' family members. He followed the man inside to a large, well-lit, beautifully decorated room with chunky wooden rustic seats covered in bright, thick tapestry cushions around tables of four and six.

The room had an orangey-brown glow, and the centrepiece was a green leafy tree, spreading its branches haphazardly across a quarter of the roof area. Each table had a large, fritted egg-shaped lamp, creating intimacy for each table. It was stunning. He was shown through an area away from the hubbub of the room into a quiet corner with mood lighting, and a cool bottle of water was immediately placed in front of him, and told someone would come by shortly to attend to him. About half of the tables were filled, but the peaceful ambience immediately struck Lando. If the food and service were as good as his first impression of the restaurant, it was just what the doctor ordered. He hoped Kadri would approve. Sure enough, a waiter arrived, and Lando said a lady friend was joining him. He asked the waiter to be super attentive to her and ordered a cool lager while waiting.

When he was halfway through his drink and had read the menu a couple of times, he started to become a little anxious as Kadri had not yet appeared. He glanced at his watch and realised she was only about ten minutes late, and maybe he had not given her enough time to get ready. Unexpectedly, a hush descended on the room, and there she was, standing in the doorway. She had the poise of a film star and was bright and radiant. She wore a long sari-style red dress with jewels sewn around the hem, the cuffs, and the neckline. It was cut in such a way that her magnificent figure underneath was not completely obscured. Her jet-black curly hair contrasted dramatically with her red dress as it cascaded down onto her shoulders. She floated over to his table behind the waiter, and every eye in the room followed her. The men's mouths were open, and the women looked on in admiration and, in some cases, a degree of envy. It was all Lando could do not to dribble. He suddenly found his manners and rose quickly as she was shown to her seat. Smiling away, she placed a little kiss on his cheek. He felt other men's eyes on him, wondering what this man had to attract a woman of such grace and beauty. Lando could not answer that question, but he would not worry about it either. They slowly sat down, and the waiter helped Kadri by sliding her seat under her.

"Kadri, you look stunning. You have brought the restaurant to a complete standstill, to say nothing of my own heart issues. I need a blood pressure tablet."

"Thank you," she replied. "This is a beautiful place. I have heard of it but never been. It has a fine reputation, and you have chosen well."

He reminded himself to give Gaji an extra-large tip. Pouring a glass of the cool water for Kadri, he asked her what she would like to drink, and she requested a glass of white wine, so he ordered one of his French favourites, a tangy Pouilly-Fuissé. They then set about the menu which could satisfy anyone's tastes.

"So Kadri. What's a nice girl like you doing in a place like this?" he said with a smile.

She played the game. "Well, some kind, well-meaning gentleman asked me to accompany him, and I accepted."

"Maybe he thought you needed feeding up, but he must have been crazy because you look just about right from where I'm sitting."

"It must be the lighting."

"Nah. So what do you fancy then?"

Kadri placed her first finger, curled up on the tip of her chin, and raised one of her dark eyebrows, which had the desired effect on Lando. He just turned to jelly and could not take the silly expression off his face.

"I meant from the menu. I must say I would like fish for a main course. I live inland in England, so the fish is not particularly fresh in most local places. What about you, Kadri? Do you have a favourite?"

"I adore fish. Why don't you pick? We can both eat the same. That would be simple."

"On one condition. You tell me if I pick something you are not happy with, as I like most things."

"That's a deal," she mouthed sensuously before receiving her wine glass from the waiter and taking a sip. "Aah. What a delicious wine," she said with a certain surprise.

Kadri noticed the corner of his mouth move up almost imperceptibly. *At least I have got something right,* he thought.

Lando scanned the menu and decided to be decisive. "OK, Kadri, any last thoughts for the main course? I think picking that one first and then picking the starter is good."

"I told you. You pick. Let us see how well you think you know me." She was taunting him, but he did not care.

"Right. Let us go for the Fried Marinated Zubaidi fish served with aromatic dill rice. I think we precede that with Mutabal– and some flatbreads."

Kadri stared at Lando in amazement. "That is simply perfect. You do know me. Where did you last have those dishes?"

"I didn't. I have no idea what they are, although judging by the picture, I guess Mutabal is some sort of dip."

"Oh dear, you have ruined it," giggled Kadri. "For one moment, I thought you had a chef inside you somewhere. Would you like me to tell you what they are?"

"Wait a minute. I shall order first, and then you can tell me what we are about to eat." He waived the waiter over and ordered two of each course, a beer top-up, and another glass of wine for Kadri as her glass was nearly empty. This boded well for later.

"So..." grinned Kadri. "Here begins the first lesson. The Mutabal is grilled aubergine, tahini, garlic salt & lemon juice."

"Like Baba Ghanoush then," interrupted Lando.

Once again, Kadri was surprised. "Well, almost. Baba Ghanoush does not have tahini and has a few other bits thrown in. How do you know Baba Ghanoush anyway?" She marvelled at him.

"Aha. Not because I am a big traveller, but in Shrewsbury, the town where I live in England, there is an Iranian restaurant where I dine occasionally, and they serve it. I love it."

"Do you take your lady friends there?" teased Kadri.

"Sadly, I am usually alone if I have gone there. Once, I went with a friend from my club."

"Oh yes, what sort of club is that?" asked Kadri, probing.

"It was a male friend, actually. He was from my karate club."

"I did not have you down as a violent man, Lando."

"I am not. I just enjoy the formality of the training in the dojo. I have had surprisingly few injuries. I had more playing Sunday league football. That game has gone to the dogs, as the refs cannot control it. Pity. I used to love it."

"So, this is a new side of you I had not imagined. A man who likes discipline!" It was not lost on Lando as she said this with a twinkle in her eye as she hung on every syllable of the word discipline.

He smiled but was not ready to go down that path. At least not yet, anyway!

The Mutabal starters arrived. It seemed like a meal in itself as the flatbreads were filling. They both tucked in. He loved seeing a woman with a good appetite ... for food, amongst other things. He smiled without realising it.

"What are you smiling at, Rolo?"

"Nothing. Oh, no one has called me Rolo for over 20 years. Maybe we should have had a shared starter," he mused as he scoffed a big mouthful. "Maybe best we do not finish it all, or else there will be no room for the main course. Although, it is good." He munched through another piece of flat bread and dip.

"I love it even though I eat it a lot." Lando looked up and wondered if she was making a rude 'double entendre.' She was not, but both started laughing and struggled to stop. A few sips of water were needed to settle them both down.

"Ok," said Lando. "Fill me in on the main course."

"Well," said Kadri, still wiping the tears from her eyes. "Zubaidi is a roundish flat fish. Very tender and flavourful. It is the national fish of Kuwait. Why, I do not know. Have you heard of Silver Pomfret, as that is its European name?"

"I have heard of it but never eaten it. Ah, here is the waiter. Yes, we have finished," said Lando to the man waiting. "Another drink, Kadri?"

"Oooh, I am not sure I should. Otherwise, I could be anybody's," she laughed. "Oh, go on then. Must have one with the main course." She still had a half glass left, so it could wait.

Lando feigned a look of surprise when she said she could be anybody's.

She smiled up at him apologetically. "I learnt that expression in England when I did an unofficial training program in England with the CIA. Hobart's controller, Harold, put me through it when I came onto the CIA payroll."

"Oh yes? You have hidden depths, then? What did you learn?"

"Oh, just some elementary self-defence, use of a pistol, transferring coded messages to my handler, IT skills, tracing information from digital sources, simple computer hacking techniques, amongst other things."

Lando's eyebrows nearly shot off the top of his head. "Good Lord. Did they teach you belly dancing as well?"

"Of course not. I learnt it initially from my mother. It is good exercise, and some believe it started as a fertility ritual, and others believe it is a dance of seduction."

"It is certainly that, Kadri. My imagination went wild when I first saw you dancing on that Sunset Excursions desert trip."

The evening wore on, and the conversation flowed, particularly after the main course arrived. It was a magical night, and Lando could not remember when he had felt so happy and comfortable in a woman's presence. Her conversation matched her looks, and time flew by. He wished it would never end, but sadly 'time and tide wait for no man'. He thought back to his school maths master who liked quoting Chaucer. As Kadri had excused herself whilst he paid the bill, the waiter complimented his choice of lady friend and asked that he return with her again as it would do wonders for the clientele at the restaurant. Lando puffed himself up, gave a bigger tip than intended, and chuckled stupidly until Kadri returned. She noticed, unsurprisingly, asking what he was looking so smug about.

"Oh, nothing of importance." He kept his face straight. "I think the waiter was gay, and he wanted to ask me out."

Kadri looked at him in shock, and once more, they laughed.

"So, what to do next, eh? Fancy a little walk, Kadri? Nothing too strenuous. Maybe a little walk by the Creek to let the food go down?"

She nodded, and they strolled out of the door, once again commanding the attention of other guests in the restaurant, particularly as the doorman treated them like royalty.

What an evening and the rest of the evening would be beyond Lando's wildest imagination, although sadly not in the way he might have hoped.

Chapter 24

Lando reached for Kadri's left hand as they ambled towards The Creek. The night was warm but not as oppressive as earlier and just about walkable without perspiration if they kept it slow. They proceeded without speaking, both comfortable in the quiet, both replete from their dinner and the relaxing effect of the alcohol.

"Where would you like to go?" said Kadri in her soft tones. "We could head for the Creek if you like. I know one or two places in the area, which I think you might enjoy."

"I'm in your hands," replied Lando. "I'll go where you go."

"I should hope so," said Kadri, smiling. "Do you fancy the Museum of Illusions?"

"I have absolutely no idea, but it sounds like fun."

"It is. The area also has many coffee shops, and I like strong Turkish coffee. Surprise, surprise."

So off they ambled down to Al Seef St. and on to the entrance of the Museum of Illusions.

"Ah, the time. The sign on the door says it closes at ten. And it is already ten past." At that moment, someone came out of the door.

"Hello. Can I help you?" The very skinny man said with a broad smile on his face.

"I think we are too late," said Kadri. "We did not know it closed at ten."

The man beamed again. "What is time on such a beautiful evening? I am happy to let you in. How long would you like?"

Lando could not believe it. This would never happen in England. He would have to be generous back.

"Fifteen minutes would be fine," said Kadri. "I wish to show my friend around as he has never seen this place."

"That is wonderful, and there would be no charge."

Again, Lando was dumbfounded at the generosity of the man. He must have somewhere to go to or a family waiting for him.

They went through the doors. They found quirky displays, puzzles, and rooms with mirrors. Kadri stood in front of one mirror and said, "Look! I look like I am having a baby."

They both looked at each other with a knowing smile. Before they knew it, ten minutes had passed, and they felt they ought to leave to allow the man to get home to his family. Lando gave him a generous tip, and the man was nearly overcome with pleasure. It was so lovely that he did that for them without asking for money upfront. He just did it .... and waited for the result.

They continued their walk and found a little coffee bar. They sat down outside and ordered two strong, black Turkish coffees. They came within 5 minutes, and Kadri put two heaped teaspoons of sugar in this one small cup of coffee. She also had a little lump of Turkish delight along with it.

"You will not keep your beautiful figure eating those things for long," said Lando as he chuckled.

"Uh-huh," she replied. "It is these things that give me my figure!"

"Should I order some more then?" laughed Lando. "Although I don't know how you could improve the current model."

Just then, Lando caught sight of a familiar figure around a corner. It was Hobart, and he was keeping out of sight but waved him over frantically. Lando made a weak excuse to Kadri and casually wandered over to Hobart.

"What are you ....?"

Hobart interrupted him, "Be quiet, and don't say a word until I have finished. This is pure chance and an amazing piece of luck. We got word that Hamza and his two buddies were in the vicinity. We found him. They are drinking coffee at another coffee bar. We can spring our trap on him as we have our pretend thief with us just out of sight. If we could do it tonight, that would be amazing. How do you feel about that?"

Lando nearly exploded. "Come on, Hobart. I am having a lovely night with Kadri. This is ridiculous. We haven't prepared ourselves or even run through a plan of action. Also, I'm just a teeny-weeny bit tiddly. I am not really in the mood for wrestling a man to the ground. I am more in the mood for wrestling a woman to the ground and certainly not for doing that outside a coffee bar. So how do I feel about it?... I think it stinks."

Undeterred, Hobart replied, "Does that mean you'll do it?"

"I guess it is Hobson's choice. I have no choice, as I'm damned if I do and damned if I don't. What about Kadri?"

"Do not worry. I shall take care of her. Remember, she is on our payroll. It would be best if we brief her very quickly at your table and tell her to go home immediately as she could be a complication. I shall ask Ahmed, the 'thief,' to escort her after he has got away from you."

"Can we have a quick recap? I have another coffee at the bar where Hamza is sitting. Your man, Ahmed, strolls past Hamza's table and grabs Hamza's purse which is where?"

"Conveniently, on the table at present."

"He makes a run for it. Hamza and his two mates give chase, probably after me, as I assume I rise immediately and wrestle Ahmed to the ground after a little run and grab the purse. He runs off, and I return the purse to Hamza, who has presumably caught up. We hope he somehow tries to repay me by inviting me for a drink or even to his home. So, what could possibly go wrong?"

"Nothing. Well done, Lando. You seem to have got it nailed. Ok, are we good to go?"

"I guess so. I still feel like a lamb to the slaughter as we are so unprepared, which goes against all my accountant's upbringing. Namely Murphy's Law."

"What is that?" said Hobart, raising a quizzical eyebrow.

"You should know. It came from a countryman of yours, an American aerospace design engineer called Murphy, who said in creating a design that 'If something can go wrong, it will.'"

"Aah, now I remember. You mean 'the buggery factor.'"

"That is another way of putting it."

"Look, we shall have Ahmed there, and I shall keep my eyes on you all the time – from a distance, of course. I shall fit you up with a wire. A little mic will be in your trouser pocket and tuned to my personal receiver." He proceeded to clip the transmitter onto the inside of Lando's left-side jacket pocket and ran the wire through the lining to the mic in his breast pocket. "We also have another three guys from the embassy in Abu Dhabi about to arrive, so we should be well covered."

"Should is not a very reassuring word… Ok, let's go with it. I assume you cannot speak to me through this contraption?"

Hobart shook his head. "Sorry, budget cuts in the company, but we will monitor every sound you make. Bit dangerous anyway having a mic in your ear as it can easily be spotted."

"There is one issue, though, that I must mention first. I have no idea what this Hamza guy looks like?"

"Don't worry, Lando. You will not need to recognise him. Just look for Abdul, who looks like a family-sized fridge. This Hamza guy has a large scar on his left cheek and is sitting with Farouk and him. All three sport dark beards and are in Arabic dress. None of which are particularly clean, but Hamza's is spectacular."

Lando felt alive and was not disinterested like he had felt for much of his life. He was swapping one bit of potential excitement, with Kadri, of course, for another, which involved wrestling Ahmed to the floor and retrieving the purse without being fingered as being involved. He knew which bit of excitement he would prefer. He walked back to his table with

Kadri and sat down, looking her straight in the eyes, and told her what had transpired.

He had to admire her. She barely blinked. Her face softened in the end, and she said gently to him, "Be careful, Lando. Remember, you are doing this for Dillon." She did not try to dissuade him. She just looked fondly at him. "I shall be fine. Hobart will look after me. I trust him."

"You trust his good intent, but do you trust his abilities in a fracas?"

"We shall have to wait and see. We should be OK."

"There's that word 'should' again."

"What?"

"Oh, it doesn't matter. Look, there's Hoby." He spied him across the street, trying his best not to look suspicious.

"He is signalling. It looks like we are on immediately, and we have no Plan B. Ugh. Here we go." With that, he stood up, placed his hand on Kadri's bare shoulder, bent down, and gave the most passionate kiss he could without being arrested as he had not forgotten which country he was in, and off he strode, trying to look as casual as possible.

He was dubious about recognising someone he had yet to meet. Still, as he went around the side of a building and spied the bar that Hoby had directed him to, he immediately caught sight of the three Arab conspirators. They could not be anyone else—one with the scar and one of the other two was so huge he looked less like a massive fridge and more like a brick shithouse. His hands and arms were like giant slabs of meat in a butcher's. He could barely take his eyes off him. He was sitting on two chairs at once, and no doubt his knackers would hang between them. Very, very dangerous and stupid, in Lando's opinion. He had a small espresso coffee cup in one hand halfway up to his mouth, which would have made him appear vaguely comical if he had not had such a frightening look on his face. Lando wondered what he ate every day to keep that size. He was like a Norwegian troll. He was not surprised he was used as an enforcer. One look at him would cause hysterical fear in any victim. Lando wrenched his eyes away from the three Arabs and sat well away from them at the far end of the outside seating area. He hoped that Hobart had briefed Ahmed to run past his table after picking up the purse so, giving Lando a head start on the Arabs, assuming they chased after him.

He ordered a coffee, and all hell broke loose within a minute. Ahmed thankfully came round the corner at the far end behind where the three were sitting and immediately pretended to trip and fell sprawling onto the table of the three 'amigos.' He raised himself, immediately grabbed the purse from the middle of the table, and bolted past Lando. Hamza immediately realised he had lost his purse and yelled 'stop thief' with some other Arabic expletives, which Lando did not understand but was likely very colourful. Lando had no idea why Hamza yelled, "Stop thief" in English, but he was probably trying to cover all the languages he knew.

As Ahmed flew past his table, he caught his eye, and Lando looked at the table of three with Abdul straining to stand up quickly, not something he was in the habit of. Lando mischievously thought a well-aimed kick to one of the chairs he was sitting on would undoubtedly send atomic shockwaves through the guy's knackers, launching him out of his seat in double quick time. Lando leapt forward, yelling, "Stop Thief" at the top of his voice, and sprinted after Ahmed, hoping he would slow down as with the food Lando had eaten, he was not in the mood for a marathon. Thankfully, he slowed enough for Lando to make one of his best rugby tackles and bring him down with a resounding crunch, and the purse flew out of his hand. Lando grabbed it, and Ahmed got up and ran off just as the brick shithouse by the name of Abdul arrived and proceeded to grapple with Lando putting two big meaty arms around his body from the rear, trying to squeeze the life out of him. He might have succeeded if all those years of karate training did not kick in. He lifted his right knee and brought the heel of his shoe right down on that slab of meat called a foot belonging to Abdul, who yelled in pain and slackened his grip enough for Lando to exhale hard to release the grip even more and drop down and give an 'empi' elbow strike to Abdul's knackers making him bend forward clutching himself after which Lando stood up quickly, twisted and brought his clenched fist like a hammer down as hard as he could on the back of Abdul's head– a 'tettsui' they called it in the dojo. Lando loved this one as it did not bruise the fingers and so could be delivered with all his strength, which he duly did. Abdul collapsed like a sack of potatoes. Hamza and Farouk looked on admiringly, and Lando handed the purse to them. Hamza reached gingerly for it.

"I believe this is yours," smiled Lando between deep, ragged breaths, still thanking his lucky stars for all the training he had done in the dojo.

"I am very sorry for my friend's behaviour," said Hamza in an oily tone. He was so grateful for his purse as although there was a little money in it, which there rarely was, he also had a small notebook of his connections and meetings with Qasim and Shazil and did not want those to get into the wrong hands. Abdul was slowly getting up with Farouk's help, who was rubbing the back of his head for him. No one offered to rub Abdul's balls, which did not entirely surprise Lando.

"I have never seen anyone floor my friend like that. I am so sorry, as he must have thought you were trying to take my purse and were somehow associated with that filthy dog who tried to rob me."

"It is of no consequence. Just doing my duty as a good citizen."

"Come and drink with us whilst you calm down, and we can repay you in some small way."

"That really is not necessary," replied Lando. He thought he would test how committed Hamza was to repaying the debt.

"Please," said Hamza. "Allah would not be happy with me if I could not repay you for risking your life to stop that filthy dog of a thief."

"Well, in that case, it would be much appreciated. I could use a long beer after that exciting bit of exercise." *Aha*, thought Lando. The first stage of the trap is set. Maybe we shall find out a little bit more about this Hamza.

"I am sorry," said Hamza. "But they do not serve alcohol here as it is not a restaurant."

"In that case, a coffee would be fine, although I would also appreciate a bottle of water."

"Of course, of course," stuttered Hamza.

They walked over to Hamza's table, and immediately Hamza introduced himself, as did Lando, but Hamza did not introduce Farouk and Abdul. That showed Hamza was the boss, but Lando had to be careful not to use Farouk or Abdul's names. However, they all shook hands and took their seats.

They chatted for a while over their coffees, and Lando learnt that Hamza lived not far away, whilst the other two did not say where they lived. Lando thought he would see if Hamza took the bait.

"Oh, I really could use a long cold beer. I'd like to know where I could get one around here."

There was a small period of almost awkward silence before Hamza spoke. "I have an idea. Why don't the four of us return to my humble abode, where I have a fridge containing a few cold beers, if you would do me the honour of allowing me to repay you the debt in some small way, I would be happy. I could find some food as well. What do you think?"

Bingo was the word that sprang to mind, and Lando struggled to keep the smile off his face. Once Hamza's residence is found, tracking him should be easy. "Mr Hamza, you flatter me with your generosity. I am constantly in awe of the Arab ways, and we in the West could learn a great deal from your culture. Yes, I would be delighted to accept your invitation."

Things were now moving along better than Lando could have hoped, and he only prayed that Hobart was keeping him in his sights. His thoughts returned to Kadri, and he marvelled at how he could have such a different evening from the one he had planned.

Hamza waved to a waiter to bring the bill. When it arrived, Hamza patted his pockets so vehemently that it became obvious he wanted Lando to pay the bill. Lando immediately said, "Don't worry, Hamza, I'll get this. It is no problem." Lando left a note on the table large enough to cover the drinks plus tip. He could see Abdul eyeing it up. He would like to take the note and replace it with the exact amount needed to pay for the coffee. Knowing Lando was watching, he decided that would not be good practice.

"Follow me," said Hamza. "We do not have far to go, my friend, and I look forward to entertaining you in my humble residence."

Chapter 25

They commenced walking. Lando kept pace with Hamza, and Farouk and Abdul shuffled behind. He felt uncomfortable at the back of his neck with these two in the rear. He could feel Abdul's eyes boring into him, and he imagined the dream of revenge written on Abdul's face. They walked for about 10 minutes, and Lando had no inkling that Hoby was following. He hoped so, as he was completely lost anyway.

As it happened, Hobart had also lost his way. Only one guy named Kamal had turned up from the embassy to help along with Ahmed. Hobart had been doing his best to follow, and even though the pace was not fast, there were so many twists and turns down different alleyways that he frequently walked down the wrong one, lost them, came back and walked up another to find them again. It was dangerous for all concerned to follow too closely, and Hoby hoped his two assistants were taking different routes, and with luck, he might bump into them. It was not to be, and Hobart was starting to panic. He was in touch with Kamal but had no sight of Lando or his three new friends. All he could hear were the footsteps transmitted from Lando's mic.

Lando kept dwelling on Abdul and Farouk being behind him and wondered what their conversation consisted of. Abdul seemed quiet, but he could only guess that he was plotting with Farouk, perhaps including slowly pulling Lando's arms off.

They finally got to what appeared to be Hamza's dwelling, and just as they were going in through the front door, which had certainly seen better days as it was almost off its hinges, Lando noticed that facing the front door, across the dusty street was a little shop called Mirzam Chocolate Makers. He had an idea in the event Hoby was lost.

"Hey, Hamza. I could do with some presents to take home. How good are the chocolates in that shop opposite?"

"Ahaa, very, very good. But I'm afraid they are closed right now. You will need to come back another time."

"I will do. What's the name? Is it Marzim Chocolate Makers?" said Lando screwing up his eyes and pretending he could not quite read the sign.

"No," said Hamza. "It is called Mirzam Chocolate Makers, and for your reference, it is just off Al Seef Street, which, of course, is a big one. The turn-off has 4 big stones piled up, and these little lanes here do not have official names. They are given names by the local people living here, so it is called Five Stones Lane."

"I thought there were only four stones," said Lando, repeating the shop's name slowly and pretending to memorise it, but he made sure it was clear to Hoby, assuming the microphone was working. "So, Five Stones Lane with only four stones in a pile. What happened to the other stone?"

"Somebody put it to better use."

I'll bet, thought Lando. *Hamza would no doubt be the culprit.*

Hamza had a slightly quizzical look but then seemed to dismiss it. He showed Lando in through his front door, and as Hamza shuffled to the fridge in his little kitchen, Lando noticed a scabbard on the side. He quietly picked it up, looked at it closely, and realised with enthusiasm that it must be the scabbard of the knife that killed Dylan! He quickly put it down with a clatter as Abdul and Farouk entered the room behind him.

"So, my friend, what would you like to eat with your beer? We have some bread and cold meats and a little cheese."

"To be honest, Hamza, I am not very hungry as I have just been out for a big meal. I will take that beer, though."

They went outside into the little yard by the front door, which boasted a small metal table, and Hamza poured him a beer from a bottle into a glass, which he thought was strange as he imagined this crowd would never use a glass to down a beer. He was later proved right as he started to feel very queasy after a few sips of beer, which had a strange aftertaste. Their voices became distant, and he began to perspire profusely. He could no longer maintain a seated posture in his chair. He felt himself passing out and wondered what the hell was going on.

At the back of his mind, he realised they were onto him. Now they were moving him and half carrying him. His legs felt like jelly, and his head was spinning, and then he passed out.

***

Meanwhile, Hobart was in a growing panic until the mic that Lando was wearing burst into life and gave him the information he needed to trace him. He called the other two excitedly and reeled off the area to get to quickly. They were all a good fifteen-minute walk away, so they had to hurry. He also picked up some of the conversations and realised something was wrong. He heard Lando slurring his words and then shuffling or dragging of feet. Not good. He ran as fast as he could. Round one bend, along the Creek, around another bend, along Al Seef Street, until he found the pile of stones. Then, up the lane, there was the Mirzam Chocolate Makers shop. He stopped twenty yards short to catch his breath. There was no sign of Ahmed or Kamal, so he decided he could not wait for them. He withdrew his Glock from the holster inside his jacket, which was drenched with his sweat, and crept up to the shop front and then turned round to see a small yard with a few glasses on a table before a door. He deliberated on what to do—should he wait for the others and then barge in with force, knock on the door, or wait until something happened? He decided to go where angels fear to tread and to knock on the door. He knocked hard a couple of times and kept the gun loosely by his side. No sound. He banged harder and then a very old man was shuffling along by. Hobart holstered his weapon.

The old man muttered, "There is no one in there, shabun. They have left." He used the Arabic term for young man.

"Oh dear, I was meeting a friend here, and I think he was taken ill," said Hobart politely. "Did you, by any chance, see where they went?"

"Yes, I did. Three very unpleasant-looking men were helping another one who seemed incapable of walking." He turned and pointed towards a large, dilapidated building. "I think they went in that direction, but I could not be sure. Definitely up to no good. One of them was like a huge bear."

That'll be Abdul, thought Hobart. He prayed he was in time. He thanked the old man, who turned round slowly and shuffled off.

Hobart made his way to the old building and noticed a pale light shining through a crack in a blacked-out window. It looked hopeful.

He found a side door, opened it slowly, and thanked his lucky stars that it did not creak. He heard a muffled conversation and noticed a foul odour drifting out of the doorway. He unholstered his Glock again, feeling its cool comfort in his palm, and let himself in. He was in a small passageway with a light coming from another doorway ahead, and the door was slightly ajar. He walked up to it, hoping those inside could not hear his heartbeat banging in his ears. He heard muffled conversations but recognised Hamza's voice as he crept up to the doorway, holding his gun in his right hand and pointing up at the ceiling.

Then he heard Farouk's voice.

"Mine will be the final torture," he said with a leer and a faint line of dribble coming from his lips. "To release your soul to beg forgiveness from Allah. You will be bent over the table, and I shall proceed to push this tent pole up your smelly white backside until you scream for mercy. You shall receive none, and then I shall push it further until you scream no more. What do you think of that Kafir?"

"Well," slurred Lando. "I went to a slightly disreputable boarding school, and this sounds a bit like the initiation ceremony my first week. But may I ask one thing? Would you mind using lubricant as splinters can be a bitch!"

Hobart could not hide his laughter, so he entered and took in the scene. Hamza was on the far side of the room, holding what looked like a rock attached to a thin piece of rope. Abdul, the man mountain, was no more than three metres in front of him, and Farouk was holding his big stick with which he was going to do unmentionable things to Lando, who was seated naked and fastened to a wooden chair. With a two-handed grip on his Glock, he immediately put a bullet straight between Farouk's eyes, who sank to his knees with a look of surprise. Then Abdul turned to face him and made a surprisingly swift move towards Hobart but staggered as his feet got caught up in the cables hanging off the battery trolley between him and Hobart. Hobart placed three bullets into Abdul's chest, which appeared not to deter him, and he ran straight through Hobart as if he was not there and continued outside. His last action on this planet was to grab hold of Kamal by the head, who had just arrived, and break his neck like it was a twig before staggering a couple more steps and collapsing to the pavement as Hobart's bullets had done their business. The whole front of his chest was awash with blood, still pumping weakly out of him onto the ground as Ahmed looked on in shock and remained frozen to the spot.

Meanwhile, Hobart had turned around to see Hamza scarpering out of a door at the other end of the room. He got off a quick shot but assumed he had missed him as he heard his footsteps on the gravel outside. Hobart thought about giving chase but knew his loyalties were to Lando, so he checked him out as well as he could as he was confused by some type of sedative and talking complete gibberish whilst tears were rolling down his face, no doubt with relief. He cut his cable ties with his trusty pocketknife, realising this tool was used for its first time, and helped Lando to his feet when he promptly fell over. He found Lando's clothing whilst Lando was rolling about the floor and marvelled that his mic and transmitter were still inside his jacket pocket. The silly asses had not even checked his clothing. He found a sealed plastic bottle of water and told Lando to drink as much as possible to wash the drug out of his body, and he proceeded to help him get dressed. They needed to get out of the building quickly, as the sound of gunfire must have been reported. He half carried Lando outside, where Ahmed was still in a daze, and explained what had happened to Kamal in stuttering sentences. He dragged Kamal's body out of sight, found an old rug and spread it over Abdul's corpse as he was just too big to move so it would not be so evident to any passers-by. He then telephoned his controller, Harold Shrimpton. Thankfully, he was incredibly calm. He would arrange a clean-up operation immediately and square it with the Dubai Security Services at the appropriate time. He required a full report on his desk by 11.00 am the next day.

That done, they had to get the gibbering wreck of Lando back to his hotel and try to make Ahmed into half a human being again.

Hobart asked Ahmed to help him with Lando as he had been filled with a drug, and doing something positive seemed to help bring Ahmed out of his shock. So off they went one slow step after another until they passed Hamza's house when Lando suddenly became agitated and refused to walk. He kept babbling louder and louder what sounded like *scaawa*, *scaaaaawa* until Hobart rested him against a wall, and Lando gestured with a floppy arm to the front door of Hamza's house. Scaaaaawa, he babbled again. Hobart almost gave up but decided to humour him. They staggered over to the front door, opened it and went in. Lando staggered over to the kitchen side, and there was the scabbard, which he grasped in his hands. He crumpled to the floor and immediately fell sound asleep.

"My God, that's what he meant," said Hobart. "Scaaaaawa was him trying to say scabbard. Sheath would have been an easier word to say!" he muttered. "I'll bet my next year's wages that it is the scabbard belonging to the knife embedded in Dillon's chest."

Ahmed gave half a smile and bent down to try to raise Lando, who was now comatose. How were they going to move him now? It was going to take a lot of work. Hobart went outside and had a look around. It was close to midnight but almost a full moon. He spied a wheelbarrow just down the road. He walked towards it and was checking out whether it would hold Lando when what appeared to be the owner came out of his front door, scratching his backside. He asked him what he was doing in Arabic and again in broken English.

"I desperately need a strong wheelbarrow to carry my friend who has had too much to drink. Would you be willing to sell me this one?" pleaded Hobart as Ahmed joined them.

The man clearly could not understand Hobart and looked very disinterested as well. Hobart then spoke a universal language when he pointed at the wheelbarrow whilst pulling a wad of dirhams out of his pocket and proceeded to count off notes until the man's look of total disinterest turned into a look of rampant interest when he hit 500 dirhams. The smiling man waved him away with the barrow and charged back through his front door.

Hobart turned to Ahmed. "Why didn't you help me out there? You know I don't speak much Arabic, and I know you do?"

"Aah, Hobart. I was enjoying it so much I didn't want it to end, so I left you to it."

"You know, I paid him 500 dirhams. That is about 130 US dollars."

"Yes—" laughed Ahmed. "And it wasn't even his barrow."

"And you knew that, Ahmed. I ought to have that stopped out of your wages. Anyway, it is up to him to square it with his neighbour. He will probably tell him he got 100 dirhams for it. I mean, look at the state of it."

As they meandered back up the hill, Hobart muttered about it doing the job and having no choice anyway. He muttered all the way to Lando's lethargic body, which was beginning to show signs of recovery. They manhandled him into the barrow and set off again with Ahmed's help down the lane towards Al Seef Street, where he hoped to pick up a taxi. He sent Ahmed back to stay at the scene until the cleanup guys arrived and to brief them about Kamal.

Hobart kept Lando in his wheelbarrow well out of sight until he flagged down a taxi whose driver was happy with the story that Hobart gave him about his 'friend' not handling alcohol very well as he had been grieving a lost friend. The man obligingly helped him into the cab, and off they went to Lando's hotel. Lando was thankfully improving and talking coherently when they arrived at the Hyatt Regency Hotel but struggled to walk very well. He stayed outside, sitting on a big stone, and asked Hobart a favour.

"Hoby, could you go inside and ask the concierge if Gaji is around? I know he can help me. He is one of the hotel's airport transfer taxi drivers. I cannot be seen by any of my students like this or any of the hotel staff, for that matter." He saw the look on Hoby's face. "Don't worry, I trust him. Goodfella."

Within two minutes, Hobart came out accompanied by the ever-smiling Gaji, who immediately asked what the problem was and if he needed a doctor.

"Gaji, it is fine. I need to sleep it off. Long story, but someone slipped a mickey into my drink."

"So, you will not want any ganja, girls or other forms of relaxation?"

"OK, Gaji, have your laugh, but I need to get up to my room without causing a stir and potentially losing my job if any of my students see me."

"Right, we can enter the hotel by a side door and use a staff elevator. I will keep a lookout, and we can get you to your room." He turned to Hobart. "And what about you, sir? Is there anything at all I can find for you? Alcohol, girls, places, knock-off watches, pubs, restaurants, girls, shisha bars. Anything at all. I'm very, very, very good at it. Just come to me and no one else."

Lando laughed almost as much as Hobart did, who politely refused but declined to comment on Gaji saying 'girls' twice.

So off Lando went with Gaji supporting him whilst they walked around the back of the hotel and entered through a side door. Lando was now perspiring profusely, mainly with the heat but also the effort of holding himself upright as well as the increased rate of his heart straining to expel the effects of the drug. They got to the service lift and up to Lando's floor, and as they walked along the passage to his room number 737, little Willie's mother, the thin, bejewelled woman, was getting into her room. She turned and looked at Lando with a mixture of fear and loathing, which was too much for Lando, so even in his present state, he could not resist another wind-up.

He shrieked towards Gaji in a loud voice, "Oh darling that was such a fun evening. We must do it again sometime," and stroked the back of Gaji's neck. Gaji helped him into the room, and they both laughed as Gaji clearly understood what Lando was doing without knowing the full story of the thin, bejewelled woman. Lando told Gaji the story about little Willie and his mother, and they both decided she was up to no good when she came into her room so late. Had she left little Willie alone? Maybe she had some secret tryst going on. All kinds of thoughts ran through Lando's head, now clearing as the sedative wore off whilst also knocking back half a litre of cold water from his mini-bar.

Gaji checked with Lando, who said he was all right to be left. Lando offered him a tip, which Gaji refused, saying, "I helped you as a friend in trouble. Somethings in my life are not about money."

Lando was sitting on a bedside chair open-mouthed as Gaji departed before he could reply. He then had a hot shower and went straight to bed, not forgetting that he had a lecture commencing at 8.30 the following day. He texted Kadri with the words, "What a night! I am fine, but I am a bit messed up in my head and need sleep. It was a lovely start to the evening and a rubbish end. Not the one I had planned. Hope you got back OK." He ended it with a hug emoji.

He got an immediate reply, "Speak tomorrow" with an emoji of a kiss. He could at least sleep peacefully, knowing she was also safe and sound.

Chapter 26

Kadri received Lando's text with relief whilst entering her apartment, as she would never sleep knowing the danger he was in. She was always ready for danger and thought back to her childhood and upbringing after her family was massacred when she was only fifteen.

Her father, mother and brother were all killed outside their church by a group of young Islamic fundamentalists who were on a mission to remove all the Christians from Turkey. She did not understand them as about 100 years ago, a quarter of the population in Turkey were Orthodox Christians; this had now dropped to well under 1%, although thousands were too scared to admit to being Christian. Her grandparents were also killed after the end of World War 1 as part of the 3 million Christians eliminated. Many also fled the country as Turkey sided with Germany in the war, bringing about a tough peace settlement. The current government was on the face of it secular, but it was still refusing to let some Christian people back in who had left the country on holiday only to be denied re-entry.

So Kadri had encountered violence through the loss of her closest family. A kind friend had taken her in, and she had stayed until she felt old enough to travel. She came to Dubai ten years ago at the age of nineteen, as she had heard from a distant cousin in Dubai about its growth and broader-mindedness compared to much of the Arab world regarding non-Islamic religions. She wished to retain her Christian roots as much in memory of her parents as for her own spiritual needs.

She had not regretted it as she had kept her head above water with her dancing work and then had bumped into Harold Shrimpton, Hobart's CIA controller, who thought she could be a great asset to 'the company.' The belly dancing income was a bit hit and miss depending on the time of year, although she learnt to fend off irritating propositions from both drunken Arab and European men, as well as women. In contrast, her involvement on a part-time basis with the CIA proved to be a great success. They had sent her to England for training, and the money they paid her was both a decent wage and paid regularly at the month's end, and she did not have to beg for the payment as she did with some of the travel companies who employed her. She was sure that quite a few of her dancing lady colleagues made significant extra money by selling themselves to their travel clients. This was not in her scheme of things for her life, although she did not judge them. She knew many of them had been entirely penniless before getting those significant bonuses and at least were able to develop a kind of lifestyle that had some level of quality. She doubted many of them did it out of choice.

Kadri had done one or two assignments on an ad hoc payment basis for Hobart, primarily small, such as cosying up to people who befriended those who could pose a threat to the United States and worming her way into their trust and finding out who their associates were. She proved to be a natural at this, and whilst Hobart had quite an aloof, privileged, cold side, he also showed a level of empathy when certain information proved challenging to come by. He had the ability to judge the truth when she told him her difficulties and never expected or encouraged her to sleep with a 'mark' to gain his confidence. They had built up a reasonable degree of mutual trust, and he had put her on a regular monthly payment, so she hoped Hobart would start to include her in more testing assignments. Her only difficulty was when it came to lying, as it did not come naturally to her. However, she felt that the greater good would be served if she somehow compartmentalised this value as she had been taught in her training in England. She coped by pretending she was just an actress delivering a line rather than telling a lie. She quickly became better at it as time went by.

She had met a few young and middle-aged men over the years from varied countries, some on holiday in Dubai and some living and working there. Whilst she had one or two relationships that lasted a few months or more, she never quite found anyone with whom she could settle down and was always aware that her dancing could, particularly when combined with alcohol, create a high degree of lust, which she was worldly enough to differentiate from love on their part. She was proud that she had never been an easy 'score' for anyone.

However, Lando created feelings in her that were different from any other man she had met. He was so clearly honest and kind and had an undeniably fit body. In her experience, those traits did not often go together. There was just something so profound inside him that she was attracted to. She had never come on to a man in such an obvious way before, but she just found it so easy because she also really liked him and, strangely, wanted to mother him. He seemed to provide the fun that her life seemed to have lacked for so long.

That said, she also could not stop herself from wanting to shag his brains out. This was a Turkish expression as well as a British one!

After her meal with Lando and their stroll to the Museum of Illusions, followed by a lovely coffee, she had harboured high hopes of another all-nighter with Lando, but that had been ruined by Hobart springing the request on Lando to immediately help with finding where Hamza lived through a very hit and miss arrangement necessitating Lando befriending this Hamza guy. She was terrified for Lando as he had no training in this type of subterfuge. Hobart quickly set it up, rang his embassy to get someone to walk Kadri back to her apartment, and told her to wait until he arrived. He would be coming from Abu Dhabi as there was only a consulate in Dubai, which did not have the available staff. Even in Dubai, late at night, some areas could be better to walk through, particularly as an unaccompanied beautiful woman like Kadri. She had waited patiently but decided to walk home after nearly an hour. She received some lascivious looks on the way, mainly from Europeans who gained their courage from being well 'dieseled up' and staggering along with equally unstable mates. She could always deal with those types, but the back alleys frightened her, so she stuck to the main roads where there were lights from shops and people around. However, when nearly home, she was accosted, for want of a better word, by a continental-looking sixty-year-old silver-haired, oustachioed, aggressive type who thought he was irresistible and was not used to taking no for an answer. She began to find his badgering in the street beyond irritating, and just as she was feeling quite vulnerable, along came a handsome knight in shining armour who had viewed the situation from his outside seat by a coffee shop.

She saw this blond-haired, beautiful, clean-shaven apparition rapidly walking towards them and, pretending to know her, he took her forearm and said in a very authoritative voice, "Ah, there you are, darling. I was wondering where you were as I was beginning to worry." The aggressive type immediately sloped off as he got the gist of the statement and realised that he was on rocky ground with someone else's wife. He did not want any confrontation with Kadri's man in whatever capacity.

He let go of her arm, and still in the middle of the street, he stood back and, putting on his best British public school manners and loud, far-back accent, said, "Please allow me to introduce myself. I am Ashley Hayhurst, and I am honoured to be at your service as I noted you were in a rather uncomfortable situation. Please call me Ash."

Kadri had been beginning to get worried about her confrontation, and the adrenaline had been flowing, ready for her need to put up a fight with the silver-haired brute. She was starting to tremble and stuttered out a 'thank you,' after which

Ashley took her by the arm again and said, "You need a damn stiff drink and a hot cup of cocoa. Come on." He wheeled her over to his table at the coffee shop.

Once seated, she was extremely grateful and thanked him repeatedly. Even though she had received limited self-defence training on her CIA course in England, she did not fancy using it in the middle of the street, causing an even greater furore.

"Ashley, sorry, Ash. I do not think we are likely to get an alcoholic drink here, and I am unsure if they serve cocoa either." She was beginning to smile.

"Do not worry. I know they have hot chocolate here, and they also have little marshmallows to float on it. What could be better?"

"Well, actually, a shot of something stronger. What is a marshmallow anyway?"

"Dear lady, all is not lost. Just wait and see." He ordered the hot chocolate as well as the marshmallows.

"Thank you so much. My name is Kadri, by the way."

"That is an unusual name. I'm sorry. To me, it is unusual as I have not heard it before."

"I am originally from Turkey. It means 'pure,' but I am anything but. Oh dear, that must sound awful. What I mean is that I am way less than perfect."

"Like the rest of us. Here comes the chocolate, which already has marshmallows in it. You can always put them in the saucer if you do not like them." The young waiter placed their drinks on the table with a couple of glasses and a small bottle of the local cool desalinated water and scooted off for his next task.

Kadri took a sip, and through a smile, she said, "Gorgeous."

"I'll say," said Ashley, grinning as he watched her face. "Oh, I'm sorry again. After what you have just faced, the last thing you need is someone like me coming on to you."

"Don't worry. I have my composure back and a bit of practice in fending off approaches nicely. Not that I wish to fend you off, but I have had a long evening and am very tired."

"OK, Kadri. Time for my '*pièce de resistance*.' I have my secret weapon here," he muttered as he leaned to his left and extracted a small flask from his safari jacket's inside pocket. "I must tell you that this is a bit special. In my family, it was known as 'granny's medicine,' as she always drank it when she had an asthma attack. It is an ancient brand of single malt whisky." He poured a slug into Kadri's hot chocolate.

Kadri took a sip, and her eyes lit up. "My God, that is good. I imagine she had asthma attacks pretty often."

"Well, she did after that. In fact, almost every night." The humour eased their chat. "It seems like a crime to put it into hot chocolate, but methinks it has nonetheless done the trick."

"Methinks? What kind of word is that?"

"Ugh. There I go again. Spouting old English. I loved English literature at school, and Shakespeare had an oft-quoted famous line using it."

"Go on. What was the line?"

"'The lady doth protest too much, methinks.' It was from his play Hamlet."

"Oh yes, I have heard of that play. Doesn't everyone die at the end?"

"Mostly yes. Miserable. Would you like some more whisky? Perhaps try it in a separate glass with just a splash of water?"

"Go on then. Just a little one." She almost felt back to her usual self.

Ashley poured a little snifter, added just a few dribbles of water, and watched her sip it silently. "Well? What do you think?" he said as her face glowed.

She smiled. Then, half under her breath, she said, "Wow, that is a bit better than a Haig Club whisky."

"When have you had that? It is not bad, but nothing compared to a fifty-year-old Macallan's."

She thought back to that fateful night of Dillon's horrendous murder and then coming back to Lando's hotel room. It was the second time in a week that a kind man had given her a strong drink to calm her nerves. She did not answer.

"Anyway, when you have finished, we must get you home as it is getting very late."

"I'm ok. I feel good now, so there's no need to *get me home*, as you put it. I am more than capable of getting myself home," she said curtly.

"Aaah! Spirited, I see. There is no way I would let a lady like yourself walk home alone at this time of night anywhere in the world. My mother would kill me. Don't worry, I am a happily married guy to a wonderful lady called Anya. We have two children, and I just want to do the right thing."

"In that case, I accept. As it happens, I have recently met a lovely guy who always makes me laugh, and we seem to have bonded. In fact, I have just been out to dinner with him. Yes, I am very fond of Lando."

"Well, this guy is a fool leaving a beautiful lady like yourself alone."

"It was my fault. I insisted as something very important came up, and he had to leave early."

"Sounds a bit dubious. I had a great friend at school called Lando. Called him Rolo. Overheard his mother call him that, and it sort of stuck. Haven't seen him in ages. We didn't half have some good times together. I needed to when away from home so long as I was at a boarding school. You have made me think it is time I got in touch with him as I haven't seen him in years. We lost touch as we lived so far apart."

"So, what is special about a boarding school? Is that because you were a naughty boy?"

"No. Not really, but I became a naughty boy away from home so much that I would have been kicked out if it hadn't been for Rolo. I owed him big time as he got me off the hook. However, that story is for another day."

"So, what are you doing in Dubai without your wife? No doubt she has the children to look after. I assume you are here on business."

"Yes, I am. Only here for a week. I work for a firm of architects in London, and we are just preparing a pitch for a substantial building design. Quite exciting. Everyone wants to outdo somebody else with either the size or the outlandish design. Makes for a bit of fun in the design, though. Anyway, enough of me. So, tell me about you. How come your English is so good?"

She told him very briefly about her Turkish background and, leaving out the CIA informant part, said she had done some training for a job in England for a few months, which did not work out. He had a look of pure admiration when she told him about her belly dancing work. It made him very excited, but being the gentleman that he was, he repeatedly interjected with compliments about how successful she must be because of her magnetic beauty. Of course, she was also still dressed in her stunning evening attire that had brought the restaurant to a standstill.

"Come on then," he said, standing up. "Let's get you back home safely. You look a little wiped out."

He paid the bill, and they walked away. They were near her apartment block near the Gold Souk, and she had no qualms about him knowing where she lived as she believed she was a pretty good judge of men after all her practice.

At the apartment block entrance, she turned toward him and gave him a big kiss on the cheek and a hug. "Well, thank you again, Ash. It has been quite an evening. Perhaps we can meet again and take you out to dinner?"

"That would be lovely. Maybe then I can check out this Lando fellow of yours, just to be on the safe side." Smiling, he gave her his card and walked off with his slightly too-long blond hair wafting in the night air. He was one of the most beautiful, charming men she had ever seen.

At that moment, there was a bleep on her phone, and she was massively relieved to see a text from Lando and replied with a kiss. She walked up the stairs to her apartment when the tiredness and stress of the evening got to her, and for the first time in her life, she flopped onto her bed and, fully clothed, fell sound asleep.

Chapter 27

Friday

It was a dreamless sleep and so deep Kadri was groggy in the morning, but thankfully, at 7.45 am, she did wake up. She showered and changed into a pair of faded jeans and a loose-fitting, white blouse that had just that element of femininity that she liked.

She looked in the mirror, had a quick brush of the hair and happily realised she did not look too bad, all things considered! A breakfast beckoned, and she emptied a bag of oats, fruit, nuts and yoghurt into a plate and scoffed it down. She was hungry, no doubt caused by all the excitement from last night. She fixed a big mug of fresh ground coffee and, staring out over the Creek, squinted her eyes against the risen sun in the cloudless sky. It was quite a night, albeit different to the one planned and she was desperate to speak to Lando. It was Friday and the official holy day. However, the change to a more westernised working week caused a little difficulty and confusion for families, as the public sector worked a four-and-a-half-day week, finishing Friday lunchtime and some corporations keeping the working week Sunday to Thursday and others Monday to Friday. It did not affect Kadri, but she was pretty sure that Lando was not working that day, so she decided to ring him.

"Yeh. Who's that?" came the reply in another groggy voice thick with sleep.

"Who do you think it is? Do you have another belly dancer on the go?"

"Sorry, just a minute." Off he went to get a small bottle of cool water out of the fridge. He walked back to where he had left his phone, though he could not think why he had not carried his phone with him. He was not yet thinking at full speed. He unscrewed the bottle top, took a couple of cooling gulps, and clarity slowly crept through his head.

"Ah, that's better. Now I can focus. I still feel pretty rubbish. Glad you got back all right, so how are you feeling?"

"Well, I was so relieved to get your text last night as I had only just got in myself. I was out like a light. Still feeling good now, so any plans for the rest of the day? Can we meet for coffee?"

Lando ran his tongue around his mouth and, at that moment, fully appreciated where a mouth like a zookeeper's boot came from. He took another gulp of water and, from three metres, chucked the empty bottle directly into the bin. *Still got it, mate*, he said to himself.

"That would be great. However, beyond that, I cannot plan as I have to go to the U.S. Embassy or, more specifically, their Dubai consulate and liaise with Hobart about last night. I believe his handler wishes to see me as well, so hopefully, I shall learn a bit more about what is going on. Hoby did request that I did not bring you as the fewer times you are seen going into the consulate, the better for your safety."

"He's more thoughtful than he looks, that guy." There was a quiet pause. "Ok, let's meet at Connigan's for a coffee as they have a really sweet balcony, and we can take it from there."

"Super. I need a shower and to chuck on a few clothes, and I shall be there in, say, thirty minutes. Will that suit you?"

"See you there at ten, then lover-boy," she said and then hung up before he could reply appropriately.

He grinned like an idiot all the same.

She was already at Connigan's when he arrived. She was seated at a table, staring out across the Creek and looking for the whole world like a poster model advertising Dubai. He had to pinch himself as he walked up behind her and briefly touched her shoulder.

"I hope that is you, Lando. Otherwise, I shall have to ask you to be gone, or I shall have you arrested."

"That would be interesting. Always fancied being molested by a gorgeous woman whilst handcuffed." He sat down. It was a very harsh law that could have you arrested for only walking down the street hand in hand. "How can I show you affection then?"

"You can always buy me a Lamborghini Huracan."

"Ha. You wish!"

"Actually, I don't. Just happy with the gentleman's presence."

"And here I am," he said, throwing his arms wide in grand bonhomie. "Have you ordered any coffee?"

"Not yet. Just been taking in the view whilst it is still cool enough to enjoy it."

"Okay. What do you fancy? A couple of cappuccinos with sprinkles?"

"Ausgezeichnet."

"Excellent indeed. I thought you were Turkish, not German."

"I am, but many Turkish know a few words in German, and many youngsters have it as a first language."

He beckoned the waiter and ordered the two coffees. "I learnt a bit at school. Surprisingly easy compared to French even though they sometimes stick a part of the verb at the end of the sentence."

The coffees arrived promptly, and few words passed between them as they took in the view of the Creek and the sky. Lando glanced at his watch and realised he needed to get to the consulate soon, or Hobart would get antsy. Between sips of coffee, they quickly caught up with each other about the previous night. Lando's protective instincts kicked in, so he omitted to tell Kadri about how close a shave he had with Hamza and his sidekicks. He said that Abdul and Farouk were now out of the picture, but Hamza unfortunately got away, and he might have been injured. Kadri listened to this open-mouthed, and when he told her about Kamal's death, she looked aghast. She sensibly did not ask too many deep questions, particularly about the meaning of Abdul and Farouk being out of the picture, as she assumed she would find out eventually from Hobart. Evidently, things were hotting up.

She told him about the kind gentleman who had helped her last night and that she would invite him for a drink with them tomorrow night if Lando could manage it. She could not see Lando tonight as she had a gig on which did not depress Lando too much as he just wanted a quiet evening after relaxing by the hotel pool. He still felt ragged after his night on 'sedatives.'

They parted company with long smiling looks and waves when Lando just wanted to grab her and give her the biggest hug and kiss possible. He needed patience, not something he had ever been blessed with.

***

Lando caught a taxi to the Dubai consulate and was about to enter when he took a call from Hobart.

"Change of plan. The consulate cannot easily accommodate us, so we are now meeting at the British Embassy in Dubai. We often work together, more than you would imagine by reading the media posts but the only issue is that a member of the British security service will need to attend our meeting. They have been briefed, and with you being a British citizen, they need to know what measures we are taking to protect your safety. Reasonable, I suppose."

"Damn right," replied Lando. "So where is this embassy? I have just got out of the taxi at the US consulate?"

"Same street. Al Seef St., a seven-minute walk, keeping the Creek on your right. Expect you in seven minutes." He abruptly hung off.

Lando deduced that Hobart was unhappy about bringing the British into this ever-widening information circle. *Why?* He could only imagine! He guessed it would restrict how they operated so that Hobart might lose a little of his autonomy. He would have to wait and see, but Lando had a strange sense of comfort knowing that British undercover operations would be involved.

He arrived at the embassy and was pleased to hear the British accents used within the building as he was accompanied on a lift going up two floors and shown into a room containing Hobart, someone he assumed was Harold and two other people. One looked vaguely technical, and the other could only be British judging by his six-foot-six ramrod straight posture, his perfectly groomed head of greying hair, a dark three-piece suit and, of course, his voice when he welcomed Lando. He was obviously 'old school' and oozed culture whilst they all shook hands.

"Hello, Lando. This is my number two, Oscar, and my name is Gerald Kirkpatrick. I am very pleased to meet you, a man who has helped our American allies in a tricky situation. The F.O. will be proud of you when this little rumpus blows over."

"I would like to say it has been a pleasure, but it has not been exactly that, although a trifle more excitement than I am used to," said Lando, putting on his best far-back accent. With typical British understatement, it was more excitement than he had felt in his whole life.

Kirkpatrick carried on. "I have been thoroughly briefed, so I would like to know how you stand on continuing your involvement in this shindig. It could get a bit messy, you see." He did not strike Lando as a typical undercover agent, not that he knew any besides Hobart. Moreover, he seemed so far removed from that type that he was probably not taken seriously. Seemed very much the Eton/Harrow and Oxbridge type mixed with very old money. He guessed it was that slightly abnormal persona that gave him good cover.

"I imagine by messy you mean a bit dangerous. We have already lost one chap, and I have been drugged, been in a gunfight, almost tortured and found myself working with Hoby here on a clandestine operation. I would like to see it all through if it is all the same to you."

Hobart winced at the use of the short form for his name.

"Yes. Kamal, God rest his soul," muttered Kirkpatrick; turning to Harold, he asked that his condolences be sent to the family after it was all over. Harold nodded with a suitably morose expression.

"We also lost Dillon most unpleasantly," said Hobart.

"Getting a bit careless with the staff, are we then?" The dark humour was lost on all bar Kirkpatrick himself. "So, we go full steam ahead, but there are two things on which I must insist. One is that I am kept informed up to the minute with every detail as it happens, and secondly, our friend Lando here is protected from direct harm as much as possible. He is neither familiar with this work nor experienced in looking after himself." Facing Lando, he said, "Although I believe you managed to render a certain large member of Hamza's team briefly incapacitated. Some good karate moves, I guess."

Lando was mildly impressed as Kirkpatrick had obviously done his homework on Lando's background. "Yes, his name was Abdul, and I am not unrelieved he has departed this world as I felt he would seek revenge at the earliest opportunity. In fact, he was about to demonstrate that with a pair of electrodes on my testicles, but thankfully, Hobart's timing on entering the room was sheer perfection."

"I heard that," smiled Kirkpatrick. "We may be able to use you directly ourselves once this little show is over. We have also heard there are inquiries in Tehran about the supply of military drones to this area, which is rather disturbing. Maybe nothing to do with this as the Iranians are always stirring up something with Al-Qaeda, the Houthis, Hezbollah, Hamas, etc., but it is curiously coincidental."

"I am due to return to England in 10 days or so as my university lectures will finish. Not sure this will all be wrapped up by then."

"Don't worry. We can clear that up with your university and the Dubai authorities. Your work visa will be good for 30 days, so no issues there."

"I should hope so. I don't want it to last that long!" exclaimed Lando indignantly. "Incidentally, are you from MI5 or MI6 or something else then, Mr Kirkpatrick?"

"I am with MI6, otherwise known as the S.I.S—Secret Intelligence Service. Please call me Gerald or GK. Don't need formalities if we are going to work together."

"OK GK. I've always wondered, what does the MI stand for then?"

"Military Intelligence. It has its origins in the military from the early 1900s."

"I hope it has moved on since then, GK," remarked Lando, needling him a little. He liked to poke the bear occasionally.

GK adopted an expression of a half-smiling grump before muttering, "I think we can move on to other, more important things."

Just then, there was a knock on the door, and in walked a middle-aged, capable-looking, crisply dressed lady carrying a large tray of tea laden with other goodies, a big smile and an even bigger chest.

"Shall I pour the tea, sir?" she purred, and GK dismissed her with a brusque wave. He did that a little too quickly, and Lando had a rather naughty thought about their relationship.

"This is one of the more important things," he said, grabbing the teapot and pouring out 4 cups. "Milk or lemon?"

All went for milk except GK, who delicately squeezed a slice of lemon in his own cup and sat back, cradling his cup and saucer like they were delicate objects recently acquired from Tutankhamun's tomb. He plainly loved his little rituals and probably a few big ones as well, judging by the tea lady's frontage.

"So," said GK. "May I sum up where we are? We have one dead Dillon and one kaput Kamal." Everyone flinched at the casual, unsympathetic humour. "Neither could be attributed to natural causes. We also have a knife, Dillon's murder weapon, coupled with other blood traces on it. We now have the knife-scabbard found in Hamza's house, so linking him directly to Dillon's murder alongside the blood traces. We have two of Hamza's criminal partners, Abdul and Farouk, now dispatched by Hobart. Finally, we have one potentially wounded Hamza on the loose who could spoil the party we want after finding the scoundrel Ashiraf. Have I missed anything?"

Hobart quickly cut in, "We also have a photograph of Ashiraf, thanks to the efforts of Dillon."

"Ah, yes, Ashiraf's picture. Of course. That is a big one. Much as I would like to circulate it around as many of our Arab colleagues as possible and our own staff, I do not think it is wise to do that. Someone somewhere will drop a clanger, either in conversation or otherwise, and he will immediately go into hiding, perhaps for months. Now Oscar, what more can you tell us about the other issues?"

Oscar, GK's number two, had been very quiet up until then, and he quickly unburdened himself with his information. "Well, firstly, forensics have analysed the blood on the knife, and, of course, as well as Dillon's blood, they have matched it to Hamza's blood from the building of the shoot-out. They found traces of blood on the floor that did not match either Abdul's or Farouk's blood type. Similarly, there were traces of Hamza's blood and Dillon's on the scabbard, so it seems cut and dried. We are still working on the DNA, but it seems virtually certain to match. That would mean that he was wounded. How badly, we cannot know, but there was enough blood to imply he would be more than a little uncomfortable and potentially seeking medical help. That might give us a lead if we can find a medic who has treated him." Just then, his phone gave a bleep, and he smiled at the screen. "Yes, a message from forensics, DNA matches all as expected."

"Good show, Oscar," exclaimed GK. "So what about other things?"

"Ah, you mean Dillon and Kamal's bodies. Their families have been informed, and their bodies are being sent to their respective countries for burial. We can do little more, and we cannot tell them the full story until it is all cleared up."

"Make sure you send the right bodies to the right families, please. If Dillon's family received Kamal's body, there would be a big flap at the FO, and heads would roll." Once again, GK managed to make a rather insensitive stab at humour.

Lando decided this was his way of processing such lurid information. "Lando, I gather you have found some interesting facts about odd goings on at the British University in Dubai. Care to fill us in?"

Lando filled him in about Qasim Sarawi, and it turned out he had been on the MI6 watchlist for some time and also about Claes Lundberg, at which GK suggested to tread carefully with what information he released there as they knew nothing about him. Still, they would do a check on him and get back to Hobart within 24 hours if they found anything perturbing.

"Well, gentlemen," he said, standing up to his full ramrod height. "I think we are about done unless anyone has anything else to add. I thank you for your summation, Lando, and please stay safe. We do not want another load of paperwork to be filled in, do we?" he said with an impish look.

With that, Hobart and Lando shook hands with everyone, and as if by magic, the crisp tea lady walked in and held the door. A big smile came over GK's face, which was not lost on

Lando. *I wonder,* he thought whilst her fresh lavender perfume wafted around the room. Hobart glanced across at Lando, as he had also picked up some vibes.

Harold, Hobart and Lando departed the building, promising to keep in close touch as they hopped into separate taxis.

Chapter 28

Lando needed to get back to bed; otherwise, he would be fit for nothing. He returned to his hotel and decided to have a swim and a beer to try to clear his head. He donned his pool gear and walked through the glass door to hit the sunshine. He quickly looked around to ensure the loony jewellery woman with her little Willie was not about and, with relief, wandered over to the bar to be greeted by Solly, who, as ever, seemed over the moon to see him.

"Hello, Mr Lando. And how are you today?" He placed a chilled glass on the counter, ready for Lando's usual 'chilled one.'

"I am fine but very tired. I have had a difficult day or two."

"Teaching can be very tiring, I am sure." He poured the drink, looking straight into Lando's eyes. Even though Lando wore sunglasses, he knew straightaway that Lando was not tired because of his teaching efforts.

Lando returned the gaze and wanted to confess all but refrained from it. "Well, teaching is one thing, but there are things between heaven and earth that I shall never understand. I need a beer, a gentle swim and a good sleep."

"Maybe a fine lady would also put you right, sir." It was a statement rather than an offer.

"One day, Solly, we shall have a proper chat when this is over." Lando ran his finger up the side of the glass to catch the foam running down and licked it. "I sometimes think you have a sixth sense when talking to people. Well, me anyway. Maybe it is because you speak to so many people or knew your share of hardship in Zanzibar and the boredom in Oman."

"You not far wrong, Mr Lando. Boredom is almost worse than living in fear."

"I couldn't agree more. You may not like living in fear, but at least you know you are alive. I am an accountant, so I should know about boredom." Lando finished his beer, signed his room number 737 and left a cash tip for Solly. He strolled over to the pool and dived in, gently swimming a few lengths, climbed out, dried himself, and, waving to Solly, returned to his room.

He had a cool shower in his central glass bathroom, which was beginning to grow on him as he flashed himself to a pretend audience around the room in all directions. He dried off, flopped naked onto his bed, and passed out for the next fifteen hours.

***

Meanwhile, Kadri found the card belonging to Ashley Hayhurst and decided to call him to invite him to share a drink with them the following evening. He answered almost immediately. "Hello, to whom do I have the pleasure of speaking?"

"It is Kadri. Remember, you kindly saved me last night from the clutches of that awful man. How could a girl forget that, or the delicious whisky, for that matter?"

"And I could not forget the prettiest damsel in distress that I have ever had the fortune to rescue, now could I? What can I do for you? I assume you do not need escorting to keep you out of trouble."

"No. Not now, anyway. I just wanted to inform you about a few of my friends meeting tomorrow evening for a meal, and I was wondering if you would like to join us for a drink beforehand?"

"I should be delighted. Where are you meeting?"

"No idea yet, but if you could reserve it in your diary, I shall give you another call tomorrow. It will probably be at an outside barbeque somewhere. You have my number on your phone now, so if there are any issues, please ring me."

"Will do, and thanks for the invite. Bye-bye."

So that was one task dealt with. She just had to prepare a little for her evening booking. She had done this one before with two other dancers for a wealthy local property developer and his guests.

***

Meanwhile, there was a clandestine meeting much further away between 5 people talking in hushed tones. This time, again in the Fadak Café on the border of Sharjah, between Qasim Sarawi, Yusuf (the go-between), the minister Shazil Haroun, Ashiraf and his well-developed African companion Bongani, the stone in his front tooth glinting like a warning signal.

Shazil started the meeting. "Yusuf, where is Hamza? We could do with an update from him."

"I do not know. I cannot get hold of him. I phoned and texted him without a reply. Either he has gone on one of his drinking binges, or else there is something more untoward going on." Yusuf acted very agitated.

"No matter. If we do not see him again, that is one less mouth to feed." Turning to Ashiraf, he said, "I gather you have some information about the supply of drones." He tried to make it sound routine, but he could not keep the excitement out of his voice. This could be life-changing for him.

Ashiraf nodded and spoke, "We have looked at possible avenues of supply, and our Iranian contacts are only too willing to be of service. They offer several types of attack drones, but we have narrowed it down to two.

"Firstly, the Bayraktar TB2. It is produced and operated by the Turkish armed forces. Contact is direct to the Baykar company in Istanbul. This can operate at an altitude of 18,000 feet. Uses internal navigation with no dependency on a GPS system. Payload capacity of 150 kg, carries laser-guided smart ammunition and has an airtime of well over 20 hours."

Both Shazil and Qasim were beginning to salivate.

"How much does one of these cost?" stammered Shazil.

"One of these would cost about $5 million, but if we include delivery, technical support commissions, payoffs, etc., this would be approximately $10 million per unit." Ashiraf was enjoying this as he knew it was outside their budget and just decided to include this model to make the next one look cheap. Shazil coughed into his coffee as he tried to take it in. "However, we imagined that you were planning on destroying it, and you really need some kind of kamikaze type of drone, which would be a little less flagrant."

"You are quite right," murmured Shazil as he was now back in possession of his brain and coffee. "I would seriously struggle to hide that in my budget. So, what is the alternative?"

"Our second suggestion is actually made in Iran. Available immediately. It is called the HESA Shahed 136. They are manufactured by the state-owned corporation HESA in association with Shahed Aviation Industries. They can be operated by a satellite/mobile phone with 4G and are easily deployed in multiples from a launch rack." Ashiraf knew immediately that he had the undivided attention of his two guests.

"What about their payload and airtime, then?"

"About 30-50 kg and travelling at over 100 mph, it will travel about 1,000 kilometres."

"So how much is one of these then?" asked Qasim tentatively, but he could not keep the smile off his face.

"About $20,000, but to you, $40,000."

Qasim raised an eyebrow.

"Remember, we are not going through the normal channels, and there are the usual payoffs along the way... including me," said a smiling Ashiraf. "Also, these have been used successfully by both the Russians in Ukraine and by Iran against Israel."

"We are only looking to send a hefty warning message. Maybe we could consider a launch rack of five of them, which would be $200,000, correct?" fished Shazil.

"I suggest another $50,000 to give the technological training and support. It is up to you, but then you will be confident of a successful outcome."

"So, $250,000 in total then?" muttered Shazil.

"That is correct and payable 100% upfront with the order." He passed a note of the amount with banking details already completed to Qasim, who winced when he realised Ashiraf must have played them. He was mentally thinking of the slush fund he had generated through the university 'ghost' students and realised that it would be bled quite dry after this. It made it much harder for him to skim personally off the top when little was left in the fund.

Shazil asked for the specifications of the HESA drone, which Ashiraf declined. "I'm sorry, but you can do your own research on this model. We do not wish any written links between us and you over this matter for obvious reasons."

Shazil stood up and nodded to Qasim to do the same. They shook hands, and Bongani gave one of his deep, resounding laughs as he looked Shazil and Qasim in the eyes. It was almost as if he was sizing them both up for a good meal. They shivered.

"I will get back to you within 24 hrs," said Shazil hurriedly as he left. He needed to move this along quickly as he was also afraid of his job after some unkind but truthful remarks from his boss, Sheikh Massoud, last week. After that, they all departed in their separate small groups.

Chapter 29

Saturday

Lando woke up bleary-eyed and spaced out. He felt completely weird, no doubt from the residue of the drugs still in his system. He slid slowly out of bed, staggered to the mini bar, and extracted a bottle of ice-cold water. He downed it in one or two large gulps and did the same with another bottle while sitting on the side of his bed. He had never slept so long in one night as long as he could remember, and he went over to the balcony doors and opened one to feel the sun's warmth on his bones. My God, that felt good. He was slowly feeling more human and looking forward to a comparatively relaxing day. He needed it. Although exciting and dangerous, this undercover business was exhausting, and he knew he needed to pace himself somehow to get through it all without mental scars. *Enough of this soul-searching,* he thought.

He grabbed his phone and texted Claes Sundberg to see if he was available for a coffee and a catchup chat around midday. He got an immediate positive response and suggested a meeting at Al Sheif's coffee shop midway between them, with just a brisque walk for each. One little thumbs-up emoji returned, and it was settled. He suddenly felt extremely hungry and realised he had not eaten for about 20 hours. He craved a big breakfast to while away some time and chill out, so he went straight into the shower and upstairs to the Al Dawaar revolving restaurant within 20 minutes. He hoped it was not revolving too quickly as his head was not yet back to normal, although it was getting there. He was shown to a seat and went to the breakfast bar to inspect the goodies. There was everything possible available: even bacon, albeit it was crispy bacon made from beef rather than pork, beef sausages, all manner of cereals, fruits and yoghurts and a chef who offered to cook him an omelette personally. This was too good to miss as Lando often cooked himself an omelette at home, but it was very much one that he would chuck lots of leftovers from the fridge into all bound together with a couple of whisked-up farmhouse eggs. Lando gave the chef 10 minutes to sit over a cup of coffee and a croissant. He took a couple on a plate and returned to his seat with a newspaper and a jug of coffee waiting. Seconds later, a waiter came along and poured him a coffee. He took a big sip and sighed as he stared across the waters, marvelling at the amazing construction work on the islands in the Arabian Gulf. The croissants were perfect; he could have eaten four of them but took it slowly. After two cups of coffee, he sauntered up to the breakfast bar, and the chef was clearly looking out for him, wishing to demonstrate his skills. So, what did Lando want in his omelette? There were about six or seven little dishes in front of the chef with odd things in them, all very finely chopped—onion, chilli, cheese and coconut he recognised but not much else. So, he pointed at the cheese, onion and chilli, and the chef poured the whipped double egg mixture into a hot frying pan, flamboyantly swirled it around and chucked a teaspoon full of each of the items into the already solidifying egg, flipped it half over and served it with well-practised panache. It looked wonderful, and Lando thanked him profusely, leaving him in no doubt that it was the best-looking omelette he had ever seen. He was grinning away like the cat that had got the cream.

Lando had always just chucked big lumps of the stuff into his omelettes, filling the stomach, but there was no comparison for the subtle taste with this one. It was delicate and filling at the same time. Exquisite. He would experiment with this back in Shrewsbury when he got home... *if he got home*, he thought a touch dramatically!

It was 11 o'clock, so he meandered off back to his room and read a book for half an hour on his balcony with his shirt off before donning his sunglasses, shirt and wallet and heading down to the foyer, waving at Gaji, who had just collected some airport guests, and walking off to Al Sheif's coffee shop to meet with Claes.

He arrived in good time, and Claes was already at a table, looking pleased to see him. They pumped hands like long-lost brothers, and Claes seemed very bright and cheery.

"You look excited, Claes."

"I am. I have some interesting stuff to share with you, but firstly, what about you? We have not spoken for some time, and I was a little worried about you."

"So you should have been. Let me fill you in on my being drugged, nearly tortured, nearly shot, seeing three killings, the blood on the scabbard, the 3 Arab ruffians, a meeting with MI6 at the British Embassy and other weird stuff." Whilst Claes showed his shock, he then decided to fill Claes in on everything since they last met, including all the supposedly confidential stuff. Lando decided he had to trust him, not just because he liked him. Claes faced him with a look of slack-jawed awe written across his face. He did not say a word until Lando had finished. He swallowed. Twice. He then whispered, "Herregud!"

"Oh my God, indeed."

"Aha. You remember the phrase then?"

Lando nodded seriously. "This is getting more and more complex and risky, and I desperately need to trust you, but at the same time, I do not want to put you in any danger. That is why I felt I had to tell you everything."

"I think that should really be my decision, don't you? All this clandestine stuff has made me realise how much I missed my time as a legitimate computer hacker. I had to keep many secrets from those I was working with. The work was often done from the physical locality of a company and not all done remotely, you know. Anyway, it is too late. I am already on board. Why don't we drink to that with a couple of double espressos?" He put his hand up to beckon a staff member and ordered the coffees alongside the café's speciality.

"Go on then. Tell me what you have ordered," said Lando resignedly.

"I do not think I will. You must taste it first. Now, I have something to share with you."

Just then, the house speciality was placed on the table alongside the two espressos.

It looked to Lando like a few small buns joined up, so he wondered what all the fuss was about. "What is it called, Claes?"

"Try it first. The name is unimportant."

"OK," said Lando, tearing one from the little collection. He placed a portion in his mouth, which just exploded with taste. "Herregud. That is just gorgeous. Give me another, quickly, man."

"Its name is Khaliat Nahal, which means Honeycomb bread. It is basically Omani cream cheese in buns sweetened by raw honey from the comb. It gets you, doesn't it?"

"It is such a lovely combination of tastes. A lot more special than cinnamon bread, that's for sure."

"I agree with you there. Now let me tell you what I have found out. I decided to set up an alternate account under a pseudonym from outside the university to do some searches inside the university. It is clearly easier from the inside, but I wish to be safer, and I am glad I did. Incidentally, I have deleted this account, so it is unlikely to be traced to me."

"So what did you find out?" interjected Lando excitedly.

"I found some strange bank accounts within the university system locked away under several password-protected doors. It sounds complex, but it wasn't if you can read the code well. These were not professionally protected, so I assume they felt no one would be interested anyway if they did not suspect anything untoward. I followed them through, and the money, 1.8 million dirhams, had then been mostly transferred to a dollar account, roughly half a million dollars, and some of the credit entries were related to our 'ghost' students. Additionally, I found some debit entries in the dirham account. These were payments to a certain Qasim Sarawi." Claes sat back in his chair with a smug look on his face.

"Qasim was skimming off the top then," exclaimed Lando with glee. "I knew I did not like that oily bastard."

"Probably, but that is not all. I found some significant other debit payments from the dollar account." Claes paused for dramatic effect.

"Go on then, Claes. Where to?"

"To a certain bank account in Tehran with a completely weird name that I could not trace. No doubt a one-off account setup for some nefarious purpose."

Lando's face dropped. "What a pity. How nice if we could have nailed the bugger who was not dealing from a full deck. That would have been too easy."

"I haven't finished. Are you ready? There was a reference on each of these transactions. What do you think it was? It was 'HAMZALISH!'"

"Hamzalish? That means nothing to me. Obviously, Hamza is that idiot, Arab ruffian. Still, he has neither the intelligence nor I feel the desire to even contemplate having a bank account, let alone the complexity of this situation."

"Agreed. But I tried playing around with some anagrams of the letters, and you will never guess what I came up with. SHAZILHAM."

"I'm none the wiser."

"There is a distant cousin of the Sheikh called Shazil. Shazil Haroun Al Maktoum. Shazil H.A.M.," Claes burst out excitedly. "He works under Sheikh Massoud, security head, and I believe he has been passed over repeatedly for a promotion, so he is effectively a security dog's body." He sat back in his chair again, breathing hard and glowing, having let it all out.

Lando was now beginning to get excited, trembling with anticipation. "Why would someone be stupid enough to put a part of his name in a transaction reference? That would be crazy."

"Not if you are as arrogant as I believe this fellow is, and he would never think it could be traced. He also feels the world owes him, as he is a distant cousin of the Sheikh and no doubt suffering family pressures as well."

"Claes, that is fantastic. I shall convey this immediately to both the Americans and the British secret services, assuming that is OK with you. They can get on it immediately and see where their investigations take them. As I am sure you know, we must be extremely careful now. Dying is one thing, but having your testicles attached to a high-voltage battery is another, and I do not want a repeat of that situation."

They laughed until they had no more tears left, after which they finished their coffee and stood up to leave. Lando asked Claes if he was busy that evening.

"No, not really," he replied. "Why? Did you have something in mind?"

"Well, I am meeting a few friends for a barbeque evening and thought you might like to come. Kadri is coming, though I doubt she will do a belly dance. What do you think?"

"Do you know Lando? I would absolutely love it. I am at a loose end tonight. Where are you planning on going to?"

"No idea at present. I think the weather should not be too warm to sit outside tonight, and maybe we could also ask for some outdoor cooling fans."

"I just happen to know of somewhere that might fit the bill. It is on the coast, and we can eat outside on the terrace. About 500 dirhams for two for very good food. It is called the Grand Grill in the Grand Habtoor Beach Resort Dubai Marina and serves alcohol as well, which helps."

"Sounds great. I love a good steak. I shall book us in as soon as I am home this afternoon. 7.30 pm then, and any different, I shall let you know." He got up, and with his worst Elton John impression ever, he burst into song. "Saturday, Saturday, Saturday, Saturday, Saturday, Saturday, Saturday Night's Alright."

"Ah yes, I know that one. Isn't it 'Saturday Night's all right for fighting?'"

"I sincerely hope not," muttered Lando as his face darkened, remembering how tough the last few days had been.

They parted company, and Lando headed back to his hotel. By the time he arrived, he was perspiring profusely. The sun was at its peak, and he wished he had brought a hat. He hurried to the comfort of his air-conditioned room and lay on the bed thinking. That makes three for dinner, so he could add one more. It would be a good time for Hoby to join them as he thought Hoby could do with a bit of R&R. He gave him a ring, and Hobart was clearly up for it, but he sounded pretty wrung out. *Good decision*, Lando thought. Do him good. He texted the details to Kadri, but before he knew it, he was asleep. An hour later, he awoke to a knock on the door and was astounded to see Kadri standing there.

"I have something important to discuss with you," she said very strangely. "I owe you something."

"Oh yes, Kadri? And what might that be? That meal we had the other night. I told you it was on me. Don't tell me you want to pay me back."

"Kind of," she said, immediately throwing her arms around his neck and kissing him long and hard.

Something in Lando awakened. Something so primaeval that it was beyond his control. Before he knew it, they were both naked on the bed, and his hands were all over her beautiful body, caressing every part with his lips. He took first one breast, then the other, gently biting each nipple to the sound of her soft groans. He moved down to her beautifully rounded abdomen and then could wait no longer and launched himself on top of her, penetrating her all in one flooky movement. It was all over within seconds, and they just lay side by side for 10 minutes, not speaking until their breathing returned to normal.

Lando broke the silence. "Paid in full."

"Aren't you supposed to say, 'How was it for you?'"

"I guess so, but I already know… it was fantastic."

She bashed him over the head with a pillow, and he reciprocated. Before they knew it, they were whacking the hell out of each other, laughing uncontrollably like children. When they calmed down, Lando suggested a shower.

Kadri looked at the glass box in the middle of the room and said, "OK, you first, Hercules."

He went through the glass door and turned on the taps, keeping the temperature warm as they had become cool from the aircon. He proceeded to soap himself slowly all over whilst facing away from the bed. Before he knew it, she was beside him, spreading the soap all over his body, and he marvelled at this picture of Venus staring into his eyes, her breath rasping as she tried to control her desires. She wrapped her slippery hand around his muscular backside until he completely lost control of his member, which felt like it was about to burst. It was a strange time to remember the words of his school's old Latin master. Carpe Diem. Yes, he would 'seize the day.' He roughly pushed her to face against the glass wall. He bent down and soaped her ankles and up her calves towards her perfectly rounded bum. He rubbed the thick lather rhythmically around each of her buttocks, then down her inner thighs until she started to groan. They revelled in anticipation of what was to come. She turned around, threading her arms under his to encircle him, allowing her nails to rake down his back as she nipped sexily on his neck. He shuddered with the pain and the pleasure, lifted her, and her legs locked around him like a vice. They moved in harmony until they climaxed together, with the water still splashing them with its sensual warmth. He trembled with spent passion and effort as he lowered her feet to the tiled floor. She could barely stand without her arms around his neck, and they kissed deeply for a long while.

They regretfully parted and rinsed themselves down, donned the hotel's white HR monogrammed towelling robes, and collapsed onto the bed.

Lando looked at Kadri and said, "That was probably the best shower I have ever had!" He knew straightaway he had made a mistake.

"What!" she exclaimed with a wicked grin. "Probably?" She poured a glass of water straight onto his head, wetting his pillow and the bed.

"Sorry. Stupid word. I meant to say undoubtedly. A brain fart, I think."

They settled down again, and as both fell into a relaxed sleep, Lando thanked God he had prepared all his lectures in good time. He did not want the whole next day to be taken up planning for the second week. He thanked God even more for the shower.

***

Before he knew it, he woke with a start and looked at his watch. It was 5.30, and the restaurant was 25 or so minutes away. He woke Kadri and told her the time, and she shrieked, leaping off the bed as she had to get home to change first. She texted Ashley to see if he was still up for a drink and that they were meeting at the Grand Grill—Habtoor Grand Resort, near Jumeirah, at 7.30 pm. She threw on her clothes, dashed out of the room, caught a taxi back to her apartment, and, whilst getting ready, received a confirmation from Ashley to say he was well up for it. She then got a text from one of her good friends by the name of Delilah, with whom she often performed her dancing gigs, asking if she was free early that evening before her two-hour evening booking in Jumeirah. Kadri invited her to join them at the Grand Grill for a drink beforehand. It was very close to her booking location, which she gladly accepted, so they agreed to go together. She would stop her taxi at Kadri's to pick her up.

Chapter 30

Lando decided to get to the Grand Grill as early as possible to ensure the booking was sound and arrived at 7.15 pm with the help of a lift from Gaji, whose face lit up, as usual, on being asked. Lando checked the table outside, which was their booking, and was shown to a table already laid up for four people. There were cooling electric fans set up by the table to blow across plates of ice when needed, and all in all, it seemed very welcoming. He was so glad alcohol was allowed in this restaurant, so he ordered a cool beer duly brimming with froth. One slurp and he was happy and relaxed, waiting for his party to arrive. He gazed around the other tables and took in the aerial view.

The first to arrive was Claes, and he had already ordered a beer, which arrived almost before he sat down. They smiled happily as they clinked glasses, and no word was said until Claes had his first mouthful.

"Ahaa," he said. "Just what the doctor ordered," smacking the glass down on the table a little too hard.

"So, you have that expression in Sweden as well? You do surprise me."

"Of course. The British have taught us so many useful things, which is mind-blowing."

Lando adopted a serious look until he looked across at Claes, who was trying hard to control his laughter. Lando knew that was another reason he liked Claes so much. Great sense of humour.

Suddenly, Hobart arrived looking very smart casual, closely followed by Kadri and her friend Delilah. No one on the terrace, including Lando and Claes, really noticed Hobart as the rooftop was brought to a stunned silence, watching the two beautiful ladies being shown to their table as Kadri introduced her friend.

"This is my friend Delilah. We have often worked together, and I invited her for a drink before the meal as she has a booking at Jumeirah Beach in an hour."

Delilah was a slim, strawberry blonde, lightly tanned and wearing a fluorescent green sheath dress that could only be described as a second skin that hugged her figure from her knees to her neck. Thankfully, she also wore a white cardigan across her shoulders that, in Lando's view, prevented her from being arrested as being too immodest, which could land her in trouble. As ever, Kadri's figure was eyepoppingly evident whatever she wore, and this time, she was all in black, matching the raven black ringlets of her hair. She had just a little piece of gold around her neck, which gave her an air of luxury. Lando warmed up in certain areas just looking at her.

Claes already knew Kadri and warmly kissed her on both cheeks with a polite comment. He then tried to do the same to Delilah but seemed completely lost for words. He appeared shocked in a good way, which Lando noted.

They sat down on either side of Hobart like a pair of Dior models from a cosmetic advert, chatting with those around them. Hobart loosened up immeasurably with such alluring women on either side of him. Once everyone had a drink, they were about to propose a toast to something irrelevant when Ashley entered through the door behind Lando, with his dashing blond hair flowing in the gentle breeze.

Kadri stood to welcome him just as Lando turned around. He gazed at his old friend Ashley, not comprehending what he was doing here, and was speechless for a second, as was Ashley. Everyone else went silent, wondering what was happening between them.

They immediately gave each other big hugs, laughing like children and bouncing up and down at the side of the table.

"Ashley Hayhurst, what the hell are you doing here?" He then looked at Kadri and realised. It dawned on both of them at the same time. "So, it was you who helped Kadri out on Thursday evening. I must thank you for that. What an amazing coincidence."

"Entirely my pleasure, old man. When she said she met a guy named Lando, it did not register with me. I even told Kadri I had a great friend at school called Lando."

"She did say a man helped her but never mentioned your name. If she had, I wouldn't have put two and two together anyway, as she said he was a very good-looking guy."

With that, Ashley whacked him on his shoulder with a pretend punch. Their conversation then descended into a catchup. It almost but not quite bored everyone else to death if it was not such a pleasure to see these two catching up on old times. Then, turning their chairs away from the table, they went into a private, conspiratorial chat, realising others would not be so interested in their history. Ashley told him he was married with two little children, and Lando told Ashley that he had been married.

"Oh dear. That is sad. How long were you married?"

"Two weeks, to be precise."

Ashley stared at him in wonder and burst out laughing. "Forgive me. Nobody is only married for two weeks. Was she Russian and wanted a work visa or something?"

"No, nothing like that. We both did it on a whim up in Gretna Green and quickly realised we were not meant for each other. We parted on good terms, though."

"Ah, well, that's all right then?" he said with a curl in his mouth.

"Yep. I was a little unstable at that time, to say the least. My parents were killed in a car crash, and I was a bit of a lost soul for a while. That is until I arrived here. It's been very exciting, though."
"Oh, I am so very sorry, Rolo. Better times to come, though, eh?"

"That's it. Always look forward."

"You had better watch it with Kadri," he whispered. "She told me she is very fond of you. That is unless she has been out with another guy named Lando, who makes her laugh."

"Really." Lando grinned like a Cheshire cat. He could not help himself. He still doubted how any woman with intelligence could possibly want a relationship with him. Here was a woman with intelligence and radiated beauty who seemingly fancied him. "Maybe she just likes a laugh," he said.

"She would certainly get that if she saw Rolo naked," quipped Ashley. At which Lando decided it was better not to continue that conversation.

The waiter came around to take their order, so Delilah got up to leave with a furtive smile towards Claes, which was not lost either on Claes or Lando. There was a mutual attraction there, and Lando made a mental note to help that relationship along the way, as it seemed like Cupid's arrow had found its mark. Ashley also got up to leave, and Lando suggested he stay if he had no other plans, which he had not, so the waiter laid up for one extra. The food order was easy, with medium rare steaks for everyone.

Hobart had been quite quiet up until now and picked up on a conversation with Ashley about his job in Dubai.

"Good to meet you, Ashley. So, what sort of building are you working on over here then?" He was ever the inquisitive one.

"I am working on a brand-new building in Jumeirah as it happens, but I have a meeting on Monday with some junior or assistant government minister. Seems strange as he wants me to visit one or two well-known buildings to assess their security arrangements, which can be incorporated into the new building."

"Why do you think it is strange?" said Hobart, perking up.

"Well, this review is normally done once the contract is agreed rather than at such an early stage."

Hobart's eyes almost bulged out of his sockets. "You don't remember the minister's name by any chance, do you?"

"It was a long Arabic name, but I picked up on one of his names. It sounded like Shabil or Shazol."

"Shazil?" suggested Hobart quietly but with a voice full of hope.

"Yes, that's the name Hobart."

"Shazil Haroun Al Maktoum sound familiar?"

"Absolutely. Do you know this fellow? He seemed a touch oily to me and wanted me, through my company, to contribute to a local charity as he said it would also help make our pitch for the job."

Hobart nearly fell out of his seat. He went all twitchy, started looking at his phone and tapped a lot of keys. Claes and Lando carried on a stilted conversation, and Kadri became very quiet and thoughtful. Ashley was not stupid and picked up a huge change in the tenor of the conversation.

"Okay, everyone. What is going on here? What have I missed? Is this guy part of some worldwide organised crime syndicate or something?" Everyone went silent. "My God, he is, isn't he?" said Ashley, his face alive with the thrill of it all.

Lando looked over at Hobart, who nodded resignedly at Lando, so Lando filled in his friend, leaving out the more lurid bits. Ashley's mouth widened, and his jaw dropped lower and lower.

Lando looked over to Hobart again. "So, what do you think, Hoby? Have I missed anything out?"

Hobart bridled again at using his nickname and decided on a little payback. "Hey Rolo, you could have bigged yourself up a bit better when you decked that big lump called Abdul Iqbal. I saw it from 50 metres away, and it was very impressive. You could have been a pro."

"How did you learn that?" asked Ashley.

"I have had a few years doing karate training. I had a brown belt. It was technically a brown and white belt, which is the last level before the black belt. I did not want to take it further as I was afraid of having to do tournaments outside my friends in the dojo."

"Well, wonders never cease, old man. You are the last person I would have expected to learn karate. Lucky for you that you did, eh? Power to your elbow, as they say."

"As it happens, Ash, I did use an elbow strike on the guy. It is very effective when applied forcefully to the knackers, and his were like cricket balls, as I recall. Took the shine off them, I think."

Hobart decided they needed to plan well to conclude this situation and suggested that they try to work as a team. He insisted on it and flashed his CIA badge at Ashley to give him more credibility. Ashley looked at it.

"Hobart G Lonsdale IV." He lingered on every syllable. "That sounds grand, Hoby. You must be from an 'old' family."

"I am actually, and now I am a bit of a black sheep as I should have joined the old family law firm, but I prefer something with a bit more intrigue. I have more than I bargained for since meeting your friend Rolo."

Ashley turned to Lando and said, "So, how did you two meet?" gesturing pointedly at Kadri.

"I was doing a belly dance performance in the desert under the stars,' cut in Kadri. 'But we sort of bonded when my friend Dillon was murdered, and Lando helped me away from the scene."

"That must have been awful for you. You were with the right man, though. He got me out of a shocking fix at school, so I can vouch that he is about the most trustworthy gent in the universe. I still owe him, but that story is for another day."

"I shall look forward to hearing it," said Kadri as she smiled at Lando.

Just then, the steaks arrived, laden with fries and surrounding salad. They were big but so tender that the knives went through them like butter, and everyone finished them in far too short a time. A few glasses of wine and beer were drunk, and everyone was well-filled by the end of the evening. No one wanted a dessert course, but a large flask of coffee was welcomed onto the table, balanced on a little burner to keep it warm.

After everyone had a few sips and the conversation died a little, Hobart voiced his thoughts on the present situation.

"Time for a bit of summing up now, guys, and may I repeat that everything in this chat cannot be shared with anyone else. This is particularly for you, Ash, as it might put you in danger."

Ashley blanched a little but dismissed it with, "We couldn't have that, could we? After all, the old mater and pater would not be happy if I was brought home in a box. Neither would my wife, for that matter."

"OK, Ash, we get the point, but you have been brought into this little group because you are in a unique position to help put this situation to bed. I would remind you that whilst involved in this group, you treat it as confidential as if you had signed your country's Official Secrets Act. Our nearest equivalent in the USA is the Espionage Act. Your Mr Shazil, a dislikeable, distant cousin of the Emir Sheikh Mohammed, with the help of Qasim Sarawi at the university, is playing fast and loose with both the funds from BUiD University as well as appearing to be involved in the funding for importing drones from Iran. Claes, we are indebted to you for what you have learned using your hard-earned hacking skills. Additionally, Lando, you have found yourself involved by chance with both the murder of Dillon and meeting Kadri and then going along with the plan to find the perpetrator."

Lando replied, "Kadri was at risk as well. Anyway, I would not have changed it for anything," he interjected, looking over at Kadri, who smiled warmly.

"Kadri is in our pay, so some danger is expected to a degree, but even so, Lando, you went above and beyond and could have been killed." Ashley raised an eyebrow at hearing that Kadri was connected with the CIA. Hobart continued. "If that had happened, then GK, your Mr Gerald Kirkpatrick, from the British Embassy would have, how do you say it in England, 'had my guts for garters.' We still have an Arab thug named Hamza wandering the streets, and he could easily jeopardise our plan to find Ashiraf and end his terror campaign. We need to eliminate him as quickly as possible. Our only hope with him is that he values his own skin more than he values any cause, so I doubt he will be planning to find Ashiraf unless there is money in it for him. He would sell out his mother for money, that one. Ashiraf, we believe, reports to a spiritual figure named Hawiya, but we do not know if this character even exists beyond someone's imagination. Removing Ashiraf would be like cutting off the head of a snake, which would be deemed a great success on its own and probably save many innocent lives. Finally, we now have Ashley's connection to Shazil, who wants him to examine the security measures in other big buildings that might form the basis of security for a building his company is designing. There is no rational reason why he would be doing this before even having a design quotation submitted or approved. I think that about covers it. Has anyone got anything to add to this?" There was a stony silence. "Okay, has anybody thought about how these things might fit together?"

Just then, Claes fired in a question. "You did say before that Shazil was a dislikeable personality, and previously, he had been regularly overlooked for promotion. Maybe he felt it was his due, being a cousin of Sheikh Mohammed, albeit a distant one. He also works directly under Sheikh Massoud, the head of security in Dubai. Is that right?"

Kadri suddenly sprung into life. She stood up and waived her arms about. "I think I have an idea. What if this Shazil was so upset that he was overlooked for promotion that he would risk anything and anybody in his pursuit of advancement? What if he was willing to sacrifice anyone for this aim? What could he do to become a hero and/or get promoted? What is his job related to? It is security. What can he get hold of? Iranian drones—let me guess, attack drones. Drones that could do significant damage and kill. Why would he ask Ashley's company to contribute to this charity? The money will be used surreptitiously to help fund the drone purchase, along with the university's secret 'ghost student' fund. Why would he ask Ashley to review the security of buildings in Dubai before he even puts in a quote for a building design?"

Everyone was holding their breath. The atmosphere around the table changed perceptibly.

Claes was the first to voice a question. "He wants to mount a drone attack on one of the buildings?"

Ashley had a look of horror on his face. "Surely no one is that evil; they would risk killing their own people just for personal advantage?"

"That is exactly why people kill," announced Hobart in a sage-like statement of fact. "They have no feelings of remorse or regret for others, and that essentially is what defines a psychopath. That is why so many CEOs of large companies are psychopaths because they can sack hundreds of people to increase their profits and sleep soundly at night. It all fits, though. I can only guess that one of those buildings would be the target, particularly with Ashley doing a security survey on some large buildings. It seems clear that mounting the attack would achieve nothing for him personally, but … if he was seen to be foiling it…" his words tapered off.

"My God," interjected Kadri, "He would become a national hero, a household name. It would solve all his insecurities in one go. I imagine he would be made for life with a massive status uplift."

"That's how I would figure it," stated Hobart. "However, we cannot know how far he would be prepared to take it. If he only foiled it through his secret service, it would probably not have the impact as the public would be unaware. I imagine the Dubai government and police would not wish the public to know about it. It could damage their reputation. However, if the attack went ahead but was largely unsuccessful due to Shazil's extra 'security' measures, then a bonanza for him." He looked over at Lando, who had a worried look on his face. "What's bothering you, Lando?"

"If he foils the plan somehow, is it not going to point the finger at him for having some prior knowledge? Should we not just inform his boss, Sheikh Massoud, and let him deal with it?"

"A good point, but we do not know that the Sheikh is not involved, although I doubt it. He will also feel responsible for allowing it to get to this stage when he was in charge. I also would not wish to reveal too much to him about what we, the CIA, have done in Dubai to come across this information. It could prove very awkward. I shall check with my controller, Harold Shrimpton, but I imagine that would be his view."

Quiet descended on the group.

Claes spoke quietly, "So where do we go from here then?"

Ashley immediately piped up. "This is all rather exciting. From my perspective, I have been requested to design a building and assess a few similar buildings' security. I assume one of those buildings could be the target, and if I assess them alongside this Shazil fellow, it might become clear which building is the target, as he would likely ask me some leading questions."

Hobart was clearly perplexed. "I am struggling here. I do not see any relationship between the security aspects of a public building or hotel designed by an architect to a potential terrorist or military situation. Surely, you are not expected to build security to that depth."

"Well, actually, the security of these buildings is paramount and does not just relate to theft, although that is the main one. Other issues, such as potential kidnapping and terrorism, are considered: professional security guards, top-grade surveillance systems, fire safety, visitor management systems, first aid, emergency protocols, etc. We also employ a specialist consultancy firm for big projects like this one because we need the physical security and monitoring areas to be built in," replied Ashley confidently. "Although I might confess that I have not come across a security system to foil a drone attack. That would need anti-aircraft canon of some sort, I guess."

"Do you know any other firms that have been asked to quote?" asked Hobart.

"No, I don't, but I doubt he will ask too many as I guess it might raise too many red flags. Asking only one, he could pretend he was just after a ballpark figure. Also, I cannot say we are happy with this request to contribute to his charity. It is not something we do as a company when it appears so obviously to be a bung, although I cannot pretend contracts in other parts of the world, including the UK, are not eased along by a kind of contribution off the books. It is much more brazen here and seems an accepted way of doing business. It would be disguised as a bung but appears to be going towards the funding of these drones."

Hobart was silent and then spoke up, "Look, Ash, your position with this potential terrorist is unique, and maybe we, that is, the CIA, can help you with this dubious contribution. We have funds precisely for this eventuality. How do you feel about continuing to help us with this situation? I can assure you we would not wish to put you in any personal danger."

Lando decided to chip in. "Come on, Hoby. You cannot think you know what this Shazil lunatic will be up to. We do not even know his plans yet. We are only guessing."

Ashley picked it up, looked at Lando, and pointed at himself with both his index fingers. "Hey up, Rolo. This guy can speak for himself. I can do what I was always going to do: assess these buildings' general security and report back with recommendations. If it is as we think, the guy will probably drop himself in it, which will be the end for me. Remember, I still owe you one from school." He had a wry smile on his face. "Cannot wait for when the balloon goes up, though."

"I am not sure what you mean by a balloon going up, but I guess it is a British expression. I hope it is as simple as you appear to make out," responded Hobart. "There is just so much we need to be on top of to deal with it without a massive international backlash, to say nothing of the potential personal and public risk."

Everyone looked a bit more serious as, up to that moment, it had all seemed like a bit of fun, but now Hobart had sown a few seeds of fear if things went wrong. No bad thing to live in a world of reality now and again. He continued with the air of a leader.

"Right. Time we drew this conversation and dinner to a close. I need a few winks tonight as there is much to do tomorrow, even though it is Sunday. If I may, I shall allocate a few tasks, and may I remind you all again not to talk about anything outside this group? Lives depend on it, not least ours."

Everyone nodded.

"Task 1. Kadri. We must get hold of this Hamza fellow. Without him locked away, we can never be sure we are not walking into a trap. I shall make that my priority for the time being. Kadri, would you please ask your friends and contacts if anyone might have seen him? Perhaps you can make up a story about him or pretend someone owes him money. That should get him out of the woodwork. Also, check a few doctors and hospitals near where he was wounded. I would not hold my breath there, but we may be lucky." Kadri nodded seriously.

"Task 2. Claes." He looked up eagerly. "Your tracking of Qasim's computer shenanigans has been invaluable. Can you keep it up? If you find the slightest thing that might be related, please let me know through Lando if you wish. Generally, if we can follow the money, we can follow the crime. I would love to know if there are any further communications, whether through bank transfers or 'cloaked' messages. Particularly anything received from or going to Iranian contacts. That means monitoring Shazil, Qasim and Shazil's boss, Sheikh Massoud. We must keep track of him until we are certain about him. Whatever you do, cover your tracks religiously. One slip, and it could be serious. Are you up for it?"

"Absolutely," replied Claes with shining eyes. Like Lando, Claes was ready for some excitement.

"Task 3. Ashley. You have indicated that you are happy to be involved. I hope that is still the case. Could I ask you not to do anything you would not normally do, whether communicating with your boss, accompanying Shazil around the buildings to assess their security or dealing with the so-called bung? We need to keep that under our hats, as would be expected, but if you could try to ask that there is a small downpayment as a gesture of good faith, that would be helpful. The CIA does not wish to lose money unnecessarily, and it would also give us a route for the money. You could liaise with Claes if we can find out the bank account. I am sorry I cannot give you a task to liaise with Delilah as well. I guess you might like that." So, Hobart was not so daft. He had picked up the looks between Delilah and Claes.

It was the first time Lando had seen Claes look vaguely embarrassed and slightly flushed as he rose to the bait. "Well, that would have been very pleasant," he replied dryly but with a wry smile that was lost on no one.

"Task 4. Lando. You need to carry on as normal with your lectures. Find excuses to speak with Qasim on Monday. You might pick up something from him by chance, but don't force it. Remember, these people have been using subterfuge for years, so their minds are tuned to anyone who appears over-interested in their work or movements. Tread carefully, my friend. Can you all coordinate through me?" he said, passing a card with his mobile number around. "But if you cannot contact me quickly enough, please work through Kadri. Also, please would you all text me and each other so we can all be in touch as and when. We now appear to be a team of five, of which three of you have no CIA training and zero background in this type of work. It scares the hell out of me, believe it or not, as I do not know how all of you will work under pressure. I must admit, though, that Lando has proved himself a natural."

Ashley smiled at his friend Lando and said, "You have hidden depths, old man. Cannot let the old school down now, can we? I hope I can be worthy of you."

"No need, Ash. Just look after yourself, and no silly risks taken."

"Got it in one," responded Hobart, quickly rising from his seat. "I'll sort the bill on the way out. Least the company can do for all your help." With that, he was gone, and the four remaining looked around at each other.

Kadri was the first to speak. "Well, we have our orders, if you can call them that. Take it from me: you can trust Hoby. He can sometimes seem a little remote, but that is his way of processing options under pressure. He has always looked out for me."

"Good to know," said Claes. "By the sound of things, we will have to trust each other fully in the coming days."

With that, they raised a final glass to each other, got up from the table, and shared a couple of taxis back to their respective homes or hotels.

On the way, Kadri passed Delilah's mobile number to Claes, saying, "She told me to pass her number to you as you looked in need of cheering up."

Claes was dumbstruck, but inside, he was ecstatic. He thought she was, in his native Swedish language, 'en absolut korkare'. An absolute corker. He could not wipe the smile off his face all the way home. A long time since he had fallen for a woman so quickly in such a short time. It was just over a dinner!

Chapter 31

Sunday

Lando had a great night's sleep. He didn't really know why because he had no right to sleep well when he and all his friends were in such a dangerous position. All he knew was that he was excited about the day and the week ahead, but he decided to focus on the short term, where he would see Kadri, have some time with her, and prepare for his lectures again in the morning.

He got up and did 50 press-ups, stomach crunches, and knee-to-shoulder raises to get himself going. He had a red-hot close shave with a razor, showered and dressed quickly. He felt pretty good, went for breakfast, and ordered another two-egg omelette with lots of little bits of something and a couple of croissants. A jug of coffee was already on the table. That should put him right for a while. During breakfast, he texted Kadri and asked her out for the day. He knew she was busy Sunday night, but they could spend some of the day together. He went over to the side in the breakfast room, picked up a newspaper and started reading the headlines. Nothing much of interest, and then he heard that little "ding" from his phone notifying him a message had been received. Kadri was free most of the day and would happily go along with whatever Lando suggested. That word, whatever, had a certain ring to it. He wasn't sure that *whatever* was literally whatever occurs as he would happily have her naked in bed all day, but maybe they should be looking at something a little less hedonistic and a little more community-orientated. He had a think about it and suggested in his return text that they go out for a little sail, maybe with a bit of lunch on board. Kadri emailed back straightaway, suggesting they focus on the sail and she would bring the lunch. She asked him to hire a boat, so they agreed to meet at midday at the west port side of The Creek.

Lando went to his room and decided he would not waste the next couple of hours dwelling on what might be. He revisited his lectures the next day and worked through all his notes, slides, and group exercises. The time went quickly, and before he knew it, he was rushing to get some appropriate sailing clothes on, which included rope-soled shoes, shorts and a good hat and sunglasses, so he was geared up and ready to go. He had contemplated donning a French sailor's striped T-shirt with a red bandana around his neck but decided that might be amusing for all of five minutes but distinctly uncool. He went down in the lift, and was in a jaunty mood. The doors slid open, and again, he faced a group of four Arab ladies in full black gear. He jumped back instinctively but recovered well and wished them all good morning.

He was walking towards reception to ask for their advice on hiring a boat, but before he got there, he noticed Gaji out of the corner of his eye and wandered over to him.

Gaji gave him a big beaming smile in his usual way and said, "Good morning, Mr Lando and how are you today, sir?"

"I am in excellent form, Gaji. I could do with your services if you are not going to the airport. How about it?"

"I am very much free, Mr Lando, for the next two hours. What do you have in mind?"

"Well, I am taking a certain young lady out on the sea for a sail. She is providing the lunch, and I must book a vessel. We don't want one that provides food; we just need a boat with a sail that has shade from the sun and is reasonably priced."

"Might this certain young lady be a very good belly dancer?"

"Of course, Gaji. I do not mix my drinks."

"I have the message, Mr Lando. I have just the person, Mr Lando. Very reliable."

"Hmm, I thought you might have."

"Very good price. He is a distant cousin and would not let me down."

"Good for you. So what are we waiting for?"

They went in the taxi to the port with Gaji on his mobile most of the way. It was not a long trip, but Lando wanted to save his energy and keep it as cool as possible. They pulled into a parking zone overlooking the bay.

"There she is, Mr Lando. I say she looks beautiful today if I may respectfully say so."

Lando saw her after Gaji did and had to pinch himself again. He exited the car and tried not to run towards Kadri, who was staring out to sea with the light breeze wafting through her hair. She wore long sky-blue shorts and a pink polo shirt, but in Lando's eyes, she could have worn a tramp's rags and still looked the business. He walked up behind her and surprised her with a gentle tap on the shoulder.

"Aha. I hope that is you, Lando. Otherwise, I shall have to call the police." She turned around, and her deep brown eyes showed her pleasure in meeting him again. Lando warmed inside.

"I see you have plenty of baggage for the boat. How many changes of clothing is that?"

"Actually, most of it is for our lunch. Which boat are we going on?"

"My God," said Lando, suddenly losing his cool. "Gaji arranged it, and I forgot to ask him who it was with?"

At that moment, Gaji's worried face appeared from behind a parked van.

"Aha, Mr Lando. It seems the beautiful lady has made your mind a little dizzy. We need to find my cousin, and I will introduce you. He is just along the way here." He gestured down the promenade whilst grabbing Kadri's bags and tried Lando's as well, but Lando waved him away, not wishing to overload him.

They came upon a relatively short but stocky man, probably under five foot, thought Lando, going by the name of Sanjay, who seemed delighted to have them both on his humble boat. They walked along a short pier and went down some steps at the side to where a lovely little mini yacht was moored. It had a cabin, much to Lando's relief, as well as a canvas-shaded area in the stern and ample seating. It seemed old-fashioned but clearly in good nick as, although Lando knew nothing about things nautical, the boat was clearly cared for, and all the little bits of brass were polished up, and all the ropes were coiled neatly in their place. Gaji checked that there were adequate life jackets before he left. *What a star!* thought Lando. Gaji said his goodbyes, which included a brief humorous threat to Sanjay if Lando and Kadri were not given a good day at sea, and Kadri and Lando waved him off as they cast off and set sail. They departed under the boat's engine power, but Lando could barely wait to get under sail.

"Right," said Sanjay, showing a mass of brilliant white teeth as he navigated around the other boats in the harbour to find his way out to sea. "What would you most like to do?" Kadri and Lando struggled to make eye contact without giving their thoughts away. The joke was not lost on Sanjay.

"Can you suggest a good way of spending 3-4 hours?" said Lando. "We would love a brief sailing lesson or at least taking the helm a few times. Also, if it is possible to do a little fishing, that would be great. What about you, Kadri? Any particular wishes?"

"I have packed our lunches," she said, patting the big cooler lunch box at her side. "And I always love a good swim before lunch. There is plenty for you, Sanjay, and you are most welcome. There is also a vegetarian option if you prefer."

"Dear lady, I should be honoured to share a meal with you both. No one has ever asked me that before," he said softly as he was indeed taken aback, and Lando thought he was close to tears. "Mr Lando, you are a very fortunate man to be escorting not just a beautiful woman but also a thoughtful and compassionate one." His English was excellent, even with an Indian twang.

Sanjay continued, "May I suggest we do a good hour of sailing and maybe a half hour to an hour of fishing? It depends on whether you want a fish you can take home and eat or one that puts up a good fight. Maybe the cobias, groupers and snappers might be biting. They are more active in the cooler waters of early morning or late evening, but we can give it a good go. We will need the right lines, though, and the cobias will give you a great fight, as they can be well over a metre in length. I would prefer not to catch them whilst we are under sail as being, I guess, the only experienced sailor. Very tasty, however. My favourite."

"OK, Sanjay, you are the captain, so feel free to give us orders as you see fit. You speak excellent English. You cannot have only learnt it at school."

"Quite right, sir. I was brought up in India, came to Europe, and stayed on a working visa in Southern Ireland for two years. I learnt much about fishing there as I stayed in a lovely coastal town in the Southwest called Killarney. Learnt a lot about Murphy's and Guinness as well.'

"Oh yes?" chuckled Lando. "And which did you prefer?'

"Oh, Murphy's, I think, but Guinness was a close second .... to be sure." He ended the sentence with a broad Irish accent, and they all laughed.

"So why did you leave, if you do not mind me asking?"

"I was made to feel at home there, and the Irish are very welcoming when they get to know you, but I was still one of a small minority of Indians there, and it was hard to find work above the minimum wage as many locals were also looking for work. I regularly corresponded with my parents and often sent money home; therefore, I had little left to live on. They told me about the growth of Dubai and how well my cousin Gaji was doing, so I took a risk. All is good now. Within 2 years, I will have paid off my boat loan, and I shall be financially sound by then."

"Well done, you. What a story. My life was pretty much mapped out as I had it all on a plate, but coming here has opened up a different view of life for me. Given me food for thought, but I cannot go into that right now," he said, looking at Kadri, who caught his eye and turned away with a thoughtful look on her face. Sanjay picked up on it.

"I hope that path leads you somewhere special, Mr Lando, as there is often pain on a journey to heaven."

"Please call me Lando, and I shall bear that in mind, Sanjay, but there is little more painful in life than boredom, and I have had my share of that whilst working as an accountant. But... I am not practising as my work is teaching at a university. Now, I am here with you, steering the ship and a beautiful woman about to feed us. Nearly in heaven now, eh? Do you have a family?"

"I do. My wife's called Farah. It means joy and happiness, and that is what she brings me. But we are not yet ready for children. Hopefully, it will be after my boat is paid off, as I might afford another skipper for my boat to give me time at home."

"Aha. You sound like a sensible man. However, as the Americans would say, life has a way of throwing us a curve ball. I'll tell you what. If you have time and wish it, I will happily prepare some alternative projections for your future business. I would need all your running costs of the boat, charge out rate, busy and slow times of the year and the cost of an assistant, and we could project your future income and whether you could afford to run another boat. Depends on demand really."

"No problem with demand, Lando. That would be amazing, but I thought you said you found it boring?"

"No, no, this is just mathematics, which I love. You could also take it to the bank if you needed another loan for another boat when this one is paid off."

Sanjay went quiet and whispered, "I had never thought of two boats," as his eyes lit up. "How much will it cost me for your time?"

"Absolutely nothing except perhaps another sail in your boat next time I visit. I would enjoy it, but look, I am really busy whilst over here. We can get started, but we may need to communicate and finish it off when I return to England in a week or two, as I guess there is no rush."

Sanjay's face lit up. "You would do that for me? Someone you do not even know?"

"You would be doing me a favour. I would enjoy it, giving me a reason to come back." He looked across at Kadri, who struggled to meet his gaze. With that, he held out his hand, and Sanjay shook it so violently that he thought his shoulder would break off.

Sanjay was beaming all over his face. "Now I shall find you the biggest fish in the sea!" He looked wistfully at the far horizon. He was dreaming again.

Kadri had not spoken but looked at Lando admiringly. She realised why she liked him. It was because he was fundamentally kind-hearted, which was certainly not a trait of many men she had been out with.

Soon, they were well out to sea, and Sanjay asked for help unfurling the jib sheet and the mainsail while steering the ship. He killed the motor, and that little surge of the wind pulling the boat gave Lando a small jolt of joy. He loved the thought of being pulled along by nature. It was like a god tugging at his soul. Even more so as he watched Kadri bending over to tidy her jib sheet. Lando hauled on his sheet to prevent the sail from spilling the wind, and off they went. They carried on in silence, revelling in the quiet, peace, and beauty of hearing the gentle hiss of the bow cutting through the water. Even though the wind was light, they were still doing about six or seven knots whilst heading towards the horizon, with the sea bathed in sunlight accentuating its deep turquoise colour. They baited a line with a small fish hooked through its gill. They dropped it in the water trailing behind and travelled like that for about twenty minutes, with Lando only taking a brief time away from the rod to get a few snaps of Kadri on the bow of the boat facing the breeze, which blew her beautiful, thick hair out behind her. He had never seen such a beautiful picture. He also took a few snaps of Sanjay as a reminder, but only after asking if he minded having his photograph taken, which he was only too pleased about. He grinned broadly for each photo, puffing out his chest and flexing his biceps to accentuate his fit physique—a short but proud man.

Suddenly, Lando felt a slight tug on the line and mentioned it to Sanjay, who looked excited.

"Don't dismiss it, Mr Lando. They often have a little nibble before taking a big bite." Lando felt nothing again for a couple of minutes and was beginning to doubt there was anything interested in his bait when he felt it again. Sanjay picked up on this.

"Mr Lando, just pull the rod towards you slightly to give the effect of the bait being alive and swimming and then let it go again."

Lando did as he was told. He felt nothing again for five to ten seconds until a powerful yank on the line almost snatched the rod from his hands. Lando stood up. "Wahey. I may have caught one."

"Wait for it, wait for it, Mr Lando. When you feel the fish take another bite, you must strike hard within a fraction of a second. That way, you will secure the hook in its mouth or lose it altogether."

Lando waited and waited. He thought he had lost it for good until he felt the fish bite, so he struck immediately. The line was pulled at speed away from the boat, and the reel whizzed around like an express train.

"Woaaaa. I got him, and he's a big bugger as well. I don't know if I can hold him." Kadri was screaming with delight from the front of the boat, her face alive with anticipation.

"Sit down in that wooden chair," yelled Sanjay, who asked Kadri to come and take the wheel and not to hold the course steady, after which he forced Lando down in his seat and pushed the butt of the rod into a hinged metal tube between Lando's feet to secure it whilst he fought with the catch. "Don't pull too hard, Lando; otherwise, the line will break. You will need to play with it to tire it out. Keep pulling it in slowly, and then let the boat drag it for thirty metres and pull a little more."

The line moved from side to side about fifty metres away, and Lando fought with the fish for about fifteen minutes, constantly hauling, releasing a little, hauling and winding in. After a while, Lando felt the fish was tired and slowly reeled it in. Sanjay waited at the stern with a gaff in his hands. The fish came to the surface fifteen metres out, and Sanjay voiced his pleasure.

"Aha, the gods have fortuned the brave. We have a great big cobia. My favourite and it is about one and a half metres long. What a beauty! You are truly a man full of good luck. Reel him in Lando."

When the tired fish came against the hull of the boat, Sanjay pulled him in with the gaff, and there it was lying on the deck, blood oozing from its mouth, too tired to flap as the spirit slowly drained out of him with his last breath. Lando had a slight pang of regret, but not for long, as he was so proud of his catch.

Sanjay was delighted and suggested that Lando pick up the fish by the line near its mouth. He asked Lando for his camera to take a photo. Lando beckoned Kadri to join him in the photo, and they settled down to recount the full story of the fight of the fish to each other. Lando started to feel a bit dizzy as he was not used to boats, and coupled with his twenty-minute battle with the fish, he was beginning to realise that fitness in one sport is very different from fitness in another. The adrenaline slowly dissipated, making him feel like a battering ram had run over him. His shoulders ached, his forearms and the back of his neck were sunburnt, and he needed a bit of shade.

Kadri spoke up. "Well, my macho sailor boys, I think it is time I did my duty and fed you all. How does that sound?"

"Great," said Sanjay. "Let us sit under the canopy and bring in the sails, and I shall set the motor to steer gently into the current. Then, we shall not drift too far off course. Here are a few cold beers as well." That brought a happy look from everyone, and with a pop from everyone's cans, as they burst open. They toasted each other, clunked cans, and downed good mouthfuls, followed by 'aah' in unison.

Kadri brought out her rich delicacies for lunch together with some French sticks and ended with a few sweet Turkish delights. They dined like kings and queens, and Lando felt as mellow as he had ever felt. Here he was in the middle of a sea, in beautiful weather, having caught the biggest fish of his life, with a full stomach and a beautiful woman who surprisingly seemed to understand him despite all his self-doubts. She just seemed pleased for Lando. Lando was pleased for Sanjay, and Sanjay was pleased for everyone. They packed up lunch and decided to head slowly home, and Kadri had a little time with the rod dangling behind the boat.

Lando shared a few stories with Kadri about his time with Ashley at Wellingsburn boarding school in the midlands countryside when, at thirteen, they met on their first day and were in the same 'house' called Radway Hall, forming an immediate bond. They had both been beaten on the backside latterly for playing tennis after house lockups. Lando still remembered the pain as he was particularly annoyed. He expected to be beaten for some trivial thing he had done wrong and had lined his shorts with memory foam. He was quite put out that he was not given a good caning as the excitement of beating the system was fun. This time, he thought playing tennis until quite late on a light summer evening could not have merited anything too corporeal. How wrong could he be? He was only wearing a pair of thin athletic shorts with a jockstrap underneath, which offered zero protection. He went into the study of the housemaster, who brandished a thick stick and proceeded to smash the hell out of his backside, and the bruises lasted for three weeks. Kadri was in stitches of laughter by this point.

"But," said Lando. "If that happened these days, he would be jailed for child abuse."

Between giggles, Kadri said, "I bet you didn't play tennis again after lockups."

"Damn right," he replied with a wry smile. "Didn't play tennis at all for a week as it hurt too much. Kadri suddenly leapt up, shouting I've had a bite, I've had a bite."

To Lando's delight, she had caught a very small snapper, and this was received with as much glee as if she had caught Captain Ahab's whale. It had been effectively lassoed around its gills, and they threw it back to live for another day. At least she had caught one so she could hold her head high, which she certainly did. She never asked Lando how he helped save Ashley's bacon at school.

They eventually landed at the dock at about 4 pm. Lando swapped emails and phone numbers with Sanjay, paid him with a good tip and promised to keep in touch about Sanjay's business plan. Then Lando and Kadri hailed a taxi and headed back together, firstly to Kadri's apartment, where she wished to sleep a couple of hours before her booking in the evening. They kissed passionately on the lips in the taxi before she left, and that set Lando's thoughts onto other lascivious things, which he quickly eradicated, and he taxied back to his hotel, where he decided to have a quick dip in the pool.

Chapter 32

Sunday Afternoon

Lando arrived at his hotel feeling quite hyped up after his sailing but knew he would need to get to bed early to be ready for lectures in the morning. He went to his room and changed for a poolside trip and on up to the pool to grab a sunbed under a brolly. He did a quick scan to ensure little Willie and his ghastly mother would not blight his evening, and he dived in and did a quick ten lengths before drying himself.

He gazed around, and to his horror, he spied little Willie with his mother, who was having a heated row with another elderly male hotel guest. Their voices were becoming louder and louder. He saw Solly leave his position behind the bar and head towards the disputing couple. Little Willie, or whatever his real name was, seemed to be cowering behind one of the sunbeds. Lando valued Solly's service for the remainder of his stay there, so he also decided to head over to the warring couple to see if he could help calm the stormy waters.

Solly reached the couple first. "Now, now, Mrs. Gumper, what seems to be the trouble?"

"What business is it of yours?" she replied. "This is nothing to do with you. This man knocked over my drink, and he was too drunk to mind where he was going."

"Now, why don't we all calm down, and I shall replace the drink immediately, free of charge."

"My word," said Lando, turning to the elderly man, "I have nearly finished my drink, so would you be kind enough to knock it over as I could do with another." At this point, the man roared with laughter, followed closely by Solly, and Lando hoped this little humorous interlude would diffuse the tension. How wrong could he be with the necklace lady?

She turned towards Lando with what could only be described as venom in her eyes and then turned to Solly. "Would you please ask this lunatic to leave? I have had several strange conversations with him, and I believe he is on a scale somewhere between weird and total insanity, and I believe it is considerably nearer the latter." She then lay back down on her sun-lounger and, ignoring little Willie, pulled the hinged sunshade cover from the top of the sun-lounger low over her face and proceeded not to speak. Lando thought she was on a scale somewhere, but he dreaded to think which one.

Solly dragged the man away to the bar, offering him another drink, which was about as diplomatic as he could be as the jewellery lady, alias Mrs Gumper, had opted out of any further discussion.

Lando decided to join them at the bar and ordered a cold one for himself. He addressed Solly while pouring the drinks, "I thought you handled that very well, Solly. She is one crazy prima donna."

Before Solly could answer, the man muttered, "Not very prima donna if you ask me, more ultima donna." They all laughed profusely. Lando had a brief view of Mrs Gumper peering out from under her sun-lounger face shade, scowling and then pulling it down again. They passed a few minutes idly sipping their drinks. The man eventually left.

Solly looked at Lando and said knowingly, "You look as if you have jumped into the fires of hell and also found heaven."

"You have no idea how close you are to the truth, Solly."

"Would the heaven by any chance be related to a lovely lady?"

Lando looked up quickly. "Aha, you have been talking to Gaji, haven't you, my friend?"

"Weeeeeeell, just a little." He smiled. "But it is written all over your face."

"Oh dear, I am that easy to read, am I?"

"No, very difficult, but I am extremely perceptive." They both laughed again. Lando marvelled at how all the temporary workers in Dubai had such difficult lives yet always found time to laugh.

Back in England, it seemed almost a crime to have a sense of humour, as one always seemed to run the risk of upsetting someone or them being upset on behalf of someone else. Wokeism gone mad. Where would it all end? Lando shuddered and put that thought out of his mind. He downed the rest of his beer.

"Well, Solly, I could do with some food at the bar. Do you do a bar menu at this time?" It was almost 6 pm.

"Just about. It will be dark in twenty minutes, so you will need to order early."

"I would just love a simple chicken and fries. Is that possible?"

"Of course, Mr Lando. I shall charge it to your room, and it will be ready in fifteen minutes, but you will eat it under spotlights. Would you like a beer with it?"

"Aha, Solly. A mind reader as well, or is that just being perceptive?"

"Aww, who cares?" he said expressively. Once again, laughing as he phoned through the order.

The meal arrived with a side of coleslaw, which was appreciated, along with a golden frothy beer. As ever, the speed of the sunset astonished Lando whilst he wolfed down his meal under the coloured lights around the pool. He waved good night to Solly and headed back to his room. He had a cool shower, was in bed by 9.30 pm, and started on his John Grisham book again. He could not continue beyond a couple of pages, and as he went to sleep, he realised he did not need adventures from a book as reality was just too full of adventures here.

Chapter 33

Monday

Lando woke up at 7.45 and had to be in the Al-Jafr Conference room to lecture by 8.30. What a nightmare! That was breakfast out of the window. He hurriedly cold-showered, lukewarm as usual, and got to the lecture room by 8.15. Lisana, looking immaculate and cool as usual, spirited a coffee into his hand and, within two minutes, had placed a plate of two croissants onto the table in front of him.

"Lisana, you are an absolute saviour. You cannot know how much I have appreciated your help on this course. You do your job above and beyond." Lisana turned her face away, but not before showing a distinct look of sadness. "I'm sorry, Lisana. Have I said something I shouldn't have?"

"No, no. It is all right. I am just not used to compliments." Lando thought she was on the verge of bursting into tears.

"Come on, Lisana. I'm a good listener. What's the problem?"

Lisana then moved from close to tears to almost helpless laughter. "I think you should have a look in the mirror."

Lando duly did so, as a mirror was on the wall behind them. "Oh my God," he said, smiling at his reflection. Several bits of flaky crust from the croissant were sticking to his chin and tie. Bad image. He quickly dusted them off and turned to Lisana. "Well, you have saved me from being branded as a slob by my students. That would not look good on my feedback form, but at least now you are smiling. I assume you are staying for lunch with the students, so what about us having a cup of coffee together afterwards if you wish? No need, of course, if it makes you uncomfortable or do not have the time."

"Actually, I would appreciate it, and I have the afternoon free."

"It's a date then… Sorry, I don't mean a date; I mean, er, er." Lando felt awkward.

"I know what you mean, don't worry." She laughed again, which suited her because she often looked serious. She looked at her watch. "About time to start, I'm afraid."

Just then, Hobart rushed in, looking a bit tired and flustered. Lando guessed he had probably been working most of the night but was still trying to maintain his 'cover' by being on the course. They gave an almost imperceptible mutual nod.

Lando started his lecture. This was on so-called 'creative accounting,' how companies bend their figures without getting into trouble. It suddenly seemed very unimportant to him, but he fired himself up to look as if he cared. He gave them a few examples to work on before their mid-morning coffee break. Hobart pretended loudly to have a need to chat with Lando about an accounting issue and so commandeered his private presence just when Claes happened outside the glass door to the conference room. This was convenient for a catchup meeting, although Lando expected little. He was wrong.

Hobart ushered Lando outside to where Claes was waiting by a couple of sofas. Hobart could not wait to speak. "We have traced Hamza, thank God."

"So quick," said Lando. "How come?"

"Kadri, God bless her, used her contacts. I doubted she would get anywhere with them as her circles are not Hamza's. Still, as luck would have it, she spoke to one of her doctor friends who had only just treated a very unsavoury Arab who appeared to have been suffering from a wound in the leg that looked suspiciously like a gunshot. He appeared not to want to go to a hospital. The doctor dressed it and warned him that he needed some powerful antibiotics as he could die as an infection had already started. He told him to come back in a few hours, and he would have the antibiotics ready. Kadri spoke to the doctor just at the right time and waited near the doctor's surgery, and sure enough, back came the Arab, and it was the smelly, limping Hamza. She texted me and followed him to where he was staying. It was in an old shed behind somebody's garage. I doubt the owner even knew he was there. We, of course, arrested him and placed him under our security."

"So, what happens now?"

"Well, we gave him a choice. He could never see the light of day again and simply disappear, as we already know he has murdered several people, or he could find himself in an open prison if he turns state's evidence. We shall also grease his palm with a significant sum of money, which is his key life motivator apart from being an insect breeding ground."

"How can you trust someone like that, though?"

"I don't, but in the short term, if he can get his hot, sticky little hands on some cash and not find himself in hell, what would you do? I trust his desire for self-survival above all else, particularly with cash also involved."

"Where is he now?" asked Claes.

"Safe and sound, and he has his antibiotics. He also has a shower, which will be a new experience for him!"

Lando and Claes looked at each other and neither thought Hamza would survive this ordeal nor were particularly bothered.

"So, he could lead us to Ashiraf then?" said Lando.

"Only indirectly, as apparently, Ashiraf works with a go-between named Yusuf."

"So, we need to tread carefully then."

"Yes. I informed Hamza that he would always need to wear a wire, and if there were any hint of him warning the other side, then we would also tell them what he had told us, and believe me, he would not want that. Their retribution would be very slow and very painful. Probably starting with the removal of his testicles and using them as an entrée for his next meal."

Claes coughed and grunted, "I wonder what he would have for pudding?" at which they all burst into raucous laughter.

"Have you any news, Claes?" asked Hobart.

"Only bits, I am afraid, but they all seem to support what we suspect. Qasim is constantly communicating in some code with this Shazil fellow, and I am trying to establish a hack into Shazil's computer, although he probably has several. I cannot believe he would do everything on his general work computer, particularly communicating with Iran, but he might give something away when in touch with Ashiraf."

"Keep up the good work then, Claes, and for God's sake, be careful, particularly around Qasim. He is one slimy fellow."

"I'll vouch for that," said Lando. "I also have it on good authority that he likes to torture and humiliate women."

"Ugh. I shall not enquire how you know that Lando, but we may be able to use it in some way in the future," Hobart replied with a frown.

"It came from the hotel taxi driver, to be precise. Hoby, we had better head back; otherwise, the students may get restless."

"OK, but you go in first, Lando, and I shall enter after a few minutes. Keep in touch, Claes, with anything new. Well done, both of you."

With that, the day proceeded to lunch without incident.

***

Afterwards, Lando and Lisana got together in a separate coffee lounge. They ordered a special Turkish coffee and some Turkish delight. It tasted so different from the chocolate-covered gloop Lando had tried in the UK. After it arrived, Lisana visibly relaxed and asked Lando about his own brief marriage.

"Well, we had this crazy idea that we would get hitched just over the border in Scotland in a town called Gretna Green. Its fame dates back over two hundred years when the laws of elopement were easier in Scotland. Her name was Georgina, and we got on very well, but there are plenty of other things to consider other than whether you get on well. It was an appealing romantic idea at the time but doomed. We were both too young."

"What did your parents think of it?"

"Well, I did not tell them until several weeks after I got divorced, so they were completely stunned for all of five minutes. A few years later, they died in a car crash, and I have been alone ever since, apart from my sister, who has a lovely family life. I believe Georgina remarried about two years later to an elderly millionaire."

"That must have been so hard on you, but it all makes sense. You are afraid of relationships because your marriage was a wrong choice at the wrong time, and then you lost that relationship and stability of your parents' influence."

"My word, I have never thought of it like that. You would make a good therapist."

"For what it is worth, I have been to a therapist. Analysis is one thing, but dealing with the issues is another. I struggle with that."

"Sometimes you must deal with stuff as best you can and wait to come out the other side. You inevitably do, but the cost can be quite high."

"Very profound. My own situation is a bit different. I am with a man I love. He is making all this money and seems to think spending it on rubbish will make him happy. It is making me miserable. Our friends here seem to be the same, and friendships can be very transient as most expats only stay in

Dubai for two to three years. We are all living in this dream world between alcoholic euphoria and fighting hangovers. It feels like I am constantly waiting for something dreadful to happen."

"I am the last person to give advice on this as I have made so many balls ups in life that I cannot remember them all, but things seem to mysteriously work out one way or another. Don't give up on yourself. That is the worst thing ever. A big question: does he love you?"

"I am sure he does."

"Do you think he is happy?"

"No. I don't."

"Would you like some advice from a once-married man? You know, blokes always want to 'bring home the bacon,' so to speak. It is what drives them to think they are doing it for their family, in this case, you. Maybe he is just disillusioned and does not want to admit it. Maybe he needs another dream. Have you talked to him about how you feel and how this life here for you guys is unrewarding in everything except for the wages?"

"Well, er, I have not talked directly to him about it. I guess it is time I did. Not sure I have the courage as it seems disloyal in some way. It is like saying the big bucks are not a worthwhile dream, and he has fallen for it."

"Just think what might be the best or the worst that can happen? The worst is that you have a big argument, but you will survive it if you love each other. The best—well, the sky's the limit. You go on to fulfil a joint dream and not one built on what the world tells us all to do or be."

Lisana went very quiet and thoughtful, staring at her coffee cup, but then a new brightness came to her face. She looked up at Lando, leaned over, kissed him on the cheek, and left without saying another word. Lando was unsure whether what he had said was even helpful for a few moments but hoped she would be courageous. One thing was for sure: she was on the slippery slope downwards if she carried on the way she was going. A good job she gave him that kiss when she was out of sight of any hotel staff member.

Another jailable offence.

Chapter 34

Lando had done his best to put himself close to Qasim without making it obvious. He had delivered his lectures, met with Lisana and now, working on Hobart's plan, hoped to see whether Qasim might let slip even the tiniest piece of information. He rang him up under the pretence of needing to check on a particular student who he thought might be on an autistic scale. Still, he sounded extremely agitated and was almost hyperventilating. This in itself was interesting, so Lando decided to hold back over going to see him. He did not want to raise suspicions. He headed up to his room.

Meanwhile, Ashley Hayhurst had been invited to take a security tour of a few buildings with Shazil Haroun Al Maktoum. He arrived at Shazil's ministry offices and noted the relatively low-quality office from which Shazil worked. They shook hands, and Shazil talked a little about the types of buildings like the one Ashley's company was bidding to design, and off they went on a brief tour of three buildings that Shazil felt were in the same league as the one they were bidding for.

They got in a chauffeured white Mercedes and set off. Shazil became very expansive as they came to the first building. "This one is called the Cayan Tower. As you can see, it looks like a twisted stick of rhubarb. At the time, in 2013, it was the world's tallest high-rise building at 306 metres high." He rattled on for another 15 minutes as they toured around it, and Ashley had a good look at the security arrangements and the viewing room containing so many camera feeds. He estimated it would need 30-40 people to man it effectively.

They drove to the next one, the Burj Khalifa. "This one is still the world's tallest structure at 829.8 metres since 2009," he said proudly as if he had built it himself. "It holds 57 elevators and 8 escalators." Again, they visited the security viewing room, which Ashley admitted was impressive. Very clear pictures, which was important if there was any form of grand theft or terrorism; they needed cameras that could have their photos blown up and placed into a police face recognition system.

The final building was the Burj Al Arab. The iconic luxury hotel shaped like a sail and is known worldwide. When they arrived, the tour with Shazil was twice as detailed, with a great many questions asked by him as to whether he could see any weaknesses in its security in terms of theft, terrorism or even air attacks. Ashley followed this line of thought and asked if air attacks seemed likely, to which Shazil replied rather too quickly, "Oh, absolutely not; it was just a personal question."

Ashley replied that military attacks were not in his remit for security, and Shazil replied, "Quite so, quite so."

Shazil brought up his request for a donation to his favoured charity, and Ashley said that his company would be pleased to help with any local charity in good faith. "Can you give me a bank account to which we might make a payment?"

"Of course." He gave him the bank account and asked that he make the reference "HAMZALISH."

"Would 300,000 dirhams be in order? It would put you in a very fine position to win the order."

Ashley was ecstatic. This was the bank reference that Claes had found in Qasim's bank account and had been used on the transfers to an Iranian bank account. He could not recall the bank account details, but the reference was the same. He then remembered what Hobart had said about making an initial payment to the charity. 300,000 dirhams was over £60,000, so not chicken feed.

Ashley looked at Shazil and said, '300,000 dirhams would be in order, but can we make an initial gesture of good faith of, say, 30,000 dirhams? We can transfer that tomorrow, but the rest would need a different level of authority and might take a day or two, but I do not see a problem.' He held Shazil's gaze, looking confidently at him without wavering. Shazil smiled and gave an exaggerated nod, indicating that it was all fine. He secretly expected to get contributions from others on the tender list.

Ashley and Shazil finally shook hands, and Ashley was totally convinced that Shazil had given the game away.

The intended target must indeed be the Burj Al Arab. Ashley did his best to seem politely disinterested in the building, not wishing to arouse suspicions, and off they went back to Shazil's offices and then to find a taxi home.

He could hardly wait to convey this information to Lando when he returned to his hotel.

It was now early evening, and Lando needed a bit of quiet time, so rather than go to the pool, he went to his room, had a cool shower and lay on his bed dwelling on life. He was relaxing when his mobile phone rang.

"Yes, Lando here."

"It's Ashley."

"Oh yes. How are you, Ash?"

"I'm good, thanks. Important news for our little group."

"Go on," said Lando.

Ashley was beside himself with excitement. "It's the Burj Al Arab. They want to bomb, attack or whatever the Burj Al Arab. Think of it. It is the one building everyone recognises worldwide, not just in Dubai. It is the building on the front of every Dubai travel magazine. It was also designed by a British firm of architects, WKA. Not that it is relevant, of course."

"My God. That would be an unbelievably well-publicised catastrophe. How sure are you that it is the target?"

"Not sure at all. But there is little doubt if you had been there to hear the stuff he said about the other two buildings and compare it to this one. Of course, I would not have picked it up if I had not been looking for it."

"What were the other two buildings you looked at?"

"We started with the Cayan Tower. That is the one ...."

"Yes, yes, the tall, twisted one. The next one?"

"The Burj Khalifa. That is the ..."

"Once again," Lando finished it off. "The tallest building in the world. So why the Burj Al Arab?"

"If only you had heard him say it. As he took me around, he even talked about an air attack when we were in the security viewing room."

"My God, he must be sure of himself. Right, we will need a meeting first thing tomorrow. I am pretty sure Hobart is busy tonight and will be coming here for my lectures in the morning anyway. I will try to make it for 6.30 am in my hotel room as I need to be in the lecture room by 8.30. I know it sounds ridiculous, but if we are all to act normally, then I cannot miss the lecture. Are you OK with that, Ash? Room number 737?"

"Absolutely. I'll be there," and he hung up.

Lando immediately texted the information to Kadri, Claes and Hobart and asked if they could meet at 6.30 am. Kadri could not manage it, but Claes and Hobart replied positively.

He ordered a light meal through room service accompanied by a lager and thought things were getting tasty, not just the food. Lando was beginning to get even more switched on. He was nervous but not remotely bored.

Chapter 35

Tuesday 6.30 am

Lando was up, showered and dressed when there was a quiet knock on the door. He opened it to Ashley, Claes and Hobart, who had arrived at the same time, and within one minute, there was another knock as his room service order arrived with coffee, croissants, yoghurt, fruit and raw honey.

"Firstly, my apologies to Hobart. I know he needs to take the lead on these meetings, but I felt it was right to set up this meeting ASAP, and here was the obvious place. Kadri cannot manage it but is informed as to the Burj Al Arab likely target and will be kept in the loop after the meeting. The information on the target building looks pretty clear, and Ashley seems confident, although not certain that it would be that building. Does that about sum it up, Ashley?"

Ashley coughed a little as he had a mouth full of croissants. He nodded and then said, "There is one other thing of importance that I have not told you yet. Shazil gave me a bank account into which he wants my company to pay his charitable donation of 300,000 dirhams."

Now it was Hobart's turn to cough and splutter. "We cannot sanction that amount. I shall lose my job apart from anything else."

Ashley smiled at him. He liked prolonging the tension. "I agreed to a 10% initial payment of 30,000 dirhams by tomorrow as a gesture of good faith as we could not sanction the full sum required without needing authorisation from above, which takes time."

"You rotter," said Hobart. "You could have started with that figure."

"Ok, Hoby. Don't get your knickers in a twist," said Lando, trying to defuse the potential for a scrap about money. "Is that the thing of importance you were referring to, Ash?"

"No, but ask Claes on this one."

Claes came straight into the discussion, "It was the bank account. It is registered in Iran. Guess what?"

They all looked inquisitively at him. "The reference for the payment is to be 'HAMZALISH.' Does that mean anything to you, Hoby?"

Hobart suddenly became very quiet and spoke in an excited whisper. "Yes, it was the same reference that Qasim used in his funds transfer to Iran. Let me see the bank account details. .... Yes, it is the same BIC Code, sort and account code. This must be the proof we need." He looked up with what could only be described as pure glee spread all over his face. There was a pregnant pause before he spoke quietly. "We have them right where we want them. Now, we need to bury them for good."

The meeting disbanded, leaving Lando plenty of time to gather himself for the day's lectures, due in 30 minutes.

***

Meanwhile, Hobart spent much time on the phone with not only his controller, Harold Shrimpton but also with GK from the British Embassy, thoroughly briefing them to ensure

Hobart's team had not breached any protocols that may get them in trouble with the Dubai authorities. GK was particularly worried. He emphasised that the sooner they could clear Sheikh Massoud from being involved, the better.

"Remember," he said. "This guy is not named Sheikh Massoud bin Rashid Al Maktoum for nothing. He is a close cousin of the Emir, Sheikh Mohammed. If Sheikh Massoud is mixed up in this, it is best dealt with by the Dubai authorities. If he is not mixed up in it, which I think is the case, the longer he is left out of the loop, the more embarrassing it is for the Dubai government and the British authorities, who will be blamed for withholding vital information. It could damage our relations irreparably, to say nothing of your own country's relations, Hobart."

"I had similar advice from my controller GK, and I shall pull every string to find out quickly."

"Also, when you have established that Sheikh Massoud is not involved, ensure you leave it to him to exact retribution on Shazil. I certainly would not like to be in Shazil's boots."

"They don't wear boots, sir," muttered Hobart.

"What's that?"

"They wear sandals, sir."

"I get the picture, Hobart, so please protect my man. I do not want to send pieces of him back to England in a box, if you do not mind. You know how much I hate paperwork."

"I understand, sir."

"Thank you for keeping me in the picture. Please continue to do so." The phone went dead.

Hobart had another weird vision of GK with that well-endowed tea lady. He wondered if this was a British thing or some kind of benefit in kind for GK. He assumed he would never know.

Just then, Hobart's phone rang again. It was Claes with more news.

"Hi Hoby, I've cracked it. I've cracked Qasim's code. It was an easy one in the end, and the idiot did it on his work computer. He used a simple cypher based on letters taken out of page numbers in a book. He hid it in his messages sent to Shazil, which were in English, making it easy to spot—with the help of a little simple code-breaking piece of software in my possession. He just inserted numbers to represent letters, and then these are ...."

"Hey," interrupted Lando, down the phone. "I don't care. Quickly, what did you find?"

"To cut a long story short, it was all in the emails between them. Clear as a bell. One is from Shazil, which refers to where the drones are arriving from in Iran, a place called Kharkushi. I found it on a map and it's by the sea. Then, it will be shipped westward across the Strait of Hormuz to the East coast of Oman. A place called Limah from where they will be launched. I checked, and it is under 200 kilometres from Dubai, so well within range. He makes reference to the Iranians, unsurprisingly not sanctioning anything being launched from Iran. He also referred to ensuring that under no circumstances could any of this information be leaked to Sheikh Massoud, as they would both be strung up from a very high pole. This seems to put the Sheikh in the clear, thank God."

"No doubt strung up by their testicles. They have a thing about testicles, don't they? Do you understand what this means, Claes? This means we can legitimately open this up to Sheikh Massoud and pass on the responsibility of dealing with the culprits involved. Claes, this is fantastic. I need to contact Hoby, GK, and Kadri PDQ so we can all breathe more easily. Right, Claes. Can you please send me the original emails and the coding so I can interpret them? I shall forward them to the Embassy and see what else we can do. What a team, eh? I don't know how we would have managed without your IT skills. Well done, my friend." The call ended.

Claes smiled as he put his phone down. He was enjoying himself. Nothing like a bit of positive validation for getting one's spirits up.

Chapter 36

Tuesday pm

Lando rang Hobart, who was over the moon about it, and he said to get hold of GK as soon as possible, preferably in person, as he always mistrusted the phone lines into the British Embassy, even though landlines tend to be more secure than digital mobiles. The problem was, where calls come through a switching system, digital or not, you could never be sure someone was not listening in.

He then rang GK during a break from his lecture to request an urgent meeting. He got his assistant Oscar. "GK has a space in his diary at 3 pm. Would that suit you, sir?"

"Absolutely, I shall be there." Lando turned off his phone and faced the rest of his day's lecture in a bit of a haze. Lisana noticed this and asked Lando if he was alright, to which he replied with a curt "Never better" and retired back into his weird zone. Lisana brought him a cup of coffee and a chocolatey pastry and decided to leave him to think. He finished the lecture session and could barely remember what it was about, and he informed Lisana that he would not be around for lunch. He hightailed it to reception and spied Gaji, whose ever-present brightness was most welcome.

"My word, Mr Lando. You look excited. Off to see your lady friend then?" The familiarity, whilst unusual from a hotel employee, was delivered without anyone near them as Lando was only too aware of Gaji potentially being overheard and immediately risking his job.

"Actually, I could do with a lift to the British Embassy. Are you available by any chance?"

"My next airport trip is in one hour, so I am happy to help. If you go outside, I will pick you up in our usual place, away from prying eyes."

Sure enough, Gaji arrived in the hotel vehicle, and Lando got in quickly and left. They had little conversation as Lando's thoughts were in a parallel universe, and Gaji could see he was not in the mood. They reached the Embassy in good time, and Gaji offered to wait for him for half an hour if he could finish in time. They agreed, and Lando rang the buzzer at the embassy door to announce his arrival and was let through.

He was ushered through to GK's office, who stood up all 6 feet plus of him and proffered his hand.

"So, what brings you here in such a rush? I hope no one else has died." There was that deadpan humour again.

"Not that I'm aware of. At least no one that I know in the past half hour. My driver did his best to knock someone off his bike a while back. He thought it was time to counter with a little bit of humour of his own."

"Good. So, what is so important then?"

Lando filled him in on all the details, and GK's face came alive when he realised that Sheikh Massoud was definitely not involved. "This needs to be handled with the utmost care as we put ourselves at the Sheikh's mercy once we inform him. On the one hand, he will be very pleased that we have brought Shazil and Qasim's dishonour to his attention and on the other hand, he will be extremely unhappy that we did not inform him sooner. We need to tread a very fine line, and I suggest you accompany me when I arrange to see him. Being outside of politics, you can bring more credence to the full story. I can also blame you a little for not bringing it to my attention sooner, and you can counter me by needing to substantiate the information more. I also think Ashley's information will have Sheikh Massoud sharpening his claws. I would not like to be Shazil or Qasim at that meeting. So, I must ask if you are comfortable accompanying me to a meeting with the Sheikh and if we can do this as soon as possible."

"Of course, I would," replied Lando.

"Right. Thank you. If you can hang on, I shall place a call with his office and see how soon he can meet us. I hope it is soon, preferably this afternoon, as I do not believe we have a moment to lose. We also have a massive potential hot potato to deal with. If the Iranians are landing their vicious cargo on the soil of the Sultanate of Oman, not, of course, part of the UAE, they will wish to deal with it themselves as it is on their own soil. Cannot say I would blame them either. Some very careful, diplomatic tiptoeing is needed here, although I believe relations between Oman and Dubai are cordial. It is still a powder keg, though."

GK asked Oscar to call the Sheikh's office and await a response. It came quickly, and, yes, given the urgency, Sheikh Massoud would be available at 3.45 pm.

***

GK and Lando rushed off to the Sheikh's offices in Gaji's vehicle, which was still outside, and Lando sent Gaji back to the hotel straight away, or he could lose his job if he was late and had no reasonable excuse.

They were escorted up the stairs to the Sheikh's office. It was impressively decorated in a mixture of modern and Arabic patterns and pictures. There were three sets of ancient crossed daggers and scimitars on the walls. The carved wooden furniture was upholstered in rich colours of red, gold and blue brocade and velvet and there were thick Persian rugs around the floor. A massive chandelier was a focus for the ceiling and a large, beautifully polished mahogany desk was to one side of the room. Sheikh Massoud rose in his white robes like *Lawrence of Arabia* from his magnificently cushioned sofa to greet them. The formalities were observed, and Lando kept his mouth shut whilst GK summarised the situation, brilliantly skirting around the issue of the Sheikh's potential involvement. It was not lost on Massoud.

He raised an eyebrow and softly said, "You cannot have truly known that I was not personally involved in the plot then?"

GK was momentarily floored, but he recovered quickly. "Well, we wished to gather more information to bring you a complete picture, knowing your time's hard-pressed and valuable."

"Well said," replied Massoud rather dismissively. "I shall not pursue the point, but you have nonetheless done your duty, and for that, I am very grateful. I shall deal with that Qasim and Shazil when it is all over. I have never liked that Shazil fellow since the day I employed him. It is my fault, though, as employing him was a family matter. He has made me appear foolish."

GK used all his diplomatic judgment in the next sentence. "If I may suggest? Perhaps if it became clear that Your Highness had been a significant catalyst in discovering and dealing with this subterfuge, my government would be very happy to support this."

The Sheikh looked at GK with a grateful, appraising look. "Well, Mr Kirkpatrick, that would indeed be helpful, and we now need to move quickly down the diplomatic route as I shall have to speak to my opposite number in Muscat to ask their advice and help in moving forward. We need to be careful."

At this point, Lando suddenly had an idea worth speaking about. "If it pleases, Your Excellency, I have one or two useful suggestions. I have a childhood friend named Chris Coghlan whom I could contact in Oman. He was a Captain in the British Marines and was contracted out by the British military to oversee the training of the Omani border guards. I believe he is based in Muscat. Beyond that, I know little else about him, but I am sure he could ease the channels a little. The second thing is that I believe I need to accompany any force that works with the Omani soldiers who will be required to prohibit any attack on the Dubai people. I am one of the few who can recognise this Ashiraf fellow if he is there at all, and he is undoubtedly the driving force behind so many of these anti-Western attacks."

The Sheikh stared at Lando for a long moment, clearly running scenarios over in his mind. "Right, that will be fine, but we must move quickly. I doubt there will be a great time frame between the drone battery arriving from Iran and the communication between Qasim and Shazil with them. That is when they will be at their weakest, and if we can intercept their communications, we can not only catch them cold but also prevent them from firing any drones. I assume Shazil has already arranged some anti-drone batteries as part of his plan, but I shall make inquiries as to their deployment and ensure they are around the Burj Al Arab under cover or onboard ships. We have a few new anti-drone guns with a highly accurate targeting system that can locate and disable drones in flight, which I hope we do not need to use, but it is comforting to know we have them available. We shall also deploy them in Oman in the desert region, hoping to bring them down there if any are launched. I need to liaise quickly with their security services, but I do not anticipate any problems. Is that all then, gentlemen? Once again, my thanks for bringing this straight to me. It will be a challenging time, but with luck and the help of Allah, we now have the benefit of surprise. I assume you can keep your friend Claes intercepting messages, which will be critical. Also, please take advantage of my car and driver as it is getting late, and the taxis will be very busy."

"I shall speak to him immediately, your Highness, and thank you," replied Lando, and they all stood up, shook hands and parted company.

They were quiet on the way back, deep in thought of what would come. On arriving home, Lando called a number in Oman that Hobart had given him to help trace his old friend, Captain Chris Coghlan. He found him in minutes. Amazingly, he was already clued up on the situation with his Omani military special services team ready to go, and he was so pleased to hear from Lando. They had years of catching up to do. Lando phoned his team, all equally taken aback by his meeting with the Sheikh. Kadri suggested meeting for an evening drink and offered to come to his hotel, which sounded like a perfect way to end the day. She arrived later at his room, and within two minutes, they were grappling with each other's clothes to get between the sheets as quickly as possible. Ah, she smelt like a bed of roses. He was certainly not bored today!

Chapter 37

Wednesday am

When Lando awoke, he turned over in bed and looked at Kadri, who was soundly sleeping. Even asleep, her face seemed to glow, and he thought no makeup could possibly improve her beauty. She must have sensed him staring at her because her eyelids flickered open, revealing her mesmerising dark irises.

"Good morning, Rolo. What are you staring at?"

"You, of course." He turned his face away, too embarrassed to think of anything slick to cover up his thoughts about the night's raptures. She had thrown him by calling him Rolo again, which only Ashley had ever done.

She suddenly smiled and raised herself up on her elbow. "That is strange. Do you know, I called you Rolo in the restaurant just for some fun."

"What is strange about that?" said Lando, getting up to boil the kettle.

"Well, when I met Ashley for the first time whilst walking home, he referred to his best friend at school, Lando, and said he called you Rolo. I just never put two and two together. How silly of me."

"Understandable, as you were probably still recovering from your encounter with that old, moustachioed dude."

"He wasn't bad looking actually, but his manner really did 'beni ürküttü.'"

Lando looked at her askance. "Wassat mean?"

"He gave me the creeps. Yes, we use that expression in Turkey!" she said with a twinkle in her eye.

Lando looked at his watch. "Argh, there goes another breakfast. I hope Lisana is up to her usual standard," he shrieked, leaping out of bed and quickly pouring Kadri a cup of tea.

"Oh, have I got competition?" she asked, looking demurely over her teacup as she supped whilst letting the sheet slide down her chest, revealing one of her magnificent breasts.

He was about to defend himself until he noticed her teasing. He was already dressed and quickly filled her in on the plan for the day. He thought he would have liked to fill her in using a more intimate method but quickly removed it from his mind.

"Basically, we are all meant to act normal until news comes about any likely attack time. We will head for Oman this afternoon, whatever, as it is 3 hours by road, but hopefully, we can fly in by helicopter, assuming our relations with Oman stay intact. We need to be there in good time as we are getting help from the Omani security services to find where these drones might be dropped off. We know it is Limah, but where exactly? Hopefully, they will find out before it is too late.

"So why are you going then, Lando? Isn't it very dangerous?"

"I shall be careful, but I am the only one who has seen Ashiraf other than via a photograph. Must scoot now as I am due to lecture in 10 minutes!" He bent down, kissed her on the forehead, and headed off.

Lisana was on hand to deal with the students' arrival. She elegantly drifted from one to another, checking that they were all right. Lando noticed that Hobart had not yet appeared and somehow doubted that he would as he had so much to arrange. Lisana already used her sixth sense to bring him a croissant and a coffee. She seemed much brighter than normal. That slight expression of sadness seemed to have left her face, and Lando remarked on how perky she looked.

"Actually, I could do with another chat with you when you have time," she replied.

"Love to, but today is not a good day. I doubt I can stay for lunch as I am expected elsewhere. I believe it has something to do with course management," he proffered a little white lie.

"OK, that is fine whenever you are free," and off she buzzed happily around the guests.

Lando was sorry to delay her, but he had to keep his time free for the rest of the day, and thankfully, the students had Thursday and Friday morning free to prepare some work to be handed in the next Monday as a part of their course.

***

The call came in from Hobart at 2 pm, near the end of his lectures, whilst briefing the class on their assignment. He apologised to the group and left the room. Apparently, it was good to go. Claes had done his stuff once more and had hooked onto a text string between Qasim and Shazil, giving the game away. Also, the Omani security forces had found the likely area

313

from which the drone battery would launch its lethal load, and he was to be ready to join the Dubai security force at a small area just outside Dubai where they had two military troop-carrying helicopters waiting to fly at 3.15 pm. Hobart would pick him up at the hotel in a half hour. He returned to the class and muttered about not joining them for lunch but would see them on Monday morning bright and early.

***

Wednesday pm

Lando went to his room and took a call from Hobart, who had duly arrived in the lobby in good time. Lando had no idea what to wear, so he just picked up some casuals with a sweater as they may be sitting around in the nighttime desert, although he believed it would be pretty balmy this time of year.

He went down to the lobby, and there, surprisingly, was Ashley, smiling away.

"What the hell are you doing here?" exclaimed Lando as they shook hands.

'My dear chap, I could not allow you to have all the fun besides besides which, you need to be looked after. If the balloon is going up, I want to be there as I haven't had so much fun in all my life."

"Ashley, this is serious business. Why are you talking in the World War 2 language?"

"Can't help it, old man. Chip off the old block, I suppose. Anyway, I have cleared it with the powers that be, but please don't ask me how."

Hobart was agitated and ushered them out to his vehicle. They drove off to their destination, and when Lando saw the Puma helicopters with UAE security forces around them, his stomach turned summersaults. It suddenly dawned on him that his life could be in severe danger. They were all given a set of army fatigues and Kevlar vests, and the field commander Ibrahim asked Hobart, Ashley and Lando if they had ever handled weapons. Hobart was comfortable with them; Lando had only ever fired Lee Enfield rifles in the school shooting team, and Ashley refused even to consider one. Hobart was already carrying his Glock pistol, and Ibrahim offered him a 30-round magazine-fed Caracal Sultan assault rifle. It had a semi and fully automatic fire facility with flip-up iron sights.

Hobart's face split into a wide grin such that Lando thought the top of his head might fall off. He felt there could be something slightly unhinged about Hobart. It must be the excitement. Lando was given a semi-automatic Caracal pistol with a spare magazine and shoulder holster and told only to take off the safety catch if he wanted to kill someone. Ibrahim told them proudly that both guns were manufactured in Abu Dhabi and were well-tested. Lando was dubious about carrying a pistol, and although he had handled and fired pistols in the past, he had never pointed one at a human being. He did not plan on using it.

They all boarded the aircraft. It was the first time for both Ashley and Lando in a helicopter, and the nerves started to kick in. Lando felt nauseous, and it took a great deal of his courage not to throw up. He regretted this whole trip—apart from meeting Kadri, that is!

The helicopter suddenly rose into the air, and off they went. It was very noisy, and they had to shout at each other to be heard.

"How long do you think the journey will be?" asked Ashley to no one in particular.

Lando replied, "Well, it is under 200 kilometres, and these birds fly at about 290 kilometres per hour, so by my reckoning, that is just over 40 minutes."

Everyone looked at him in astonishment. Lando just nodded in a sage-like way and pretended his knowledge and calculations were an everyday occurrence. No one spoke until he confessed to asking Ibrahim in the quiet. At that point, he received several manly punches on his shoulder and a few laughs, even from the professional soldiers on their aircraft.

They duly arrived close to their destination, went into hover mode, and slowly put down behind some dunes out of sight of prying eyes. They disembarked, and Commander Ibrahim gave them pep talks about upholding the highest standards and having confidence in their training.

"Remember," he said firmly, "we must walk for at least a half hour in complete silence until we reach the expected meeting with the Omani security services. We pray to Allah that they have found out the exact place from which they plan to launch the drones, or we shall not be welcome home again."

Ashley was the only one of the three of them who seemed to be remarkably calm. He kept close to Lando as they marched, if you could call it that, through the thick sand. After a while, Ibrahim lifted his hand in a fist, and everyone stopped and crouched. There was a soft hoot that sounded just like an owl, which Lando later learned was a Desert Owl sound. Ibrahim replied with a similar hoot of his own, and immediately, the troops were all surrounded by men in military uniforms.

The next thing everyone did was clap each other on the back. Ibrahim smiled at the group of three Westerners. "The Omani Security services," he said, still smiling. "and, having twisted a few arms, they know for sure the launch site."

Suddenly into view came this stocky, swarthy man in a camouflage uniform. Lando at once recognised his old childhood friend Chris Coghlan, and they swapped big man hugs with each other. Lando introduced him to Hobart and Ashley, and he then removed a map from his chest pocket, opened it out and showed Ibrahim and the three of them the site of the expected drone launch.

"How did you find this out, Chris? I assume you did not just guess," interjected Lando.

"Had to apply a little pressure on one or two locals already known to us with dubious sympathies. We tried financial inducement, which yielded little, then a more physical inducement. They could not stop talking to us after that."

Lando decided not to enquire of any specifics as there were things in life that needed to be done that the ordinary man would not be prepared to do, and Lando was one of them. They sat around for over two hours. It felt longer. Lando was beginning to wonder if their information was incorrect. They chatted about many things to take their mind off the waiting.

Ibrahim told them there were a couple of lookouts in radio contact who would let them know when any dubious deliveries arrived in any of the nearest bays. Addressing Lando with feeling, he said, "I gather you have met this Ashiraf son of a pig."

"No, I have not met him, but I saw him at close quarters, and his face had a distinct look of menace. He was short, walked with a limp, and wore thick glasses. He also had a small dark beard. I gather you have had a look at the photograph we circulated."

"Yes, I have. One question?" said Ibrahim quizzically. "Why do you think he will be here at the launch? He does not need to be here and only puts himself in potential danger."

"An excellent question that I asked myself. Apparently, he is very hands-on when it comes to his terrorist acts. Whilst no one has seen him, not only does he allegedly supervise all the details in the planning, but he also has a thirst for being there at the kill. Once he sees the drones launch, he will no doubt travel to Dubai to gloat over the devastation caused. That is one of his weaknesses, so, surprisingly, he has never been caught."

Suddenly, there was a slight crackling of static on Chris's little transceiver. His eyes lit up. "They have landed ashore with what appears to be a package fitting the description. Only a dozen people with it, so they do not look as if they expect trouble. There is one enormous guy with them, which is interesting, together with a very short fellow with a limp."

"Why is that interesting?" asked Lando.

"Because there are often large people involved in military-style operations which are not worthy of comment. This guy was apparently worthy of comment, and the guy with a limp sounded like it could be your man, Ashiraf."

"Let's hope so," whispered Lando.

Things were coming to a head, and quickly. Everyone hunkered down in the shallow, sandy trenches that they had prepared. They heard equipment being assembled a hundred yards away and waited for permission to attack. Neither the Omani security services nor the Dubai special ops heard confirmation to proceed. Something was awry with the communications. Ibrahim realised they must have been using a signal blocker as he could not contact either his men or, indeed, the telephone command and control centre. Chris and Ibrahim chatted quickly and decided to lead an immediate attack irrespective. They stood up from behind the dunes and ran full speed towards the little group of terrorist Arabs, nearly ready to fire their payload. As soon as Chris and Ibrahim knew they were spotted, they shouted their men on and opened fire, spraying towards those near the equipment. Three went down immediately, one screaming. The rest of the squad ran forward as well, and all hell then broke loose with the staccato sound of automatic fire echoing around the dunes in the half-light of the sky.

Hobart, Ashley, and Lando jogged forward and crouched, trying to take cover behind whatever they could. Out of the darkness, two of the ruffians ran towards them screaming Allahu Akbar, and Hobart let rip with his semi-automatic, almost cutting one in half with a dozen bullets. Still, he took a bullet himself full in the shoulder. The ruffian then turned towards Lando and was about to pull the trigger on him when Ashley threw himself at the hairy Arab, his forehead connecting directly with his nose, knocking him out cold just when his gun went off. Ashley got up and realised he had been shot twice. Once into his chest, thankfully saved by his Kevlar vest and once clean through his left arm. He saw the blood seeping out and, with his eyes rolling up, collapsed slowly to the ground, out cold. Lando quickly applied a compress to the wound and tightened it with a tie before looking up and immediately recognising Ashiraf.

Ashiraf turned, saw the recognition on Lando's face, and ran towards the drone launch pad. As he did so, Lando saw the massively wide figure of an African man advancing towards him. He had hands like meat cleavers and a row of white teeth, one of which glinted with what appeared to be a diamond. The man looked at Lando, and a deep rumble of a laugh started in his belly, and moved upwards, exciting from his mouth like a roar.

"Ha …… Ha …… Ha …… Allah has placed you in front of Bongani for his pleasure."

"Oh yes?" replied Lando. "And who might you be?" He could think of nothing sensible to say.

"My name is Bongani."

"Oh really? I had a goldfish by that name. Does it mean something?"

"It means 'grateful.' Ha …. Ha …. Haaaaa." There was that deep laugh again.

"And what are you grateful for, Mr Bignini?" Lando deliberately mispronounced his name to try to irritate him. It did not seem to work.

"I am grateful to Allah for giving me this meal today."

"Am I missing something," said Lando, looking around. "I see no meal here."

"You are my meal." With that, Bongani moved deceptively fast for one so musclebound and grabbed Lando around the neck. Lando felt life draining from him, and he could not breathe. He struggled to use an elbow strike but managed it. He struck Bongani on the nose, but that just made him laugh. The next thing, those vast white teeth came towards his face, and his mouth opened. My God, he might be eaten alive by this foul mountain of a man. He felt like a puppet in this man's hands. He knew his position was critical. However, all was not lost. Lando's hands were free even though he was being shaken like a rag doll. He managed to reach inside the rear of his waistband and remove his Caracal pistol that Ibrahim had given him. He pulled the trigger, and nothing happened. Of course, it didn't. The safety catch was on. Bongani laughed again, threw Lando to the ground, and advanced towards him with increasing momentum. Lando realised just in time, knocked off the catch and "boom …… boom …… boom." He let

Bongani have it three times straight in the face. Lando will never forget the expression of shock on Bongani's face as he sank to the ground senseless, spurting blood and brain matter in all directions, although there could not be much of that with this fellow.

Lando looked around just in time to see Ashiraf at the controls of the drone battery. Whatever he did, two drones launched straight upwards and then headed across the desert. Lando shivered. My God, he had launched them. Ashiraf then took off with astonishing speed away from the firefight near its end.

The full moon shone down on the scene. It was like something out of Dante's Inferno. Bodies everywhere. They were glinting with fresh blood, and few were moving. Two of the security forces appeared dead, and another three were injured. They were in good spirits, though, as their battle was over. Lando went over to his friend Ashley, who had surfaced and was sitting up chatting with a soldier who was applying a medical treatment of some sort. He looked up with his drawn, pale face and saw Lando.

"Hey, Ash. How are you? What were you doing getting in the way of a bullet? You had not even got a gun on you."

"Thought you needed looking after. Got a good story for my kids now, which I can dine out on for years."

Lando looked at his friend and realised how close he had come to death. He struggled for the right words to say at this time as Ashley had put his whole body on the line for Lando. He had dived in without thought for himself and taken a bullet to the chest, thankfully hitting his protection vest and one into his arm.

"Thank you, my friend," were the only words he could come out with as he looked at his pale face. Through clenched teeth and a tear in his eye, he said rather too loudly, "Are you in pain?"

Ashley smiled. "Actually, old man, my arm aches a little, but my chest is excruciating. I might have a broken rib. How is Hoby? I gather he caught one."

"He is not in a good way. He took a nasty one into the shoulder, so he will not be chucking any baseballs for a while. It is serious, though, and he was in a great deal of pain, although they have dosed him with morphine, so he is a bit woozy. There are two of our guys dead, and unfortunately, Ashiraf amazingly got away, for now at least, and managed to launch two of the drones."

"Good Lord," grunted Ashley.

"Well, Ibrahim has already spoken to the other security unit based in the desert with the anti-drone gun, and we expect to hear whether they have brought them down. He has also been in touch with Sheikh Massoud, who has warned the anti-drone batteries surrounding the Burj Al Arab."

Ashley was beginning to fade as a combination of his adrenalin wearing off and the pain in his ribs was taking its toll. Just then, Ibrahim came over and told them that one of the drones had been brought down on the desert path, and the other was thankfully stopped by the anti-drone gun on board a ship right in front of the Burj Al Arab. Most of the guests assumed it was just fireworks.

Ibrahim was glowing. "The Sheikh sends his deepest congratulations and sympathies for those lost or wounded, but he is very pleased with the result. It has already hit the TV news, and Sheikh Massoud was able to sell it as an exceptionally well-coordinated operation and a diplomatic success with Oman, as well as acknowledging the British and American involvement."

Lando was dubious. "The press in our country would be very suspicious about what has happened here. I cannot think anyone would really believe a news item so positive."

"People believe what they want to believe," retorted Ibrahim. "That is why we have a smile on our faces."

"We still have not nailed Ashiraf, which was my reason for being on this mission," grumbled Lando. "Pity. He remains free to carry on his violent antics."

Ibrahim looked across at the approaching Captain Chris Coglan. He had a beaming smile on his face. "So, what do you think of your first taste of action then, Lando? It was your first, wasn't it?"

"Yes, it was. We were commiserating about losing sight of Ashiraf. It was a big negative about this operation apart from those we lost. We could lose a lot more now."

"Don't be so sure. We interrogated one of the wounded prisoners. Apparently, Ashiraf planned to go to Dubai after the attack to spread discontent. He will probably try that anyway if only to negate the positive State PR coming out of the failed attack. We have an associate's name there. He goes by the name of Yusuf."

"Aha," exploded Lando. "I know of him. He was the go-between for Ashiraf and Hamza, assuming he was the same Yusuf."

"Hamza?" Chris looked up.

"Doesn't matter. What else can we get off him?"

"Nothing. He is dead."

Lando looked at Chris, who did not look him in the eye and decided not to pursue the point.

The evening had taken its toll on everyone, and they all shook hands, and the Omani security services departed. The Dubai special forces team, along with a few of the wounded on stretchers, including Hobart and Ashley, as well as Lando, climbed back onto the helicopters and headed for home. As they journeyed over the starlit desert in silence, apart from the engine noise, the moon looked twice its normal size as it shone across the sandy, wavy landscape, and Lando felt good to be alive. Really good.

Chapter 38

Thursday 2 am

When they landed under the moonlight, as they removed their fatigues and handed them over, medics were already waiting for them. Hobart and Ashley were examined and loaded onto an ambulance and driven off without sirens to what appeared to Ashley like some backwater military hospital. However, when they got inside, the care could not have been better, and they were both attended to speedily without form filling, questions or superfluous care. Ashley had his cracked rib confirmed by an x-ray, so he was told it would take some weeks for the pain to go completely. His arm was cleaned and stitched up, and he was given precautionary antibiotics. The nurse struggled to take her eyes off his handsome face with the lengthy blond hair, and he played on it unmercifully. There was a taxi waiting for him outside to take him back to his hotel, where he slept like a baby, having used the antibiotics as canapes to precede cleaning out the whisky contents of his minibar and making a phone call to his family.

Hobart, however, was not so lucky. He was told he needed an operation on his shoulder and was immediately put under general anaesthetic, where they put a metal pin in his shoulder. He would have to stay in overnight at least and would need physio for a few weeks, but as he said before going under, "It could have been worse." When he came to, he was astounded to see his controller, Harold Shrimpton, at his bedside with an admiring expression.

"You are definitely destined for bigger things, my friend. I believe congratulations are in order. Bloody well done," he said in a low voice, showing what appeared to Hobart to be a look of regret or envy on his face. Hobart doubted that Harold had ever even been in a gunfight.

***

Lando arrived exhausted at his hotel at about three in the morning. He got very strange looks from the staff in reception, who must have thought he had been out on the town, seeing how ragged he looked. He realised there were other more important things in life to worry about. He headed for his room, threw off his clothes and leapt into the shower. He kept the water on warm and stayed under it until he was nearly asleep, dried off, and managed to text Kadri the briefest of messages so she would know he was safe before he fell asleep.

He woke up at about 10 am and, for a moment, thought he had missed the start of his lecture. Then, he remembered with relief that the students had the morning off to finish their assignments. He was wonderfully relaxed and realised this was a hangover from the euphoria from the previous night. He showered again and made breakfast in time, ordering some beef bacon, a couple of eggs, a waffle and lashings of coffee.

He returned to his room and got on the phone. He briefed Claes on what had transpired, who was very concerned for Hobart until it was fully explained. He then rang Kadri and had a long, intimate chat before ringing Ashley to see how his wounds were faring.

"They are healing nicely, old boy. Couldn't be better."

"You sound pretty chipper for a man who was shot and could have died."

"Why shouldn't I be? Think of the stories I can tell my kids …. and the grandkids, for that matter. I shall be a hero in my family. In fact, by the time I embellish the story a bit, my wife, Anya, might let me off stacking the dishwasher for a few days."

Lando smiled with relief that his friend was so upbeat. He was still amazed at how he threw himself at the Arab ruffian in front of Lando without thought for himself.

"Maybe meet a bit later, eh Ash? Plenty to chat about."

"You bet," he said, ending the call.

As soon as their connection closed, Lando took a call from Hobart.

"How are you, Lando? Good night's sleep?"

"Fine Hoby. More important, how are you? How are they treating you in hospital?"

"They are not. I have self-discharged. Far too much to do. At home and full of painkillers, but I need to ride it out."

"Are you sure that is wise?"

"Probably not, but I cannot miss out at this late stage. I'm ok, though, so thanks for asking. Phoned my parents in the States. They nearly hit the roof and immediately told me to resign and take up their offer in the family law firm after taking the bar exam. No chance of that. Never had so much fun…. ever.

Even got the chance to use an automatic rifle in anger. What could top that, eh? My controller, Harold Shrimpton, was by my bedside when I woke up after the operation. He said he would put me up for a CIA valour award. Not that I care much about it, but it would certainly do my career in 'The Company' no harm."

"Sounds like you are healing fast, Hoby."

"I would heal faster if we could nail that Ashiraf bastard."

"We have a lead, Hoby, through that landfill called Hamza. Ashiraf is likely to head to Dubai to stir up anti-government feelings following his part in the failed attack. His go-between is a man called Yusuf, who I have not met, but Hamza could arrange that if he wants to remain alive."

"Aah. Now, you have cheered me up a great deal. Let's get on with it then. Perhaps we can meet to coordinate how we permanently nail this asshole."

"That's more like it, Hoby. A bit of anger will do you the world of good."

"Maybe so, but let's you and I get together at the American consulate in an hour. I shall enjoy conducting a little interrogation of Hamza." The phone conversation ended, and it dawned on Lando that despite the euphoria of surviving the successful armed operation, the whole situation would only be wrapped up with the neutralisation of Ashiraf.

Within the hour at 1 pm, Lando found himself at the consulate, and he was escorted by a security guard along a seemingly endless corridor and down two levels of stairs to a big studded closed door. He knocked a couple of times, and the door was opened eventually by another guard who looked at Lando with a half-smile on his face. Inside sat Hamza at a table, head slumped down, shaking as if he had a violent fever, with a rather ghastly bespectacled man with a thin black moustache cradling a box of hypodermics in his arms by the table. Hobart was behind him, arm in a sling, whispering to Hamza close to his ear.

"Now then, Hamza, look up and tell me if you recognise the man who has just come in."

Hamza slowly raised his head, and recognition crossed his face. He muttered something which sounded to Lando like a cuss of some sort.

Hobart was enjoying the tension in the room.

"So, I take it that you recognise him. You killed his friend Dillon, did you not? How do you think he feels about that, then?" Hamza said nothing.

"I think he may like to introduce you to one of these little friends in the box. All except one are filled with scopolamine, which, as you may know, will help you tell the truth; something very foreign to you, I know. The odd one out is a lethal injection used for capital punishment. It should contain pancuronium bromide, which causes muscle paralysis and respiratory arrest, potassium chloride, which stops the heart, and midazolam for sedation. However, we have doctored this a little. We have removed the sedation and replaced it with a new chemical compound that will seem like fire burning through all your veins. Your eyes will bulge out of their sockets until they bleed, your bowels will immediately turn to water before they empty involuntarily, and the pain in your ears will be so bad you will beg for an early death." Lando almost felt sorry for Hamza, who looked up pitifully until he remembered the savage death of Dillon.

"Now, Hamza, will you please tell us how to contact Yusuf? I am sure you can help us here, and it will be good for your soul."

"You are a foul son of a rabid dog, and I will tell you nothing." He then spat on the floor near Lando's feet.

"So, Lando, please step forward and have the pleasure of injecting our friend with the scopolamine. It is the end hypodermic."

Lando moved towards the box before the ghastly bespectacled man with the thin moustache. He grabbed the end hypodermic and jammed it in Hamza's forearm before he could move.

Hobart moved forward quickly, shouting at Lando at the top of his voice. "You fool. I said the one at the end. Wrong end. That is the end nearest me, not the end nearest you. That is the one with the lethal poison in it."

Lando immediately rose to the bait. "How was I supposed to know? You just said the one at the end. Is he going to die then?"

"Yes, and horribly as well!" He then winked at Lando, who realised it was all a ruse.

Meanwhile, Hamza looked at the two of them in a state of shock. "What have you done? What have you done? Please,

please don't let me die. I would have told you anything. There must be something you can do. I will tell you everything. May Allah have mercy on my soul."

"The poison will take about two minutes to take effect unless you are unlucky, and Lando has, by chance, found a vein, so spill the beans and make it fast. I have an antidote, but we must get it from the office upstairs. Daniel," he said to the man with the hypodermics. "Go upstairs and get it from the office."

Daniel slowly got up and dragged one foot slowly after the other. Hamza was now in a rage. "Quicker, you son of a pox-riddled alley cat. My life depends on it." Hobart slapped him across the face to re-establish who was in charge.

"Now talk. And fast. Where can we find Yusuf?"

"Quick, quick with the antidote. I can feel it moving up my arm. Where is that foul-smelling man who resembles the ball sack of an aged hyena?" He started shaking again. "Yusuf has a small house where he lives independently, but you will never find it. However, I can find it. I can lead you to him but for a tiny crossing of my palm."

Lando had to admire his ability to negotiate even under the threat of death.

"All right then, Hamza," said Hobart. "We shall see what we can do, but your information had better be good; otherwise, nothing."

Daniel entered the room.

"Quick, quick," said Hamza. "Give me the antidote now."

"Information first. Where is Yusuf? Which area?"

"He is in Sharjah near the Alekhlas Mosque off the Corniche Road. Beyond that, I cannot describe it as I need to walk it. Quick, give me the antidote." The sweat was pouring down his face and neck. Hobart looked at Daniel and nodded.

"There is none," said Daniel.

Hamza looked aghast. The colour drained from his face. "Then you will never find Yusuf after I die." He stared at Hobart with pure venom, and then he replied matter-of-factly.

"Actually, Mr Hamza, I do not believe we need the antidote this time as no antidote is needed for an injection of water."

The dawn of realisation spread across Hamza's face. "You illegitimate son of a syphilitic goat. Now, I will never trust you." He did, however, appear to calm down as the fear went out of his eyes. Lando was also relieved that he had not contributed to killing Hamza despite his violently unpleasant nature.

Hobart paced around the room. "Now we must leave ASAP." He looked at his watch. "It is 6.15 pm, and we do not have a moment to lose, and the light is fading. My car is outside. You Hamza, Lando and me to go. If we send in a load of troops, Ashiraf will get wind of it and fly the coop again. We need to move with stealth. He has evaded capture so often that we must assume he has many friends in the area and has a sixth sense about those near him. We can leave nothing to chance. Hamza, you stay in the handcuffs. Lando, here is an automatic pistol. Please keep it safe. Right, outside everyone and make it quick."

They quickly left the consulate, and Lando took the wheel of the car whilst Hobart kept an eye on Hamza in the back.

Things were moving fast, and Lando was once again wound up tighter than a camel's arse in a sandstorm. He was nonetheless as high as a kite. He was not sure enjoyment was the right word, but he felt he was becoming addicted to the thrill. Dangerous.

They arrived at the border of Sharjah within fifteen minutes after sunset and cruised in without needing to show any ID. They quickly arrived on Corniche Rd, which, not surprisingly, ran alongside the seafront. They found the Alekhlas Mosque, and Hamza told them to park nearby. They got out and walked, with Hamza at every second looking like he would bolt. Finally, after walking down several narrow alleys that twisted and turned, they arrived near a small residence with lights on in one of the downstairs rooms. "That is the one," said Hamza. "Yusuf lives there." Immediately, Hobart turned and swung his pistol in a fast ark and caught Hamza behind the ear with a sickening thud. He went down like a sack of potatoes. Hobart staggered back himself.

"Are you all right, Hoby?" asked Lando with genuine concern.

"We could not have him messing up the plan, could we? I must say I am feeling more than a little queasy. I think the painkillers must be wearing off as my shoulder aches like a bitch." He then vomited violently and leaned against a wall. "Don't worry, I am OK. Just a bit of stress overload."

"O.K., but you could be in a bit of shock or PTSD or something of that nature. Let me know immediately, please, if you feel like fainting, although in my experience, people do not faint slowly."

"I said, 'don't worry,' and I meant it. My training should kick in," he breathed irritably.

Suddenly, another room was lit up, and two men were talking animatedly to each other. Lando peered through the window from their vantage point.

"I can confirm, Hoby, that one of those men, the one on the left, is our man Ashiraf, and the other, I have no idea but can only assume he is Yusuf."

Considering how rotten Hobart must have felt, Lando was amazed at his speed. He marched quickly up to the open window and fired three bullets into Ashiraf, one into the gut and the other two into his head. After a look of pain mixed with hate on his evil face, Ashiraf crumpled to the floor in a pitiful heap. He then shot the other man, presumably Yousuf, making a perfectly placed round hole between his eyes before he collapsed, quivering on the ground.

Job done, thought Lando. No messing around there.

Lando was surprised at how little emotion he felt for these two people who had been responsible for so many deaths. He had just effectively witnessed an assassination and felt absolutely nothing. No sadness, no remorse, nothing. Did that make him a psychopath? He hoped not, but right now, his thoughts turned to Hobart, who was clearly in some distress with closed eyes. Lando held a plastic water bottle to his lips and watched as Hobart slowly sipped. After a couple of minutes, Hobart opened his eyes and smiled.

"Thank you, Lando. Thank you for everything. Between us, we have completed our assignment." With that, he passed out.

Lando quickly got on the telephone with the British Embassy and was put through to GK, who was thankfully working late. Lando filled him in, and GK was highly elated that Ashiraf had been neutralised. He immediately instructed Lando to wait with Hobart until a vehicle and a medic could be sent to him.

Lando checked on Hamza, who was thankfully still out cold. Within fifteen minutes, a roomy vehicle arrived with a doctor and a CIA operative who secured Hamza. It had been ordered by the American consulate with whom GK had spoken. They were driven back gently, and the doctor administered a painkilling injection, which seemed to bring Hobart around quickly. Hobart expressed the request that he be taken home and not to any medical establishment despite the doctor trying to persuade him otherwise. Lando and the doctor helped Hobart out of the car and into his apartment, propping him up in the lift on the way up although he had slightly improved.

"A good night's sleep is all I need," he muttered as they helped him undress and get into bed. He fell soundly asleep again.

Lando checked with the doctor about Hobart being left and the doctor said he would get a nurse over immediately to stay the night. It was, he said, exhaustion caused by the general trauma he had gone through in the last thirty-six hours, combined with the pain in his shoulder. He should be all right.

They parted company, and Lando stayed until the nurse arrived and returned to his hotel. Despite his tiredness, he found it very hard to sleep. He was trying to process everything that had happened, and it all seemed like a strange dream. It was neither a nightmare nor a dream. It was just some crazy experience that hit Lando squarely on the forehead like a whack from a cricket bat. The main assailant had failed in his attempt to cause death and destruction. He had been dealt with, never to repeat his crimes, but what about Hawiya? The so-called spiritual leader seemed to have again vanished like a ghost, or rather, he had not appeared, and no one was wiser about whether he was even real.

Chapter 39

Friday am

It was Friday morning, Holy day in Dubai, when few people worked. Sheikh Massoud did, though, on this Holy day. He was waiting in his sumptuous office for the arrival of Qasim and Shazil. They had been invited or rather escorted to see the Sheikh as he had some exciting news for them. They arrived separately at his offices without being able to speak to each other, so both were in the dark about what the Sheikh might know and hoped that they might not have been implicated in what was now a broadcast headline on both Al Arabiya and Al Jazeera TV channels. When they both entered his office through separate doors, it was like an old British farce, with one looking surprised at the other. They did not need to speak as their expressions gave it all away to the Sheikh and outgushed their pitiful attempts at blaming the other.

The Sheikh thanked them for arranging the anti-drone defences around the Burj Al Arab. He had dealt with it within thirty minutes of being informed of the plot by GK and Lando. There were some willing tongues loosened in record time. He also thanked them both for enhancing his political and personal position, and he said goodbye to them on this most unholy of Holy days.

Neither were heard of again, although the Sheikh provided for Shazil's family. Many women of a looser variety in Dubai were not remotely upset at the loss of Qasim's custom.

***

GK phoned Lando to ask him for a late morning cup of coffee if he fancied it and to have a final debrief, to which Lando agreed. Whilst in his taxi, he rang Claes, Ashley and Kadri and suggested an early evening meal, and they all jumped at it, not least because they all wanted to chat with Lando about his military exploits in Oman the previous 36 hours. Claes asked if he could bring one other along to join them.

"It wouldn't be Delilah by any chance, would it?" Lando probed.

"Well, as a matter of fact, it would," Claes replied.

"Good for you, Claes. She would be most welcome. What about meeting tonight at my hotel at, say, 6.30 pm in the Al Dawaar restaurant? This one's on me, or rather my expenses!"

"Great. I often wanted to go there but never quite found the right occasion. Hasta la vista, baby." With that, he put the phone down. Lando chuckled and marvelled at how saying Arnie Schwarzeneggar's pet phrase in a Swedish accent seemed to ruin it. The time and place were passed to Ashley by text, and then he rang Kadri.

"How are you, Kadri? How's...."

She cut him off immediately, "No, no, no. You're the important one. I have been worried about you since your Superman trip to Oman."

"We'll catch up tonight. All is good, and I am fine." He gave her arrangements for dinner.

"That's good. Maybe we can catch up more intimately afterwards, as I will be in situ at a certain hotel reception."

Lando waited a few seconds too long before replying questioningly, "Now, let me think about that?" At which she slammed the phone down, giggling all the time.

Lando found Gaji in reception, and he was happy to take him to the British embassy for his meeting with Gerald Kirkpatrick.

GK stood up to his full height with his right hand held out in a most welcoming gesture and waved him to an armchair. He rang a buzzer, and the ample-fronted tea lady walked in, smiling as usual with a tray of tea, coffee and delicate chocolate-covered biscuits. Lando mused that they were ordered from England, especially for GK. As she left, he half thought that the tea lady was also requested in the same way, but he quickly shelved the idea as his imagination could run riot if he let it.

"So, Lando, firstly, well done. You have done a magnificent thing, not just for your country. Please tell me about it from start to finish. Coffee or tea, by the way?" GK was pouring it himself.

Lando filled him in on every detail, from the trip to Oman to accompanying Hobart to eliminate Ashiraf.

GK nodded approvingly at each element of the story before asking, "Now, Lando, how did you feel about killing that solid rhinoceros called Bongani? I assume he is the first person you have killed."

"Yes, it is the first person and hopefully the last. I have to say it frightened me. It frightened me because I felt completely unemotional about it at the time and since. I knew it was him or me and reacted like an animal for self-preservation. I wondered if that made me a psychopath or if I could grow to like killing people."

"I am pleased to hear it. Not everyone acts the same. Some people have nightmares for years about it. So, no, you are not a psychopath, as you presumably do not wish to carry on killing people without regret. That is another reason I want to talk to you. Should the opportunity arise, would you be prepared to work for us again? This might shock you, but your characteristics cannot be taught. They are inbred. We would put you on a small retainer, and you would be free to turn down anything asked of you that did not sit kindly with your morals or values."

Lando was flabbergasted. He sat back in his chair and tried to sip his tea without spilling it as his hand was trembling slightly. Excitement was boiling up inside him again. He felt that sense of purpose and validation that had eluded him for most of his life until now.

"So, what do you think?" said GK, nudging him along.

"GK, I am touched by your confidence in me, but there is no telling how I would react in a different scenario."

"Let me be the judge of that." With that, GK stood up and implied that their meeting was ending. "Can you let me know before you head home? I must set things in motion to get all the Home and Foreign Office approvals. Also, we have heard from Sheikh Massoud that your dean, Justin Cocker, had personal dealings of the fiscal kind with that Qasim fellow. We believe it was no more than some dirty little kickback and that he knew nothing of the subterfuge between Qasim and Shazil. We can use this to our advantage if we want you released for a particular venture. You will not have a problem with him from now on."

Lando nodded positively, and they shook hands. Lando left with Gaji to return to his hotel. He was not surprised about the dean. He returned to the swimming pool for an afternoon swim and to say goodbye to Solly at the pool bar.

He got to his room, grabbed his swim shorts, and headed to the pool. Solly was polishing his glasses and cleaning his bar top with his ever-present white teeth reflecting the sun.

"Hello again, Mr Lando. I have not seen you for a day or two. Would you like a beer?"

"Yes, please, Solly. That would be perfect."

"I have heard great things about you, Mr Lando. I believe you have avenged the death of your friend."

Lando looked at him in awe. "How on earth do you know that?"

"I have ways," he said conspiratorially, tapping the side of his nose.

"Just call me Bond," said Lando. "James Bond." Once again, Solly's laughter boomed out across the swimming pool area. "I am leaving for England soon, although I am not sure exactly when, but I have enjoyed meeting you."

"You are very welcome, Mr Lando. I am on holiday from tomorrow for ten days, so I will not see you again, but may your God go with you as you are a very kind man."

"Solly, you have done a lot to make my stay here bearable as I have had to cope with some challenging situations. Perhaps you will accept this little gift from a grateful person." He handed Solly an envelope with a significant sum of cash. "Before you say anything, I appreciate that you might be embarrassed by the contents, but it would be my honour if you accepted it on behalf of your family."

Solly, for once, was completely speechless, and without even examining the contents, he said nothing other than a thankyou with his eyes.

Just then, a nightmarish vision appeared by the pool. It was the bejewelled woman, Mrs Gumper, with little Willie. She strutted around the pool, barking orders at any waiter within shouting distance without really knowing where she wanted to sit or on what. He casually trusted it did not end up being his face. He shuddered and contemplated giving her a piece of his mind and decided it would not help, realising that some battles were not worth fighting. It was best avoided, given that she clearly thought he was some level of lunatic, so he slinked off to his room.

Kadri arrived at 6 pm, a half hour early, intending to surprise him, which she certainly did. He opened the door, clad only his towel. He was met by the glorious apparition of Kadri, who took one look at his well-muscled body and immediately threw herself at him, dragging him to the bed and ripping off his towel in one single movement. It took Lando all of three seconds to respond with possibly the fastest hard-on he had ever sported in his life.

The silk of Kadri's dress dragging across his engorged member seemed to drive him to new states of rapture. Despite this, he was able to help her out of her dress without shredding it and buried his face between her magnificent breasts and sucked her nipples until they were as hard as hot marbles as she moaned in ecstasy. She then rolled him over and sat up, straddling him; he glided into her like an express train going through a tunnel. They climaxed together within two minutes, yelping like two wild dogs at night.

"My God, that was good," whispered Lando into her ear.

"Good!" she said. "Good! Is that the best word you can think of?" Too often, he picked a thoughtless word. She grabbed a pillow and leathered him with it for the second time in their relationship. Then she launched the duvet over him, all the cushions, followed by a chair and a bedside table, while he laughed until he was nearly sick. They lay back exhausted.

The rest of the evening was a blur. They rushed to the restaurant and received some appraising looks from the other guests, who smiled knowingly, but all had a lovely time. Seeing Claes with Delilah made Lando's heart much better. Claes seemed tremendously at ease and happy in Delilah's presence, and she seemed much the same. Ashley was his usual upbeat self, and then Kadri asked him what it was he had to pay back Lando from his school days.

"A fair question, I guess. The problem was that I had always been a bit of a rabble-rouser, and I think it is fair to say that if I got into any more serious trouble at school, I would be out. I had been 'gated' twice already, which means you are not allowed through the school gates or, in fact, often the house gates, sometimes for a weekend, which was a pain and incredibly dull. In one instance, I was beaten over the backside with a big stick four separate times for the same incident. I was beaten by the bedroom monitor, who then sent me to the house monitor, who beat me again, then sent me to the housemaster, who beat me again and then sent me to the headmaster, who beat me again. I believe I made the record of beatings for the same incident, which still stands today."

"Do you think it will ever be broken," piped up Kadri, fascinated.

"No chance. You can't beat anyone now in this namby-pamby society. Probably a good thing, I suppose, but there was a belief in a short, sharp shock treatment in those days."

Kadri jogged him along. "So come on, what happened then with Lando?"

"Well, we were, as you know, good friends and Lando and I were on a flat roof of our house at about 11.30 pm re-enacting a scientific experiment, whilst wildly pissed, of course. A light shone across the breakfast room from a window below, and as we were a bit piddled, we had a pee off the roof. As it went through the light from the window below, it shone into the stream of pee but not out of it, so it dragged the light along to the ground." By this time, everyone was screwing their eyes up with laughter.

"Go on, go on," said Claes, beating the table and laughing. "So, what was the scientific experiment then?"

"Fairly obvious, I would have thought. T.I.R. Total internal reflection. The light from the window shone into the pee stream, and rather than going straight through, it bounced off its internal wall of pee and so it was carried to the ground."

"So, it was reflected internally," said Claes, barely able to get his words out.

"Yes," said Ashley, "but Lando kindly took the full rap even though they knew someone else was on the roof with him as there were twin streams. Even Rolo could not do that." He gazed over at Lando, who was grinning like an ape. "Yes, the little wimp had a clean record, of course, so it seemed logical that he took the rap. I would have owned up to being a party to it, but Lando insisted. Hence, I have always wanted to repay him; otherwise, I would have been chucked out of school. Mater and Pater would have been more than a little cranky, not least because my old man went there and donated to the school."

"Well, you certainly paid me back, Ash, as putting your life on the line for me was a bit special, to say nothing of you being wounded. You could have been killed."

"I didn't think about it at the time. I was just very angry with him. Maybe if I had thought about it, I would not have leapt at the squalid little man."

Kadri cut in."But that is the point, Ash. You didn't think about it. You did it instinctively, showing you to be a genuine friend. A big thank you from me as well for saving him."

"I could see you were happy when you both arrived this evening. You were looking, dare I say it, a little 'in flagrante delicto.'"

Everyone roared with laughter, and Kadri and Lando looked at each other rather coyly. Just then, Lando's phone rang, and he realised it was a Facetime call, and it was from Hobart.

"Hoby!"

"Quite right, it is me. I gather you are having a get-together without me. Not sure I approve of that. Anyway, this is just a message to all of you and from my controller, Harold. A big thank you on behalf of the United States. It was a very successful outcome both diplomatically and politically."

Everyone around the table raised a glass to Hoby. Lando took up the silence.

"Hoby, can we meet before I return to jolly old England?"

"Of course. I am back in my apartment again and much improved. I shall be right as rain in a few days, so keep in touch, as I need a serious chat with you anyway."

"Sounds ominous. I'll call you tomorrow. Nighty night then."

"Nighty night then?" exclaimed Ashley. "You sound like my Nanny." The gathering, with one accord, flung their rolled-up napkins at him.

The evening ended on a high note, with no one wishing it to end and everyone heading off to their quarters, hoping they might all meet again. Lando asked Kadri whether she thought Claes and Delilah might get it together, and she replied that Delilah was captivated by Claes, so why not? Lando said he had not seen Claes so content since he had been in Dubai. It was a feel-good point for the evening to end with, although Lando had further needs, which were never far from his mind, and Kadri detected them.

"Rolo, we need a chat," she said in the taxi to his hotel.

"You don't want to come back?"

"Of course I do, but we still need a chat."

They arrived at the hotel and went up to his room. He went to the mini bar, removed a couple of Haig whisky miniatures, poured them out, and added a dash of water.

They clinked glasses and took a sip each. "Go on then," he said.

"You and I are pretty good together, aren't we?" she looked up enquiringly.

"Of course. Without wishing to copy a much-used phrase, 'You are the best thing that has ever happened to me,' I think I could be falling in love with you."

"And I am extremely fond of you, but ...."

"Oh yes, what is the but? I am unsure I am going to like this conversation."

"Lando, you and I come from such different cultures. We have met in the exotic setting of Dubai, been put in situations of extreme tension, excitement and fear and come out the other side. That is not a recipe for a normal life. Additionally, Hoby has asked me to join the CIA permanently as a salaried employee, provided I pass the relevant tests and training. He has promised that will not be a problem for me. It will be the first permanent job I have ever had. I also enjoy the work, and it feels so marvellous I can hardly describe it." She had tears of mixed emotions rolling down her cheeks.

Lando placed his finger gently upon her lips. "You do not need to justify yourself. You have shone a wonderful light into my life which will never be extinguished."

"Hey, Lando. Do not be sad. We still have the night before us."

With that, they made love gently and sensitively and slept like babies, holding on to each other throughout the night.

Chapter 40

Saturday am

When Lando awoke in the morning, she was gone. Her side of the bed was all rumpled, and Lando put his face into her pillow and deeply inhaled her scent. He would never forget it. He felt sad but knew she was right with everything she said. Her upbringing had been extremely tough, and he had the opposite. Everything had been too easy. They both had many issues to work through and who knows what the future might hold. One thing he knew for sure, he was still not bored. Having been bored much of his life, he knew nothing could be worse.

He got up, had a lovely tepid shower, and went down to the breakfast restaurant.

He had a plateful of everything and could barely move when he got up to leave the table. He had two days free before lectures again on Monday, so he set about filling them. Firstly, Hobart wanted to see him. So, he fixed it for late in the morning. Secondly, he needed to meet Sanjay, the boat captain on his fishing trip, who needed some help doing a bank presentation to expand his business. He just needed to confirm that his offer of help was good. Thirdly, he needed to do his preparation for the remainder of his course before returning home. He rang Hobart, and they met on the waterfront under a cafe umbrella, not far from where he met Sanjay for his fishing trip. He would try to combine the two if he could contact Sanjay.

Hobart was looking good. His shoulder would be in a sling for some time, but it was immediately apparent that his energy had returned.

"My, my, you look better, Hoby," said Lando as they shook hands.

"Feeling much better, thanks. Feeling great. All is good in the Hobart G. Lonsdale IV world today. As I saw you coming, I took the initiative and ordered you a cappuccino. Hope that was all right?"

"Yes, absolutely, bang on. It's great to see you, Hoby, and I am so glad you are on the mend. Looked very dodgy for a while. Nasty wound. Ah, here comes the coffee."

"Cannot beat coffee in the sunshine staring at the boats."

There was a gentle silence for a minute, and Lando realised that Hobart was brewing up something.

"Lando?"

"Yes, Hoby?"

"Lando, we get on pretty well, don't we?"

"Like a house on fire, Hoby. Whether you were English or I was American, we could have been friends at school."

"My feelings precisely. I do not get the feeling you like lecturing in accountancy. Am I right?"

"Not exactly. I am not passionate about the subject, but I do enjoy teaching. I care, I suppose. It's probably because I identify with many students who find it a bit dull. I try to make it light and relevant. It could be worse. I could be teaching veterinary students to express a dog's anal gland."

"Strange comparison. I never really thought about it that way. However, I have something a little more interesting for you that I wanted to discuss."

"Oh yes, and what might that be, Hoby? Chasing gunrunners around the Statue of Liberty, perhaps?"

"Not quite but close," laughed Hobart. "Actually, I wondered if the opportunity arose, you fancied doing any more work with the 'Company,' so to speak?"

Lando nearly fell off his chair. "Hang on. This boring accountant has just had one offer from MI6 and another from the CIA. Are you having me on?"

"I was aware that GK had already spoken to you."

"Why am I not surprised by that? I suppose I might as well get myself shot up as my relationship with Kadri cannot last, no thanks to you, I might add."

"Ah, she has told you I recruited her then. She will be a massive asset to us, whether in this region or another. My request to you would be purely ad hoc and probably only over the next 2-4 years, or else it would be defunct. GK would be happy with it as the Company often works with MI6 when we have a mutual interest. What do you say?"

"I would say that I have not yet confirmed that I will work with GK for MI6. But I would only say yes to you if working with you alone, as I am not about to be paid for by someone I do not know from the 'Company' in another country."

"Understood, but who said anything about pay?" said Hobart indignantly with a severe look on his face. Lando looked at him, and they both chuckled.

"That is wonderful, Lando. With your travelling abroad for lectures, that is a good cover, and we can arrange these things easily with your employers."

"So GK told me."

It was starting to get very warm, and Lando was perspiring away as they talked. He suddenly spied the diminutive figure of Sanjay, the fisherman, wandering along the promenade. He waved to him, and Sanjay walked over with a broad smile.

Lando turned to Hobart, "Please excuse me, but do you mind if Sanjay joins us for a few moments? I promised to meet him before I went home." Hobart nodded approvingly and ordered another coffee.

Lando chatted for a few minutes with Sanjay, who could not believe Lando had even remembered him and, even more, was about to fulfil his promise of help.

Lando confirmed that Sanjay had his email and telephone number and that they would communicate in a fortnight after Lando had settled back home. Sanjay went off whistling and smiling, believing that Lando had been sent from a far-off galaxy to help him through life.

Hobart turned to Lando. "That is why I want you in my corner; you truly care about people. Too many in the Company only care about their promotion, which gets in the way of rational, beneficial decision-making."

"Well, Hoby," he said in an American drawl. "You sure know how to give a guy a good time."

"That is the worst American accent I have ever heard."

"Hoby, can I give you a lift back as my taxi awaits? I assume you are not driving."

"That would be great,' said Hobart, "provided you do not call me Hoby again.'

"All right, just for today."

Hobart was dropped off at his flat, and they parted company with a big hug. Not a common occurrence in Hobart's life.

Chapter 41

Final week

Lando's last week passed with comparative ease, although he struggled to maintain focus after what had transpired in the previous week. The students had submitted their assignments when he went in on Monday, and he coached them through the rest of the syllabus that week until the final Thursday lunch.

It was generally a well-received course, although Hobart unsurprisingly did not appear for that week, but his recovery was going well. Lisana was amazingly professional throughout and came to see Lando after the final lunch session, asking for a quick word, so they went into a private area with a cup of coffee.

"Hey Lando, that was a great course, but I could tell you were very distracted last week but got it together again. How did you think it went? I want to give feedback from your perspective and my own."

"Considering certain course-unrelated situations I had to deal with, I think I coped reasonably well, but I must tell you I have never faced such problems before in my whole life. Woke me up, however. Your help has been amazing, particularly in how you looked after the students, and me for that matter, so thank you."

"It was my pleasure. It really was, but thank you for your advice about my marriage issues.

"Oh yes, what was that? I cannot remember," said Lando, trying to make it easy to draw her out.

"You suggested I have a heart-to-heart with Jim, my husband, on whether he is happy in his job."

"Ah yes, of course. How did you broach it?"

Lisana moved around in her seat slightly uncomfortably as she relived the scene. She sipped at her coffee and took a deep breath. "I had prepared a lovely evening meal for him, and he was opening a bottle of wine as usual, and I suggested we did not drink that night. I said I was worrying myself sick about how much we were both drinking, and I did not understand why we did. I asked if he was unhappy either with me or his job. He was so silent, and I could tell I had touched a nerve. He looked at me with tears and said he could not possibly be unhappy with me. In fact, he hated his job, and he was doing it all for me. You were right, you know. He just wanted 'to bring home the bacon.' We had a great heart-to-heart talk, and I said I did not care about the money we made; I just wanted to see him happy. Why didn't we return to the UK and start our own business? His face lit up, and he immediately shared all the ideas he had dreamed about, particularly starting a smallish residential conference centre, but he had been too afraid to share them with me. I said I would have loved to start anything like that with him, and he hugged me, and it felt like a whole weight had been removed from the two of us. We did open the bottle of wine, though, and toasted to our future. He reckoned that if we stayed in Dubai another six months until after his bonus came through, we would have enough saved to get the business off the ground. In short, he looks so, so happy. We are both exercising hard together in the gym and swimming, and he is like a new man, and so am I."

"I seriously doubt that. Please stay as the beautiful lady you are. Anyway, I am very pleased for you both. It will not be without hardships, as starting new ventures can be a fraught time. Always pleased to help with the figures, of course, if you need a business plan in the future. Be my pleasure."

Lisana looked Lando straight in the eyes. "I sincerely wanted to thank you so much for helping me find the courage to be honest with him. To see him excited again is wonderful." With that, she made her excuses to leave, stood up, and threw her arms around Lando, giving him a long, thankful hug, which made him feel like he was on top of the world.

Hobart arranged a final get-together on Friday with Lando, Kadri, Ashley and Claes. Lando struggled to look at Kadri as he remained powerfully drawn to her. However, he knew they would not sleep together again before he left. She was warm to him throughout the evening, though, so who knew what the future might bring? He vowed to keep in touch with Ashley, who was leaving Dubai the day after Lando. There were embraces all around, contact details all swapped and vague plans for all to meet again in the next couple of years. His final lingering hug from Kadri was still full of possibilities, however.

The next day, he was taken to the airport by Gaji to catch his flight home, reminiscing in his mind about the whole experience of the trip. He left Gaji with a very generous tip, who was still trying to sell him something dubious before he arrived at his terminal. Gaji was an amazingly crazy and happy part of this whole trip. It was like nothing he had ever felt before, and he had discovered traits about himself that he was still unsure of. Who was the real Lando Westwood?

Chapter 42

His plane landed at around 8 pm on Saturday evening at Birmingham International, and he hired a taxi and arrived home in Shrewsbury at eleven o'clock. He went to his drinks cabinet, poured himself a large 12-year-old Aberlour scotch with a dribble of water, and sat down, toasting the preciousness of life before bed. He slept ten hours straight, waking at 10 am, forgetting that he was home until he recognised his bedroom curtains as his eyes flickered open. His memories came flooding back. What a trip! What a bloody trip! He had never felt so alive as he was right now.

He got up, and the sun shone without a cloud in the sky. He had an ice-cold shower to wake himself up, which it did, and he went downstairs to make breakfast. He had got nothing in, so he wandered down the street to the little family-run café called Rivellino's, named after a former Brazilian footballer who graced the pitches of the world for many years. He sat in the window, waiting for his order, overlooking the sunny street and picked up a newspaper already on his table. Then it arrived. Dry cured bacon, two eggs, sourdough toast and some great coffee. The taste was unique and far removed from the crispy beef bacon he had sampled in Dubai. It was a great start to the day, which went well until he had a run in the afternoon in the Quarry Park through Percy Thrower's old garden in the Dingle. It was picturesque. However, he quickly tired and realised he was pushing himself too much after his travels. He walked the last mile back to his house. The rest of the day was a bit of a haze as he kept falling asleep, waking up to put the TV on, and falling asleep again. He could not remember a single programme he had watched. He did not eat the rest of the day.

He was up bright and early on Monday, ready for action at the old University. He motored over and was in his office in good time, drinking a coffee when the door flew open. Who should it be but Gary, full of everything he had done the last couple of weeks and all the gossip circulating the business school?

"Hey, boyo. Our esteemed Dean Justin has got into trouble with the financial arrangements with the British University in Dubai or, more precisely, with some guy named Qasim. They cannot get hold of Qasim, and Justin has been sweating on whether he still has a job. Do you know anything about that because I assume you dealt with these people?"

Lando thought better of admitting anything as he assumed Qasim was now as dead as a doornail. All he said to Gary was, "One day, Gary, I shall tell you what I know, but I am guessing there is a bit of backsheesh flying around. Right now, I only want to settle back into a simple lifestyle."

Gary looked at him sideways with a deep frown, realising there was so much more to this story than a bit of backsheesh. "OK, boyo. How about we catch up in the Dog and Doublet over a pint this evening after lectures? Six o'clock good for you?"

Lando nodded and smiled at Gary's enthusiasm to have Lando back in the fold. The day wore on, but he had yet to speak to the Dean. He wondered how this information about

Justin had got out, and then a thought occurred to him. Hilda Clench, the dean's secretary. She had Justin over a barrel through compromise somewhere in the past, both personally, because he probably liked it over a barrel, or his desk anyway, and probably also politically within the University machinations. If she knew something about what the Dean was skimming from the contract with BUiD, the dean would be even more compromised. Maybe Justin had not been putting out the way Hilda liked it, leading her to spill the beans. *Hell hath no fury like a woman scorned*, he thought.

Six o'clock came rapidly, and Lando walked down to the Dog and Doublet and strode up to Gary at the bar, who was already ordering a couple of pints from the alluring Amber. Lando had forgotten what a warm, reddy brown her hair was. She saw him staring at her and spoke. "Hey love, I have not seen you for a while. What are you looking at me in that strange way for?"

A month ago, Lando would have blushed and got tongue-tied. Gary knew that and had a big smirk on his face. Lando then spoke as if his voice was from someone else.

"Hi Amber, I was just thinking how beautiful your hair was. It is like the rest of you, completely captivating." If Gary had been sitting on a bar stool, he would have fallen off it as he was so surprised.

"Why, thank you, Lando. That is the loveliest thing anyone has told me for a long time. Have a free bag of my pork scratchings."

"Is that a euphemism?" Lando asked, and the two stared ahead, open-mouthed, processing what Lando had just said.

Maybe Lando imagined it, but Amber's cheeks seemed to colour up slightly. He leapt in while he had a chance.

"Amber, do you like the movies?"

"Yes, I love them, actually."

"A director's cut of *The Abyss* is showing this week at the Odeon. How would you like to keep me company?"

Amber looked him in the eye and smiled excitedly, saying, "You mean the James Cameron film? That is one of my favourites. Yes, you are on. I have Thursday night off. Is that any good?"

"Great for me, too. Here's my number if your plans change, but text me where I can pick you up," said Lando, leaving his university card and casually taking his pint and the free bag of scratchings to their usual table.

Gary's jaw had to be almost scooped off the floor. He was dumbfounded as he took a sip of his beer. "Where did all that come from, Lando?" he said admiringly.

"Gary, I have no idea, but I think I have won the bet. What was it? Could you arrange a date with Amber or gain entry to Mensa? I believe the prize is mine, and you will now buy my Friday lunches and beers for a month."

Gary grimaced and then raised his glass to him. "Fair and square," he said as he swallowed his pride. "You must still take the Mensa test before I pay out, boyo."

He thought he would take the Mensa test anyway, just for the hell of it, but without telling Gary when. He would only rub it in if it did not go well. He appreciated that he had newfound confidence after his trip to Dubai, which was helped not only by facing up to the violence he encountered but also by his relationship with Kadri, which had lifted his self-esteem to previously uncharted waters.

He now planned on upping his training at the dojo to go for his black belt.

Previous fears seemed to have left him.

About the Author

Richard France always loved mathematics and spreadsheet modelling, which, outside of his university career, took him abroad to the Middle East and Africa. So, he utilised his background to write novels fusing exaggerated aspects of real life with his daydreaming about exciting and darkly humourous adventures for his main protagonist. He has three children who have grown up more than he has, and lives in the countryside of North Shropshire, England, with his longsuffering wife, Anna and a dog called Buddy.